That's Amore!

FOUR NOVELLAS OF EROTIC ROMANCE

edited by Marilyn Jaye Lewis

First Magic Carpet Books, Inc. edition July 2004

Published in 2004

Manufactured in the United States of America
Published by Magic Carpet Books, Inc.

Magic Carpet Books, Inc.
PO Box 473
New Milford, CT 06776

Library of Congress Cataloging in Publication Date

That's Amore! Edited by Marilyn Jaye Lewis
ISBN # 0-9726339-9-5

Book Design: P. Ruggieri

THAT'S AMORE!

Four Complete Novellas of Erotic Romance

Edited by Marilyn Jaye Lewis

CONTENTS

AUTHOR'S NOTE:

COME FLY WITH ME

Jackie de Martini

PART ONE

'Let's leave our hut dear,
get out of our rut dear,
let's get away from it all…'

CHAPTER ONE

Paige Allen could count on one hand the number of times she'd flown in an airplane: exactly three. And the most recent time hadn't been since the trip to Paris, when she and George had gone on their honeymoon. Back then, they'd flown Pan Am – an airline that had been out of business for twelve years already. At age thirty-two, it was safe to say that Paige Allen, a first grade schoolteacher from eastern Pennsylvania, was not very worldly, but that was all about to change.

Flying Aero Mexico this time, Paige was traveling First Class, a thing she'd never dreamed she would really do, least of all without George. But here she was. It had been a long flight from the international airport in New Jersey to Puerto Vallarta on Mexico's Pacific coast – eleven hours and fifty minutes, to be precise, but flying First Class felt as effortless as flying in the comfort of one's own living room. The spacious, reclining seats, the individual movie screens, the unlimited supply of gourmet food and wine, all made a nearly twelve hour-long flight seem practically enjoyable... except for one unavoidable thing.

'Why don't they open the lousy door already?' It was Penny, Paige's impatient niece. 'We've been on the ground for at least ten minutes. This is insane. Haven't they kept us trapped in here long enough? I'm going *crazy*.'

At age fifteen, Penny Allen was much worldlier than her Aunt Paige. Thanks to affluent parents, Penny was a seasoned traveler. But along with her exposure to those finer things in life that affluence often brings, young Penny had acquired a sense of entitlement out of proportion to anything Paige had ever witnessed.

'Honey, try to be patient. I doubt they're keeping the door locked just to torment you. I'm sure there's a perfectly good reason for it – something safety-related, no doubt.'

Being a first grade schoolteacher for more than a decade had instilled in Paige Allen a level of patience unknown in most ordinary grown-ups. Even the flight attendants, whose jobs also required unusually high levels of tolerance, had begun to show visible signs of agitation when forced to contend with Penny's incessant whining for twelve non-stop hours.

It had started early in the journey, with Penny's dissatisfaction in the food. 'I don't like this,' she'd told a stewardess. 'It tastes funny. I want something else.'

Her knack for avoiding those magic words, please and thank you, had sent up a red flare to the entire first class cabin that here was a spoiled brat; a potentially irksome situation on such a long flight.

It fell to Paige then, the task of smoothing out Penny's rough social edges, but she didn't resent it, she tackled it with grace. Having no children of her own, Paige loved her niece and for the most part, enjoyed her company. It didn't keep her from privately regretting the questionable parenting skills of Penny's mother and father, but now wasn't the time to be ruffling the feathers of any family members, especially any on poor George's side.

Six months ago, George Allen, Paige's husband of twelve years, had quite suddenly succumbed to a fatal heart attack. The Allens were a small, tight-knit clan. The unexpected loss of George, a respected college professor, a soft-spoken, congenial man of only fifty-eight, had devastated all of them, not just Paige – although the last thing Paige had ever expected was to be a widow at age thirty-two. Perhaps she had grieved George's death more than anyone else; still everyone who'd known him had mourned the loss keenly.

'There we go!' Paige exclaimed cheerfully as the plane's hatch opened. 'Finally. I'm suffocating.'

Paige ignored the remark. Frankly, she was near suffocation herself, if only figuratively. But they weren't out of the woods yet. They were still a good hour's bus ride from their final destination, a small fishing village north of Puerto Vallarta. There, Paige and her precocious niece would spend an 'enchanting holiday week' in a secluded, romantic villa together – and everything would be Primera Clase. It was a Christmas vacation George and Paige had planned on for a long time. They'd scrimped and saved in order to do it all first class. It had been a dream they'd dreamed together, had paid for in advance, never once suspecting that George wouldn't live long enough to enjoy it.

Rather than let it all go to waste, and since Paige desperately needed a vacation, the family had decided it would be a perfect Christmas break for Penny, as well. It was hardly the romantic getaway Paige had been dreaming of all those years with George, but for her, being with family especially at the holidays, was better than being alone.

For first class passengers, getting from the airplane to the bus that would take them up the coast to the quaint Villa Corazon resort was relatively uncomplicated. Puerto Vallarta's international airport was modern and sophisticated. The same couldn't be said for the bus ride itself, unfortunately. It was a hot, bouncing, jolting, and grueling trip that frequently skirted the jungle. Still, the sun was setting and the colorful sky over the Pacific was glorious.

Sheer exhaustion had stemmed the tide of Penny's constant complaining, at least for the moment, and Paige was free to stare out the open bus window at the beautiful sights passing by and let her mind wander.

It had been a tough year for her. Losing George, suddenly facing the future alone, tackling a new school year with feigned enthusiasm – it had all taken its toll on Paige. She was worn out, a little empty, and tired of the things that used to feel satisfying when she was happily married. As much as she missed George and the Christmases they'd spent together, it was still a relief to be so far away from the sameness of home and to be in such a lush, tropical paradise. It was unlike anything Paige had ever seen outside of the movies.

Penny, on the other hand, was unfazed by the splendor of it all. In her short life she'd already traveled to places like Ixtapa, Belize, Acapulco, and three of the Hawaiian Islands. Coming from a small town in Pennsylvania, Penny was presently at an age where she was more impressed by big cities and the promise of fast living and excitement. And since she'd never once had to shell out a dime for any of her elaborate vacations, she had no way of appreciating the upscale amenities Paige and George's combined incomes and thrifty diligence had managed to secure for them.

When the bus at last reached Villa Corazon high in the hills, and the passengers disembarked, the perks of a first class vacation returned; the already gentle, respectful staff soon bordered on the obsequious as they showed Paige and Penny to one of the Grand Villas. Set higher up in the hills than even the deluxe or superior villas, the Grand Villas were afforded absolute privacy and the best views – three hundred and sixty degree vistas that looked out over the ocean as well as the jungle. The views were hard to fully appreciate at night, but the villa itself was breathtaking.

While still secluded from the other villas, it was primarily an open dwelling made of whitewashed concrete and splashes of ceramic tiles and a high, thatched roof. Each of the main rooms had at least one wall that opened onto the night air, which explained the mosquito netting draped securely around both beds and the Tiki-style torches that blazed bright on the terraces. One terrace had a gentle waterfall and a plunge pool that appeared to be carved out of solid stone. The other terrace – the one that looked out over the ocean – served as the dining area and was just off the villa's fully equipped kitchen.

'*Señora. Señorita.* We hope you enjoy your lovely stay at Villa Corazon. *Feliz Navidad.*' The bellman that had lugged the cumbersome baggage up the winding path to the villa respectfully retreated back down the hill, without so much as anticipating a tip. Even the gratuities had been pre-paid.

'Wow,' Paige declared, both overwhelmed by the exotic beauty of her surroundings and a bit out of breath from the long trek up the winding path. 'This is just wonderful, isn't it, Penny?'

'Yeah, but I'm starved. When are we going to eat?'

'Food… that does sound good. Mind if I take a quick shower first? That dusty bus ride just about did me in.'

With her characteristic impatience, Penny nevertheless resigned herself to waiting until Paige had showered and dressed. Then the weary travelers made their way down the hill to the Villa Corazon's one and only restaurant. It offered authentic Mexican and Italian fare, and both cuisines were Paige's favorites.

'I can see already that I'm going to put on ten pounds before this trip is over!'

The lively restaurant consisted of a single, medium-sized room with a generous scattering of wrought-iron tables. In anticipation of the upcoming holidays, the room was festively draped with strands of twinkling Christmas lights and ethnic religious decorations. There was tropical greenery everywhere and the floors and walls were laid with colorful, hand-painted tiles depicting the local scenery. Paige and Penny were welcomed by a smiling young hostess and led, rather ironically, to a romantic candle-lit table for two.

In one corner of the room, a small boisterous crowd was gathered around a group of tables.

'Guests of the hotel?' Paige asked the hostess.

'*Si*, a wedding. It takes place tomorrow evening. The *señorita* there in the middle with the long blonde hair? She is the happy bride.'

'A wedding!' It might have been the hunger, the exhaustion, or the bittersweet memories of her own wedding to George; whatever had triggered it, Paige had to fight back a tear.

As the hostess went back to her station, Penny looked appalled. 'Aunt Paige, you're not going to cry, are you?'

'I might, honey,' she kidded her. 'I always cry at weddings.'

'But this isn't a wedding, this is just dinner. And we don't even know those people.'

Paige smiled wistfully and blinked back her tears. She tried in vain to recall if she'd been that unsentimental when she'd been fifteen. 'You don't have to know someone personally to feel their happiness, Penny, or their pain for that matter.'

'I know, but I just want to eat now.'

'Me, too. Don't worry,' she assured her. 'I'm not going to embarrass you by being a cry baby. Now, what are we going to order? Everything looks so yummy.'

Penny let out a sigh of despair.

'What, honey? What is it?'

'Nothing. It's just that you always talk like you're still in the first grade. It's kind of weird, you know. You don't talk like a regular grown-up.'

The comment took her aback; still Paige gave it some thought. Her niece was probably right. 'I'll make you a deal,' she suggested. 'If you promise to try to enjoy yourself for the rest of the trip, I promise to leave my classroom behind. I won't let a single first-grader cross my mind until after the New Year. Is it a deal?'

With reluctance, Penny agreed. 'All right, Aunt Paige, it's a deal.'

*   *   *

After the leisurely and too-filling meal, the last thing Paige felt like doing was winding her way back up the hillside to the villa, but there was no other choice. She and Penny trudged up the hill slowly, as if with weights around their ankles. On the torch lit path that led to the Grand Villas, they passed several of the wedding guests who'd been at the restaurant, including the bride and groom. Understandably, they were in much rowdier spirits than Paige and Penny, and not just because they'd ordered several rounds of margaritas during dinner. It was nearly Christmas after all, and the happy promise of a wedding was just around the corner for them.

'Congratulations,' Paige offered, as she passed the bride and groom. 'The hostess at the restaurant mentioned that you were getting married tomorrow. What an idyllic spot for a wedding. You must be so excited.'

The pair stopped and accepted Paige's warm regards. It was their shining hour that awaited them, their moment in the sun. When would they ever again be this special, that strangers would stop to congratulate them?

Penny rolled her eyes and kept trudging up the path.

'We've been planning it for over a year already,' the eager bride replied, her long blonde hair and the warm yellow glow from the lit torches making her look barely old enough to be out of high school. 'It seems like forever. It's hard to believe it's finally going to happen tomorrow!'

'Well, good luck,' Paige said, as she politely continued on her way. 'I'm sure it'll be just wonderful.'

As she caught up with Penny, she wondered if she'd sounded too much like a first-grade schoolteacher. Then her thoughts got lost in the impending wedding, even though it wasn't her own.

Those kids must be rolling in money, she thought. A stay at the Villa Corazon at Christmas was expensive enough, adding a wedding to the mix must be costing them all a fortune.

*   *   *

Later that night, tucked into one of the queen-sized beds with the mosquito netting secured around her, Paige found that she was actually too wound-up to sleep. She lay awake instead, reliving her memories of her wedding to George. The wedding had been a very modest affair. Back then, Paige had been a full-time student on scholarship, just a few credits shy of graduating from the local teacher's college and George had been one of her professors. They weren't poor exactly, but their financial resources were lean. The wedding had been held in a local banquet hall. The hall's ambiance couldn't have been further from the Villa Corazon's, but Paige and George had been blissfully happy, none the less.

Paige's family had opted out of participating in the wedding. They had already seen Paige go down the aisle once, with less than stunning results. That time, she'd been fresh from high school, only seventeen, and her first husband, Jeff, had only been a year older. Everyone, friends and family, had urged Paige to give it time, to reconsider, to not rush into anything; that she and Jeff were too young to know what they were getting into.

But rush in, they did. The marriage had lasted six months and then had been annulled. In Paige's mind, her marriage to George was the 'real' marriage. It was as if the first marriage had never existed, as if the wedding had never taken place. But to her parents' bank account, the wedding between Paige and Jeff and the elaborate reception that had followed had undeniably taken place and they were in no mood to spring for another wedding, so Paige and George were on their own.

Funny, she thought. When was the last time I thought of Jeff?

Her memories of Jeff Palmer were always troubling. She'd loved him like crazy, that was undisputed, but they'd fought like the proverbial cats and dogs. Perhaps her attraction to George had never been so hotly passionate, as her attraction to Jeff had been from the moment they'd laid eyes on each other in the hallowed halls of Franklin High. But her marriage to George had been stable, peaceful, secure, the way she knew married life should be – if a marriage had a hope of surviving. Two level-headed adults, approaching life soberly, that's how a successful marriage was achieved.

It had never once occurred to Paige Allen that passion – the lusty, unbridled kind of passion, the kind that reached ecstatic highs and tortuous lows – could ever be part of the formula for a relationship's success.

A quiet heart, a quiet mind, she told herself.

Then before she knew it, she had quietly drifted to sleep.

CHAPTER TWO

T he morning sun, with no concrete wall to block its grand entrance, spilled into Paige's bedroom and woke her at dawn. She opened her eyes and was immediately greeted by the tropical splendor of her surroundings; a world of lush, riotous colors that she hadn't been able to fully appreciate when she'd arrived the night before.

'No way am I sleeping through this,' she whispered to herself, not wanting to wake Penny who was sound asleep in the other bed. Paige wasn't quite ready for the onslaught of adolescent angst; there would be plenty of time for that later. First, she wanted to savor the solitude of the early morning on her own.

She grabbed her cotton robe and crept quietly from the room.

The 'fully equipped kitchen' boasted about in the Villa Corazon brochure was not an exaggeration. It was stocked with the basics for the heartiest American style breakfast, as well as a wide array of bright fruits and vegetables. Right now though, all Paige wanted was a cup of coffee to linger over out on the terrace. From there, in the morning light, she discovered the full range of her breathtaking view of the Pacific Ocean.

Directly below her villa was a private stretch of beach belonging to the resort. As Paige drank her coffee, she watched members of the hotel's staff readying the beach for the upcoming wedding. A fluttering white canopy was erected, its poles anchored deep in the white sand. Chairs were set out, decorated in clusters of flowers and white ribbons.

'I am not going to spend the day watching this,' she quietly cautioned herself. 'I can't spend this entire vacation crying over what I had with George. I'm here to put the grief behind me.'

In a way, it was unfortunate that her trip to the resort coincided with a wedding. Still it reminded Paige that she would welcome someone new in her life. She wasn't sure she could picture herself getting married again, but a significant 'someone' to spend time with, to talk to, that would be all right. She was lonely, she knew that. But she couldn't imagine anyone in his right mind wanting to spend time listening to her talk about missing George, or about everything she'd had with George when he was alive. Realistically, a new relationship for Paige was probably still a long way off.

'Aunt Paige, hey.'

'Well good morning, Penny. You're up bright and early.'

'I'm starved. What is there to eat?'

'As far as breakfast goes, there's just about everything. But unless you feel like cooking we should probably head down to the restaurant. I'm not interested in spending my vacation in any kitchen.'

'Oh.'

With that eloquent reply, Penny disappeared into the bathroom. Within moments, Paige could hear the shower running. She guessed that she should probably get dressed and prepare to head down the hill to civilization. Effective communication was not one of her niece's strong suits; Paige needed to rely on psychic intuition much of the time.

She went into the bedroom and threw on a cotton sundress and a pair of sandals. It seemed to take forever for Penny to emerge from the shower. There was plenty of time for a second cup of coffee out on the terrace.

Below, a banquet table had been brought out to the beach and draped in a white tablecloth. Paige watched as a tower of champagne flutes was erected on the table.

Congratulations, she thought, silently toasting the lucky couple, wherever they were, and recalling how she and George had had little money to spare on champagne, but at her first wedding, her wedding to Jeff Palmer, the champagne had flowed freely.

It was a night to remember, that first night, the night of their honeymoon. Being alone with Jeff, finally, had been the most exciting night of Paige's life.

Wait a minute, she stopped herself. Jeff was the most exciting night of my life? Didn't I mean George? She finished the last of her coffee and stared down at the lively activity on the beach below. Well, didn't I?

* * *

The restaurant seemed hopelessly understaffed. Perhaps all hands were needed to set-up for the wedding. Paige tried to be understanding about the slow service but Penny's impatience was getting intolerable, even for Paige. She felt like offering a prayer of thanks when their breakfasts finally arrived.

'Well, Penny, what do you feel like doing today?'

'I don't know. Go swimming, I guess.'

'Did you notice the view of the ocean from our villa?'

'No, but I want to swim in the pool.'

'My goodness, Penny, you can swim in a pool any day back home. Wouldn't you rather swim in that beautiful ocean?'

'Not really. If you don't mind, after breakfast, I'd like to look for the pool.'

Paige resisted the urge to roll her eyes and sigh. 'Sure, honey, whatever you want. It's your vacation as much as mine. But I think I'm going to spend some time on the beach today. This is my first time seeing the Pacific Ocean, you know. Don't you think it looks much bluer than the Atlantic?'

'I guess so. I never really thought about it. I haven't spent too much time on the Atlantic.'

That was really saying something, Paige thought. Eastern Pennsylvania was not that far from the Atlantic coast, yet this kid was more familiar with the Gulf of Mexico, the Caribbean, and the Pacific. Paige wondered what that must feel like, living a life of relative privilege and not even knowing it.

After breakfast, they went in search of the hotel's private pool. It looked almost as breathtaking as the ocean. It was one of those infinity pools that seemed to drop off the edge of a cliff and flow right into the Pacific beyond. The pool area was landscaped with rocks and plants and trees. There was an area by the deep end that seemed to wind its way into a grotto of some kind. And by an end of the shallow side, there was a bar that swimmers could swim right up to and order drinks. Even with the ocean so near at hand, many of the resort's guests were already flocking to the pool.

'Do you think you'll be okay here by yourself? I can always go to the beach later.'

'I'll be okay, Aunt Paige. I know how to swim. I go to the pool by myself back home, all the time. Come on let's go back to the villa. I want to get my swimsuit.'

Paige was so used to being surrounded by six-year-olds that she felt uneasy letting Penny go to the pool on her own, but she figured she was probably over-reacting. The pool had a lifeguard, and besides it would be nice to spend some time alone on the beach. Even Paige preferred the quiet of her own company sometimes to being with children of any age.

*   *   *

The warm sun beating down on her, and the rhythmic pounding of the waves against the beach put Paige into a deep sleep in no time. Luckily, the noise of the busy staff setting up the wedding nearby woke her before she got burnt.

She turned over and idly watched the other people on the beach. She had nowhere to go, nothing planned. She could do just this for the rest of her vacation and it wouldn't bother her a bit.

Twice, she wandered down to the water and waded into the waves. There was nothing but beauty everywhere she looked. It was both tranquil and entrancing. Paige was sorry George was missing it.

Fearful of overdoing it in the sun on her very first day of vacation, Paige forced herself to head back to the protective shade of the villa when it had reached high noon. She sat out on the terrace instead and from up there, continued to watch the hypnotic waves of the ocean return continuously to the shore.

Within the hour, Penny came charging up to the villa. She seemed bursting with energy and good spirits – for a change. 'Aunt Paige, I met the coolest man at the pool!' she exclaimed.

Paige felt immediately alarmed. Oh no, she thought; she definitely did not say 'a boy.'

'God, you should have seen him.'

'What do you mean by 'a man,' honey?'

'Some older guy, not as old as Uncle George was, but old like you are. And he was so gorgeous. Aunt Paige, he could have been a movie star. He's from New York.'

'How do you know that?'

'Because he told me. He asked me where I was from; he thought I knew the bride and groom. I guess he's here for that wedding. And I think he's rich.'

'I see.' Paige was trying to keep her panic at a low simmer. Clearly this was a harmless exchange between two hotel guests. If Penny's parents had been here, Paige wouldn't have raised an eyebrow. But they weren't here. She was in charge, responsible for the safety of her precocious niece. Her alarm was rising again.

'How did you happen to strike up a conversation with such an old man?' she asked as casually as she could.

'I was waiting for a drink at that bar in the pool and so was he.'

'A drink at the bar in the pool?'

'A diet coke,' Penny explained condescendingly. 'Please, Aunt Paige. Just because it's a bar doesn't mean you have to drink booze.' She said it as if she'd decided that her aunt would never be more than a first-grader for the rest of her life.

'Well, excuse my error, Penny. It just sounded funny. Did this man have a name?'

'I don't know. He didn't tell me and I didn't ask.'

'Is he here with his wife?'

'I don't think so, he didn't look married. There were women hanging all over him when he got out of the pool. He had black hair and black eyes, and he was tall and really built. Not like a body builder, or anything, but just really handsome. He talked to me for about twenty minutes!'

This can't be good, Paige thought. 'Well, what else did you talk about?

Twenty minutes is an awful long time to chat with someone without even finding out his name.'

'He just asked if I was here on vacation from school and junk like that.' Penny's voice trailed off and she succumbed to a rather dreamy expression. She seemed smitten by this older handsome stranger from New York. Paige decided there and then that she wasn't letting Penny out of her sight for the rest of the vacation.

By late afternoon, Penny was chomping on the bit to go down to the beach and watch the wedding. It was to take place at five-thirty.

'Honey, you weren't invited. It wouldn't be polite.'

'But you don't have to be invited! As long as we don't sit in the chairs, we can sit on the beach and watch the wedding. Everybody does it! They were all talking about it down at the pool. They have weddings here all the time.'

'I don't want you bothering people, perfect strangers.'

'I won't bother anybody. Come on, let's go.'

Penny was in such a state that Paige felt the pressure to consent. 'I don't think I could really handle going to a wedding right now, Penny.'

'Aunt Paige, *please*.'

'All right all right. We'll go down to the beach. We can watch the ceremony, but that's it. After that, we're going to go have dinner and leave those people alone. Are we on the same page about that?'

In Penny's excited state, an inch was as good a mile. 'I promise. Just the ceremony and then we can go. I just want to point him out to you. That's all.'

'Penny…'

'Come on, you already said yes.'

A mariachi band had begun playing. It was a tender, swaying, swooning sound that drifted up to the terrace hauntingly. Paige couldn't resist the romance of it. 'You just stay close by me, Penny Allen, you hear?'

'Okay.'

The two made their way down the hill to the beach. Most of the hotel guests were either gathered casually on the sand or dressed formally and being shown to the chairs under the white canopy.

It was no use; Paige would be in tears in no time. But it was a wedding, after all, who could fault her for getting so emotional?

She and Penny sat close to a group of people who seemed as enchanted with this idea of a wedding as she did.

'That's him,' Penny whispered. 'Up there, toward the front. He's sitting down already.'

Paige tried in earnest to catch a glimpse of this man who had so effortlessly captured her niece's heart, but all she saw was the back of a black head of hair on a man wearing a tuxedo. He didn't turn around. Soon he was obscured completely by the other wedding guests.

As twilight set over the ocean, the mariachi band played a soulful melody that seemed to stop everyone's heart it was that poignant. The whole beach was quiet and suddenly there she was, from seemingly out of nowhere as the sun set behind her in brilliant hues of crimson and pink and gold, the bride sailed onto the beach in a small white boat, guided by local fisherman. As was true of all brides, especially those who wore white gowns of lace – miles of lace, with all the accoutrements – she looked like she'd stepped out of a fairytale. The crowd gasped. The guests under the canopy stood and watched her walk slowly across the beach and then down the aisle to her groom.

From where they sat, it was impossible for Paige and Penny to hear the actual exchange of vows, but it was still moving to watch and Paige was glad she'd finally let Penny persuade her to come.

The ceremony was brief. When the bride and groom made their way back up the aisle, a cheer arose from the entire crowd. The Mariachi Band launched into a lively, raucous number. Paige nudged her niece. 'Come on, Penny,' she shouted above the music. 'Let's go get something to eat. You want to go back to the restaurant?'

'Aunt Paige, please, can't we just stay for a few minutes?'

A guest leaned close to the two of them and said, 'Excuse me for intruding, I couldn't help but overhear you. The restaurant is closed right now because of the wedding – it's a tradition. It won't be open for dinner for another hour or so.'

'See, Aunt Paige? Come on, we can stay for a little while.'

Penny's whine was grating, even though it was nearly drowned out by the band. 'Penny, we had a deal.'

'I know, but just a few minutes, it's not going to hurt anyone.'

An explosion of fireworks shot up into the lingering twilight, the battering of booms and pops fighting the blaring music of the mariachi players. It was clear that the crowd on the beach intended to stick around and join in the festivities, or at least be on the outskirts of them. One of the bars, Paige soon learned, was in fact a cash bar that had been set up on the beach for just this reason – to serve the hotel guests who weren't actual guests of the wedding party. Everything was conspiring against Paige. Another guest inquired loudly, 'What are you drinking? I'm going to make my way over there, no sense in both of us fighting the crowd.'

'Oh thank you,' Paige replied. 'That's very considerate, but I'm not drinking just yet. Thanks, though.'

Penny was tugging sharply on her arm. 'That's him. There he is.'

The handsome stranger had come out from under the canopy with a young woman on his arm. But they were making their way to the crowded champagne bar in the other direction.

Penny was pulling her along.

'Penny, stop it. This is rude. We don't know those people.'

'Let's just say "hi", please? Come on.'

The band played on, with that swelling blare that only a mariachi band can achieve. Overwhelmed by the merry atmosphere that was swallowing the whole crowd, Paige was led along in the direction of the champagne bar. How bad could it be? She consoled herself. He clearly had a date on his arm. Penny meant absolutely nothing to this man. She was panicking for no reason. It was irrational. Penny was just a love-smitten child that was all. No real harm in it.

Before Paige could utter another word in protest, the man emerged from the crowd with his date and his champagne and was standing right in front of her.

'Paige?' he shouted. 'Paige Thompson?'

Paige was nothing short of flabbergasted. '*Jeff?* Jeff Palmer? My God, what are you doing here?'

'I'm at a wedding, how about you?'

'Oh my God,' she stammered again in shock. 'I just can't believe this. I'm, well, I'm here with my niece on vacation. And I'm Paige Allen now!'

He looked down at Penny, who was speechless. 'Ah – Penny, isn't it? We met at the pool today. She said she was here with her aunt. Naturally, I had no idea you qualified as an aunt. How long has it been Paige, about ten years?'

'More like fourteen.'

'Fourteen!' Jeff let out a bright shout of astonished laughter. 'Where does it go? Oh, Doreen, this is Paige and her niece, Penny. Paige and I used to be married. Can you believe that? Funny we should meet again at a wedding.'

Penny looked white as a sheet. 'Aunt Paige,' she cried out over the music. 'I didn't know you were ever married... I mean, except to Uncle George.'

'It was a short-lived affair,' Jeff said.

Doreen, his date, looked nonplussed. In a flat, un-festive voice, she said loudly, 'I didn't know you were married, either.'

'Well, we sure were, weren't we, Paige?'

'Yes, we were, when we were young and crazy.'

'I'd like to think I'm still young,' Jeff joked. 'But I know for sure I'm still crazy. How about you, Paige? You look great, you know? How's life treating you? Are you here with your husband?'

'No,' she managed to reply. 'He was supposed to be here, but, well, he couldn't make it.'

'Nothing serious, I hope.'

'No,' Paige lied, 'nothing serious.'

Penny's jaw dropped open. She stared at her aunt in exasperation. 'Uncle George is dead, Aunt Paige That's pretty serious.'

Paige smiled uncomfortably. 'Well, yes, that's serious. I just didn't want to put a damper on anyone's mood.'

Jeff looked at her quizzically, uncertain how to reply. 'Your husband's dead?'

She nodded her head. It was all feeling too crazy. She was supposed to be on this vacation with George, but George was gone, and here she was at a wedding, a loud, wild wedding on a beach – with Jeff. Was she dreaming? Was this happening? 'He had a sudden heart attack six months ago,' she tried to explain. 'But we were already booked on this trip so I brought my niece. I needed the time away.'

'I'll bet you did. That's terrible. I'm so sorry to hear that.'

'Well... thanks.'

'Listen, Paige, how long will you be here?'

'Through New Year's Day.'

'I'll be here for two more days. Let's get together for a drink or something, okay? I'd love to catch up with you.'

'Okay,' Paige agreed. 'I'd like that, too. We're staying in one of the Grand Villas at the top of the hill. Come by tomorrow, if you want.'

'I will!' he exclaimed, to Doreen's obvious dismay. 'I'm in one of the Grand Villas, too. That'll be great! Paige, it was so nice running into you.'

'Thanks. It was nice for me, too.' Paige watched Jeff and Doreen make their way back to the wedding party and felt an odd elation; it was exciting seeing Jeff again. She never would have suspected she would care one way or the other.

Penny was still in shock. 'Aunt Paige, I can't get over you! You have a secret life!'

CHAPTER THREE

A secret life? Not really. For Paige it was more a mistake and a heartbreak that she'd wanted to put behind her. She'd been too young. Seventeen was not a suitable age for getting married. Paige looked across the table at her niece, who was busy eating her dinner in the relatively quiet restaurant, and realized with a mild sense of horror that it would be equal to Penny making that trip down the aisle in just two years!

No wonder everyone had begged us to think it over, to postpone the wedding until after college, she realized, getting the broader picture now. We were barely adults.

Looking back on it, Paige had only the vaguest memory of what all the rush had been about. To wait four years to marry Jeff Palmer had been out of the question back then; she wanted nothing else than to be with him night and day. And it wasn't just because she'd wanted to have sex. She'd been attracted to Jeff Palmer like a magnet, unable to withstand the powerful force of that attraction. When they came together there were always sparks – both the sparks of passion and of a collision. Paige and Jeff always seemed to crash into the wall of each other's stubborn streaks head on.

It wasn't until they'd actually tied the knot that it became clear the two were on entirely different paths, especially when it came to their careers. Paige had graduated high school a year early and had a full scholarship to a local teacher's college that she was to begin attending in the fall. Her family had limited resources and she saw a full scholarship as her only chance to get a good education without having to hold down a full time job at the same time. Jeff, however, came from a more affluent family. He had an uncle in New York City who owned a successful business firm and Jeff had been accepted at Columbia University. Jeff's family wanted him attending an Ivy League school at any cost, while working at his uncle's company as a sort of Junior Executive where there was a bright future in business awaiting him.

The full effect of these 'minor' conflicts had escaped the happy couple's awareness before the wedding, but the entire summer was engulfed in fights over whose future was more important. When fall came, Jeff Palmer was indeed in New York City attending Columbia and going home on weekends to be with Paige. She in turn had begun classes at the teacher's college. The stress of that arrangement tore the love right out of their marriage. Even though both of them looked forward to the weekends with eagerness and lust, the weekends would arrive and would never fail to be non-stop shouting matches. The only times the newlyweds weren't fighting was when they were in bed making heart-crackling love.

But sex wasn't enough to keep them together. After six months of that draining, demanding schedule, the marriage sputtered to a halt. Jeff was too overloaded with schoolwork to keep going home every weekend – only to argue. His studies were suffering. But Paige didn't take kindly to the constant pressure to quit school and move with Jeff to New York. Why weren't her career goals given the same importance as Jeff's? Just because he stood to earn more money than Paige, it shouldn't mean that she didn't deserve a shot at a fulfilling career.

That was the story of how a marriage can end. However, it overlooks why a marriage happens in the first place, all the fireworks, the legions of butterflies let loose in one's belly, the erotic swoon.

Paige had kept the memories of why she'd married Jeff in the first place, buried deep beneath her memories of why the marriage had failed. But seeing him that afternoon, fourteen years later, had ripped the lid right off those buried treasures and left her heart nearly gaping open.

Could it be possible that Jeff Palmer was even more handsome now than he'd been back then? Paige couldn't believe it. He'd matured into quite a work of art, the perfect specimen of masculinity.

It was the first time in months, since George's funeral, that the emotional burdens Paige carried inside her felt lighter; her thoughts were centered on something uplifting, something intriguing.

'Aunt Paige, you're not listening to me.'

'I'm sorry, Penny, did you say something?'

'Only that you look like you're a million miles away.'

'I guess I am, honey, I'm sorry. This must be very tedious for you.'

'Not one little bit. It's incredible. I wish I were you, I wish I'd been married to that man. I can't believe you left a man like that. What were you thinking of?'

'My sanity, I suppose. But it's not something I'd expect you to understand. When you look at Jeff, Penny, you're seeing the handsome, personable, and successful man.'

'Well, what the heck do you see?'

Paige laughed. 'To be honest, the same thing, but that's not what I meant. I meant that I was married to him, so I saw other sides to him, sides that were harder to live with.'

'Like what?'

'For one thing, we were opposites, we fought constantly. We argued all the time. I guess we were both stubborn; we wanted different things from life. Things that didn't have any common meeting point and we took it out on each other – our disappointment.'

Penny was clearly turning these comments over in her brain, trying to make sense of it, how marrying a man as handsome as Jeff Palmer could include any of these undesirable things, or how any of these undesirable things could carry more weight than being married to a man like Jeff Palmer.

'Besides, the marriage only lasted six months, honey. We were just kids, barely older than you are. My marriage to your Uncle George was a much more rewarding relationship and I'm sure Jeff has had more rewarding relationships in his adult life than his marriage to me could have been, I was only seventeen.'

Penny choked on this added revelation. 'You got married when you were only seventeen? Your parents *let* you?'

'It wasn't so much that they let me, it was more like they were trying to get out of the way of a steamroller. To put it mildly, I was determined.'

Paige stared down at her plate of half-eaten enchiladas and the glob of rice and refried beans congealing under cold, melted cheese. More memories flooded her, things she hadn't thought about in years. Penny was right. How was it possible that her parents had allowed her to get married at such a young age, paying for the wedding on top of it? Paige no longer thought of herself as that strong-willed, hardheaded person who had lived in her parents' house. She barely remembered that girl. The years with George had mellowed her; she'd become someone else, a woman in less of hurry to get to that all-important somewhere. First, there had been the rush to get out of high school as quickly as possible, then the rush to marry the boy of her dreams. Soon, the push toward college and a career trumped the rush to be married and it became her next all-consuming goal.

Then there was George and the urgency stopped, just like that. That alone had led her to believe that George had been her destiny.

But now here I am alone, and I'm only thirty-two. That can't be all there is to destiny...

'I just can't picture it, Aunt Paige, even though I'm really trying to. I can't see you as someone who could ever be demanding about anything. You're always so agreeable and, well, I don't know, quiet – like a little schoolteacher mouse, or something.'

'A little schoolteacher mouse? Wow.' Whatever vague excitement Paige had been feeling over the chance to get re-acquainted with Jeff suddenly plunged down to the depths of self-consciousness and self-doubt.

A schoolteacher mouse, and here he was, obviously a successful New York businessman.

Probably very successful, she thought.

And for all she knew, judging by the way the women had fawned over him at the wedding, he was one of the world's most eligible bachelor's. Jeff

Palmer had clearly matured into a man who was out of her league. Now the mere thought of having a simple conversation with him unnerved her. It was intimidating, all that success.

CHAPTER FOUR

I am a little mouse, Paige thought dismally, as she sat on the terrace the following morning and watched the ever-returning waves washing up to the shore. Down on the beach there was not a trace of the wedding from the night before remaining. Where's that girl I used to be, she wondered, the one who met Jeff Palmer head-on; who matched his iron will with a will of my own? How did I become so timid?

Had safety done it, the sameness of everyday life? The calm predictability that had come from years of having the same job in the same school, living in the same house, driving on the same roads everywhere she went? This trip to Mexico was the first enjoyable detour her life had taken in a long time. The detour of George's death – if it could be called something as trivial as a detour – was a high dive into the unpredictability and uncertainty of permanent change. It had been harrowing, but she'd handled it – and not timidly. Still she'd tried as hard as she could to get her life back into the sameness of her old routine as quickly as possible. She'd tried to squeeze her now-single life back into the safe boundaries of where she'd once lived so contentedly as a married woman. It had been an uneasy feeling, admitting to herself that those old outlines of the life she'd had with

George had become insufficient, that there was nothing but emptiness, no feeling of 'there' there. When school had started up again in the fall, she'd been unable to ignore it, that feeling of emptiness; the class of new and eager little six-year-olds before her no longer ignited her enthusiasm for teaching. Instead, they seemed to drain her of her mental energy. All these children who, year after year, took from her the basics of what they'd need for the rest of their lives and then went off merrily in search of that – of the *rest* of their lives. They weren't 'her' children, they were only her students, temporary boarders in her psychic space; new faces replaced the old, year after year. She and George had never had children of their own. She had vaguely thought she'd wanted at least one child, but she loved teaching, she loved her job, so they'd kept putting it off…

Paige heard the distinct sound of footsteps on the stone path leading to her villa's front door. The now familiar squeaking wheels of the house-keeping cart did not accompany the sound, so it wasn't the maid. Still in her robe and nightgown, clutching her cup of morning coffee, Paige went to the door to find out who it was, but somehow she knew it was going to be Jeff.

She had the door open before he could even knock. He stood on the stone step in front of her, looking a little startled. 'Wow, I wasn't sure you'd be awake yet, but you sure are!' He had that handsome, self-possessed smile on his face – the one that had bowled her over the day before. 'Were you guarding the door or something?'

'No,' she spluttered, feeling a little embarrassed, a little transparent. 'It's just that it's so quiet up here. I heard you coming up the walk.'

'How did you know it was me?'

'I didn't, really, I just guessed.'

That affable smile lingered on his face, keeping her off balance as he took in the early morning sight of her; her hair a little mussed, her feet bare; how sensible she looked in that simple cotton robe.

'I was heading down for breakfast and I thought I'd see if you two wanted to join me.' The smile persisted until Paige couldn't help herself and she smiled back.

'Well, how nice of you to think of us, but I'm afraid Penny's still sleeping. Isn't your friend up yet?'

'Who? Oh, you mean, Doreen? I have no idea. She has her own villa, down the hill a ways. We're not here together, we just know each other. We both work with the groom back in New York. Well, they both work for me, would be more accurate.'

Paige didn't doubt it. It fit in with her somewhat inflated idea that Jeff Palmer owned the world.

'It was very thoughtful of you. I wish I could but I need to wait until Penny's awake.' She hesitated. 'Do you want to come in and have a cup of coffee?'

Even in the tranquil quiet of the early morning, Jeff's exuberance seemed to infuse even his smallest comments. 'It sounds like fun, Paige! But, you know, I feel like I'm imposing. It's so early. I'll come by later instead, how's that sound? We can have a cocktail or something.'

'That sounds really great, Jeff.'

'Okay, then! I'll see you.' He gave a little wave, turned, and sauntered back down the path in the direction of the restaurant.

He walks like a man who has the world in the palm of his hand, she thought, like he doesn't have a care. Had he always walked like that? She couldn't remember.

Paige watched him until the path disappeared into a swell of jungle trees and tropical flowers and she couldn't see him anymore. Her heart was pounding.

Gosh, he's sexy, she thought. And then she looked quickly around herself to make sure she was alone, as if she'd said it out loud, a flush of nervous heat blossoming across her serious schoolteacher expression.

She glanced down at herself as she stood there in the open doorway, in the early morning sunshine. Her boring old robe! Why had she let him see her like this?

'Damn it,' she cursed herself quietly. She went back in and closed the door.

* * *

For the rest of the morning and most of the afternoon, Paige's thoughts kept returning to Jeff Palmer. Try as she did to keep the whole reunion in perspective, she was shocked to discover just how eager she was to see him again.

Penny wanted to play tennis in the morning and Paige accompanied her to the hotel's private court. She didn't play tennis herself. She only went to keep her eye on Penny – and find out if maybe Jeff Palmer had taken up the game in the years since they'd been married.

Apparently not for he was nowhere in sight.

At lunch, Penny wanted to go out into the surrounding town and try a different restaurant for a change. Paige decided it was too risky. 'What if we catch an amoeba, or something horrible like that? Tourists are always getting sick in Mexico.' It sounded like a reasonable excuse, but really Paige wanted to eat at the hotel's restaurant again in hopes that Jeff might be having his lunch at the very same time.

No luck there, either.

This is crazy, Paige told herself. I'm acting like I did back in high school, when every move I made was a calculated effort to run into Jeff Palmer. Besides, I already know that I'm seeing him later today. Why am I acting like this?

She wondered if maybe she wasn't more than a little curious to see who might be keeping him company.

'Am I jealous?' she said out loud.

'What?'

'Nothing, honey, I was just thinking.'

'Aunt Paige? Can I ask you something?'

'Sure, honey, what is it?'

'Do you like to ride horses?'

'Not especially, no. I think I rode maybe one horse in my entire life, and that was probably more than twenty years ago. Why? Do you like riding horses?'

'I love to! And there's a group of riders leaving from the hotel this afternoon. They go riding in the jungle! Can I go, Aunt Paige, please?'

'In the jungle? I don't think so. Who are these riders anyway?'

'It's a group from here at the hotel – the hotel sponsors it.'

Paige saw the earnest look on her niece's face. And Penny's dire tone wasn't lost on her, either. The kid is probably having a terrible time, she realized. I've been nothing but a schoolteacher this whole trip, even after I promised I wouldn't be. Paige relented. 'All right, Penny. I suppose it'll be okay. As long as there's someone responsible from the hotel overseeing the trip. And don't wander off alone, you hear me? You stick with everybody. I don't want to have to tell your parents that I lost you in the jungle somewhere.'

It was like night and day, the transformation in Penny's expression.

'And Penny,' she added. 'I'll be sure to check with the concierge about some other restaurants to try, okay?'

'That would be great! Maybe we could even go shopping.'

'I don't see why not.'

It wasn't until after lunch, when Penny joined the horse riding bunch gathering in the lobby, and Paige walked back to the villa alone, that Paige realized the timing was perfect. She would have plenty of privacy now. She could get herself ready for Jeff's visit.

In fact, I'll call him right now, she thought. I'll see if he can drop by while Penny's gone. That way I won't feel so conspicuous.

Paige was well aware that when it came to Jeff Palmer, Penny was still all eyes and all ears, every curious fifteen-year-old inch of her.

When she reached the villa, Paige went straight to the phone and dialed the front desk.

'I need to speak to Jeff Palmer, please. He's a guest here.'

But much to Paige's chagrin, Jeff was not in his villa and before she could protest, the front desk had him paged.

This is attracting too much attention to me. Now I feel like a fool.

'Jeff Palmer here! Who's this?'

Too late; it was Jeff's energetic voice on the other end of the line.

'Jeff, hi, it's me, Paige.'

'Paige is having me paged?' He found this very amusing.

'Sorry to bother you, Jeff. I didn't think they would page you. I was only trying to reach your room.'

'It's not a problem. I'm just hanging out with my friends at the pool.'

The pool again. Paige wondered why some people even bothered to spend a vacation at the beach. Then she pictured Jeff, every gorgeous inch of him, lounging by the pool with all his beautiful, rich girlfriends from New York. Why am I letting this intimidate me so much? She wondered. I am not just a little mouse.

'Paige honey, are you still there?'

Honey? Why would he call her that all of a sudden? 'Yes,' she stammered, 'I'm still here. Sorry. I was only calling to tell you that my niece has gone off horseback riding for a few hours, and I thought you might like to stop by sooner rather than later, but I don't want to disturb you.'

'Please, Paige, what are you talking about? You're not disturbing me. I'm just hanging around the pool with people I can see any other day of the year back home. I'd love to come up. Just give me a half hour or so. I'll go get dressed.'

When they'd hung up, Paige's heart soared through the ceiling. Have I really been this lonely? She wondered. Who would have thought I would ever feel like this again?

* * *

Unfortunately, Paige's vacation wardrobe left much to be desired. It had never occurred to her while she was packing back in Pennsylvania that she would wind up wanting to look seventeen again.

She had very little time to pull herself together; she didn't think she could do it. She thought of all those women at the pool, they probably had impeccably stylish wardrobes, even here on the Mexican Riviera. She flung herself down on the bed and stared up at the ceiling – or at the rustic underside of the thatched roof. 'Who am I trying to kid?' she blurted. Then she suddenly felt as if she was being unfaithful to George, too, and she felt even more foolish. 'My God, it's just drinks, Paige,' she tried coaxing herself. 'He's just stopping by to say hello, for old times sake. Why am I letting myself get so frazzled? It's just Jeff Palmer. The man I swore I never wanted to see again.'

But now here she was fourteen years later more than *ever* wanting to see him again. 'I'm just lonely, that's all. That's what this is. Jeff is more like an old friendly face now, a long lost high school romance. I'll only look stupid if I try to be something I'm not or try to make more of this than it is. I can't compete with those girls of his from the city.'

At last, she found her resolve. She went to the closet and picked out a perfectly casual sundress, a nice bright white one with colorful flowers all over it; something she'd worn a hundred times before and felt comfortable in, perfect for the middle of the afternoon. 'Good old Paige Allen – that's what this dress says,' she encouraged herself, hoping that it would somehow work in her favor.

* * *

True to his word, it was no more than thirty minutes and Jeff Palmer was once again at the front door of Paige's villa. She'd barely had time to feel liked she'd pulled herself together and suddenly he was there, knocking.

'Paige! Look at you, you look great.'

She had to stop herself from gushing, 'I do?' like an insecure school-girl, as if it were a thing she'd rarely heard said. 'Well, thanks,' she managed instead. 'As always, you're looking pretty great, too.'

It was more awkward now between them – alone like this – than it had been down on the beach the evening before. At least Paige felt awkward. She wasn't sure if it was all coming from her or not.

The mid afternoon sun was streaming into the Villa, bouncing off the colorful ceramic tiles and making the open airy rooms seem alive with their own vibrancy.

'That dress is really great on you, Paige. All those colors – they really make you look so, I don't know, healthy... happy? What's the right word? I'm not really sure how to say it. Is it okay to say you look happy? I feel so bad that you've lost your husband, even though I didn't know him. I can't keep from thinking about it, you know? You're too young to be going through something like that.'

'Well, I agree with you on that, Jeff.' Paige led him over to the sitting area. From there, the views out to the ocean and to the mountains in the distance were unimpeded by jungle growth. It was a vista that appeared to go on forever. 'George was a lot older than me – he was fifty-eight. But that's still awfully young to just go like that, so suddenly without any warning – he had a heart attack. It's sad, but there are still reasons for me to be happy. I've had time to get a little distance from the shock. What are you drinking today?'

'The usual.'

'Which is? My God, Jeff, do you realize that when we were married we were both too young to legally drink!'

'Were we *ever* really that young?'

'Can you believe my parents actually let me get married at that age? That's what I can't stop thinking about, how young I was and I thought I was so ready for life.'

The ice between them had broken. Jeff followed her over to the kitchen area where there was a fully stocked bar, and not just a mini bar. Grand Villas were set up to feel like home.

It turned out Jeff's 'usual' was a vodka and tonic, with lime but no ice. 'I'm not willing to risk it,' he said. 'This whole trip, I've been avoiding the ice along with the water.'

'Have you been to Mexico before?'

'Once or twice, but when I travel it's usually for business and I go to the Far East or Europe for that. I'm a bit of a workaholic, frankly. You're seeing me in a very unusual light. I am not usually relaxing anywhere.' He laughed at himself good-naturedly and followed Paige out to the chairs on the terrace. They sat down with their drinks. 'How about you?' he asked. 'Do you come to Mexico often?'

Paige shrugged. Here was her perfect opportunity to just be who she was and not pretend to be anything else. 'I never go *anywhere*, Jeff. I've just been a first grade schoolteacher who's spent holidays relaxing at home with my family. George and I weren't poor, or anything, we just didn't travel. We saved our money. And when we did feel like we wanted to a trip somewhere, we saved up for this particular vacation for a long time because we wanted to do it first class. I guess you always travel first class, huh?'

'Business class, mostly, which is kind of the same thing.'

Paige was drinking white wine. She studied her glass, feeling at a loss suddenly. 'We really ended up in two different worlds, didn't we, Jeff?'

'I don't know. I don't really know what your world is like.'

'Quiet, safe, always the same except for the occasional trauma… Do you ever make it home to visit your folks?'

'No, they moved. They live closer to me, now. Do you ever come into New York? You should come see me.'

'You know that I've never been big on the city, I was always that way.'

'But you never really tried it. You need to give it a chance.'

'I'm happy where I'm at, you know. It's quiet and it's home.'

'That's exactly what you were saying fourteen years ago, you know that?'

'Well, I guess it's just always been true.'

'Or easy.'

'Easy?' Paige was taken aback. 'What does that mean?'

'It's easier to say the same thing over and over than to find out for sure if it's how you actually feel.'

'Some people just aren't city people, Jeff.'

He conceded. 'True.'

Tension set in between them – if only the slightest hint of it. Still, Paige found the feeling undeniably familiar, the beginnings of a thin argument that could, if they put their minds to it, turn into an all-out war. It's what they'd always done best with each other in their younger days: disagree, and loudly.

Jeff was the first to break the mood. He chuckled, making light of it. 'There's something very familiar about this, isn't there?' he asked. 'Last night after I saw you, you were looking so sweet and so pretty, and here you are some young girl's aunt and everything, and a widow on top of that of all things, and I was trying to remember just why it was that we broke up. I only remember feeling happy with you, but now I'm starting to remember.'

Paige was touched. 'You remember feeling happy with me?'

'Of course, I do, Paige. You were the big love of my life.'

Paige didn't want to admit that up until yesterday, all she ever remembered was the fighting.

'Why exactly did we split up, anyway?'

'Jeff, you really don't remember? It was for this very reason – I didn't want to go to New York.'

'That's kind of ironic.' He got up from the chair and wandered over to the far end of the terrace where that view of the beach below was spectacular. He drank his vodka and tonic.

Paige watched him thoughtfully while she sipped her wine. He thinks I'm sweet and pretty, and I was the love of his life, she marveled. She would never have bet money on it, that he would have said something like that. She had trouble believing it was true. Yet he'd sounded genuine, this man who had the world on a string and could be in the company of any woman he wanted.

Why is it that I'm so reluctant to go to New York, even for a visit? She wondered. It's because of all those wild things I see on TV and in the movies. Or is it?

'So you're a schoolteacher,' he announced suddenly. 'Congratulations on that, by the way. I know it was important to you; your goal. Do you like teaching?'

He walked back over to where she sat but stopped at the table and studied her while she spoke, as if maybe trying to get a more complete picture of her.

'I do, I like it. Well, I've enjoyed it very much until recently. Since George died, I'm starting to feel as if I'm only going through the motions.'

'That's natural, don't you think? I'm sure it'll pass. You've been through a tough time.'

'Yes, probably you're right,' she agreed half-heartedly.

'You're not buying it?'

She smiled. 'I don't know, Jeff. Do you ever reach that point where you feel like you don't know anything at all and probably never did, even though you'd always felt so sure of yourself, of what you wanted?'

'Nah,' he kidded her. 'Everything's perfect in my world.'

'It's that New York City factor, I suppose. It makes everything perfect?'

'That's right, that's what it is. It's like a magic charm. That's why you should come check it out – get a little magic charm in your life.'

'Maybe I might.'

'Now *that's* resolve if I ever heard it – you want a little more wine?'

Without waiting for her response he went to get the bottle from her refrigerator. 'What are you doing about dinner?' he asked, refilling her glass.

'I hadn't thought that far. I guess I'll wait and see what Penny wants to do. She'll be back by then.'

'Ah, yes. Penny. Funny how quickly I'd forgotten about her.'

I wonder what that means, she asked herself. 'You're welcome to have dinner with us, if you want. Although you might not like being around kids, I don't know.'

'Kids are okay but Penny's hardly a kid anymore, is she? It might be nice. I'm so tired of that crew I'm here with – the same damn faces. And then after the New Year, we'll all be right back together at the office. Sometimes I feel like I see them twenty-four seven, that I don't have any other life outside of work. It was so great running into you last night, Paige. I wanted to ditch everybody and go off and have dinner with you.'

'You did?'

'I sure did. But that would have been a little rude – even for me.'

'Are you in the habit of being rude?'

'No, but I am their boss. I mean, I do pretty much whatever I want most of the time.'

Then Paige recalled Doreen, the muse-like woman who had been on his arm at the wedding, her gossamer evening dress, her stunning appearance. It was hard to imagine that the company of a woman like that could get tedious. 'I would have loved to have had dinner with you last night,' Paige confessed. 'I probably bored poor Penny to tears. I was thinking about you all evening, in fact, remembering everything, the good as well as the bad.'

Jeff looked at her and, for a moment, hesitated. 'Yes, there is that,' he finally said.

'What?'

'The bad… I tend to forget all about the bad and remember only the good about us.'

'You do?'

'Sure, why wouldn't I? So what if we were just kids? I still hold it up as the one relationship I'd *wanted* to be in, that I'd felt passionate about. Everything else kind of pales in comparison to those early days, when love was less calculated – for me, anyway. I don't know.' He sighed, sounding a little defeated. 'Maybe my memory plays tricks on me as I get older and more successful.'

Paige's curiosity was soaring now. She wasn't sure if it was the wine making her feel lightheaded or something else. 'What do you mean it plays tricks on you, in what way?'

'The usual way.' Jeff finished his drink and set the empty glass on the table. 'I don't want to insult you, Paige. I feel like, you know, you're a widow now and I should talk to you in a different way.'

'That's silly, Jeff. Just talk to me.'

'Okay, I'll say it. The sex with you was really great, Paige. Even though we split up, it wasn't because the sex had gone bad. And I think I hold it up as the high watermark of sex, you know? If we'd split because we were seeing other people or because the thrill was gone, or something like that, I bet it would be different today. But that's not how we ended, is it?'

Paige felt her face flush hot. It was a combination of the jungle heat, the wine, and her undeniable lust. A kind of lust she'd never, ever once felt with George. It felt scandalous to admit it even to herself, as if it would sully George's memory somehow. But there was no disputing it, when it came to the very embodiment of lust – of all-consuming lust – it was always her private memories of Jeff Palmer; that was how Paige defined great sex.

'I've often wished that I would run into you again,' he continued. 'But I admit, not for the most chivalrous reasons.'

Paige was now in a bit of a panic. As flattering as it was to hear, why was he bringing this up? Was he expecting her to trade confidences with him? She was unaccustomed to hearing this kind of talk from a man, least of all from a man she still found so attractive. If they started talking openly about things like this, about desire and lost love and secret yearnings, how could it lead to anything but sex? Was she ready for that? True, she'd taken this vacation to paradise to escape from her everyday world. But sex with Jeff Palmer, when she had her niece to worry about on top of everything else? It just couldn't happen. That was farther from her everyday world than she was prepared to go.

'I hope I didn't insult you, Paige. I think I'm making you uncomfortable.'

'It's okay, I mean, I'm not insulted. It's just that –'

'I know,' he stopped her. 'Timing is everything. I should keep these things to myself, they're too personal. We don't really know each other anymore and you've been going through a lot lately, I know. It's just that, well, I'm leaving tomorrow and I was afraid I might not see you again for another fourteen years. I didn't want to leave here without telling you that I still think about you sometimes and that I'd really love for you to come see me in New York. You're not that far away, you know.'

'I know.'

'Listen,' he said. 'Thanks for the cocktail, but I think I should take a rain check on that dinner. I don't want you to feel pressured by me or uncomfortable having me around. How about we make a date to have dinner together in New York, on me? Sometime soon, what do you say? Are you game for a trip to the city?'

'You know, Jeff, I think I am. I think I'd like that very much.' New sensations… maybe that would be her resolution for the upcoming New Year.

She walked him to the door and he kissed her lightly on the cheek before saying good-bye.

'Promise me you'll get in touch?'

'I promise.'

She was disappointed to see him leave so quickly, but in truth, it felt like a reprieve. It was suddenly clear to her that she had feelings for this man; highly flammable, explosive feelings that she didn't know quite how to handle. Buying herself some time to sift through all these sudden emotions was the safest way to go, and even though she was very willing to test the waters and try new things, safety was still good old Paige Allen's middle name.

CHAPTER FIVE

'The conversation with the flying plates,
I wish I were in love again...'

What better way to herald the birth of spring, Paige told herself, than to pack a bag and go to New York at last?

It had been three month's since Christmas, and her idyllic vacation on the Mexican Riviera seemed like a lifetime ago. Now her spring break from teaching was finally within the realm of possibility; it wasn't too far off on the calendar, just a few weeks away.

I could finally see New York, she told herself. And then maybe look up Jeff...

For now, it was the only way she could approach it psychologically, as if going to New York could possibly mean more to her than a chance to see Jeff again, to have that dinner together that they'd both promised each other. In truth, she would have gone to Timbuktu, if that's where Jeff and the dinner invitation were waiting.

For the first few weeks in January, Jeff Palmer had been the talk of the

Allen family. What, with Penny being unable to keep herself from gushing the news of Paige's prior marriage to a very handsome, wealthy businessman that they'd met at Villa Corazon. She'd told everyone who would listen from the moment they got off the plane. And to Paige's dismay, but not to her surprise, everyone was listening.

The Allen clan reacted to the news as if Paige had somehow been unfaithful to George throughout their entire marriage by having been married once before. But Paige knew better. George had been well aware of her brief, tempestuous marriage to Jeff Palmer long before Paige and George had tied the knot.

Besides, she reminded herself now, her past wasn't anybody else's business anymore. She was single again. She didn't have to answer to anybody.

In the safety of her comfortable, familiar kitchen, Paige picked up the phone and dialed information in New York. Within moments, she had Jeff's home phone number. But then she discovered that having the number and dialing it required two very different types of resolve. If it were anyone else on earth besides Jeff Palmer, Paige could convince herself that a casual dinner between old friends was all she was after. With Jeff though, deep inside herself Paige knew she wanted to share much more than a dinner with him. She wanted to have sex with him again. To the point that she had steadily begun fixating on it ever since she'd come back from Mexico.

She looked at the kitchen clock. It was only four in the afternoon. If she hurried, she could call him before he got home from work and with any luck, get his voice mail and then it would be up to him to call her back.

For some reason, it made her feel more secure this way, like taking the initiative in baby steps. She dialed Jeff's number and did indeed get his voice mail.

'Jeff, it's Paige,' she chirped cheerily. 'I was thinking of taking my spring break in New York and I was wondering if you'd be in town. Give me a call, okay?' And then she left her number.

'There,' she said with a profound sense of relief. 'It's done.' And to fortify that sense of relief, she poured herself a modest, pre-dinner cocktail.

This dating nonsense is exhausting, she thought. Between her marriages to Jeff and George, Paige had done very little in the way of dating or mating. Asserting herself was not second nature to her – especially when it came to the highly attractive and equally opposite sex.

*   *   *

The phone startled Paige from a sound sleep. Confused, at first she thought it must be the middle of the night – but then why was her bedside lamp still on and the TV blaring?

I must have fallen asleep while watching television.

The phone rang again. Paige found the remote and clicked off the TV. 'Hello?' she answered sleepily.

'Paige! Don't tell me I woke you! It's not even nine o'clock!'

Her stomach jumped. Here it was, she recognized that enthusiastic voice. 'Hi, Jeff,' she said brightly, trying to sound composed, alert, and most of all, not sleeping. 'You got my message.'

'Yes, I did, just now. I just got in. So you're finally going to do it, you're coming to Sin City?'

'I thought Sin City was Vegas?'

'Yeah, well, we run a close second. So you're really coming? And we're having that dinner together, right?'

He remembered. This was both exciting and unnerving. Now she couldn't be quite so cavalier about why she was going to New York, without making a fool of herself, that is. 'Well, I did promise you. So, how are things?'

'Things are great! But I'll tell you what. Can we make a date to speak on the phone tomorrow night? Will you be around? I'm actually still working over here, technically, anyway. I've got company and we're getting ready to have some espressos and a little gelato and all that end of the night stuff.'

'Sounds tiring,' Paige said. If it sounded so *tiring*, she wondered, than why did she feel so left out? 'I mean, it's late to still be working, isn't it?'

'Ah, this is nothing. Some nights I'm still at it past midnight.'

Still at what, exactly? She thought.

'So will you be around tomorrow night? Can I call you back?'

'Sure, Jeff. I'll be here. I'm always here,' she added, as if she had an uncontrollable need to make her life sound boring.

'It'll be great to catch up,' he said. And they made plans to speak the following evening.

After hanging up, Paige felt angry. At Jeff, for having his own life, and at herself, for letting her stomach do somersaults over a man who did, indeed, have his own life.

Even though it was only nine o'clock, Paige turned off her bedside light and tried to fall back to sleep. But all she could do was lay there and stare up at the ceiling, remembering that woman Doreen and the other women from his office. How many of them were with Jeff right now, making themselves at home in his apartment, partaking in the espressos, the gelatos, and all that end of the night stuff?

*   *   *

The phone woke her from another sound sleep and this time it was the middle of the night. 'Hello?' she said, dazed from the remnants of a vague and complicated dream.

'Paige? Ah, shit, I knew I would probably wake you again. But I'm finally alone here and I thought I'd take a stab at calling you back.'

'Jeff?'

'Yes. It's me, Jeff.'

'What time is it?'

'About one a.m. Should I hang up and let you get back to sleep?'

'No, don't hang up.' She hoped she wasn't sounding too eager. 'I'm awake now, sort of.'

'So you're coming to New York? When?'

'In about three weeks.'

'You want to stay here at my place? I've got plenty of room, you know – practically a whole guest wing. It would save you a bundle and I'm in a great part of town. I have a loft in Tribeca.'

'I'm not really sure what that means. I don't really know New York. Are you sure you want to put me up? Isn't that a bit of an inconvenience?'

'None, at all. Paige, I would love to have you here. It'll be like old times. Well, I'm not sure what I meant by that. I guess we fought a lot in the 'old times.' And what's there to fight about now, right?'

'Right.' She suddenly felt foolish about the jealousy, how it had overwhelmed her when they'd spoken earlier. God, what was the matter with her? Why had she over-reacted? 'If you're sure it's all right with you, then I'd love to stay at your place. I'll only be there two or three nights, or, days, I mean.'

'Two or three, is that all? Well, you know you can extend that if you wind up feeling like it.'

'I wouldn't want to overstay my welcome, especially after all these years.'

'Well, you never know what's going to come up, right, Paige?'

She wasn't sure how to answer that. The tone in his voice had shifted dramatically. It sounded more intimate – or maybe it was just her heart playing tricks on her. After all, she was in bed alone, in the dark, his voice was the focal point now of all her senses.

'Paige? Are you still there?'

'I'm here,' she replied quietly.

'I thought I'd lost you.'

'No not at all.'

'So we'll leave it open then?'

'Leave what open?'

'How many days and nights you want to stay with me. We can leave that open, right? Once we see how it goes?'

His words were laced with innuendo. Paige was sure of it. 'Okay,' she ventured cautiously. 'We'll leave that open – the days and, well, the nights. We'll see how it goes.'

'Uh-huh.'

For a moment, there was silence on the line. Paige's heart was pounding. It had literally been years since the last time she'd felt like this – so much on the verge of giving herself away. She'd nearly forgotten the erotic delight of it, revealing her cards to her opponent and finding she held a winning hand.

'Well, I'd better let you get back to sleep now.'

'Are you sure?' Even Paige heard the fine edge of panic in her voice.

'Why? Did you want to talk about something?'

'Well… I don't know.'

'What's on your mind, Paige? You can tell me.'

God, his voice sounded great in the dark, warm and masculine and in control; he was a hundred miles away and yet the nearness of his voice seeped into her inner ear and then slid clear down to her clitoris and the vibrations of his words lodged themselves there, nudging her. Had his voice always had this effect on her clitoris? For the life of her, she couldn't remember.

'If you won't tell me,' he continued, 'should I hazard a guess? Does it have something to do with what we were almost talking about that afternoon on your terrace at Villa Corazon? The cocktails, remember?'

'Yes, I remember,' she said.

'You know, I've given it a lot of thought since then, what I said to you that day. And I asked myself was it really true, is it still like that? How exactly do I feel about Paige Thompson – or, Allen, excuse me. And you know what the voice keeps saying?'

She was almost afraid to ask. 'No, what is it saying?'

'The voice keeps saying that, more than anything, I want to make love to you again. Can you imagine it, Paige? You're so… grown up now.'

'We both are.'

'That's right. We both are.'

The silence that ensued seemed to indicate they were both imagining it now – sex as grown-ups. And the seventeen-year-old girl who was still inside of Paige somewhere was breathless, she was that overcome by her own arousal.

'I guess what I'm saying,' he continued quietly, 'is that, well, I was wondering how you felt about that, you know? How does the very grown-up Paige Allen feel about having sex with me again, after all these years of not being married to each other? I have to say that I've been thinking about it constantly since I ran into you at Christmas.'

'You have?'

'I have.'

'Oh, God…' Her already breathless voice disappeared into a helpless groan.

'And when I got your message today, saying that you were finally coming to town, that you were finally going to do it after all these years. Well, it seemed like a sign to me and I felt I just needed to say it, to tell you what's been on my mind. That's why I couldn't wait until tomorrow to call you back.'

'I see,' she said, because she couldn't figure out how to say what she was really thinking. She wasn't sure how to get the words out without exposing herself completely, her lust and all its flaws. She knew he was a more experienced lover than she was and it worried her. Maybe his expectations of her were too high. She'd had only a handful of lovers since they'd separated and then so many years with only George. What if in real life she couldn't compare to the Paige he'd built up in his head? Then where would they be if even their memories became tainted?

'Is that a good 'I see' or a bad 'I see?''

She stumbled on her reply. 'I think it means I feel the same.'

'Well, that's a safe answer, isn't Paige? But I'll accept it. I'm not going to get choosey or anything!' And then his good-natured laughter broke the erotic spell. 'I'm really glad you're coming. I'll be looking forward to it.'

Before she knew it, he had wound down the conversation and they had said goodnight and hung up. She was once again lying alone in the dark, staring up at the ceiling and brooding – only this time her aching clitoris was in need of immediate attention.

If he was the one doing all the confessing, she wondered, why do I feel so exposed?

*   *   *

The days that followed did nothing to relieve the constant torment throbbing in Paige's clitoris. She couldn't leave herself alone – which contrary to what she'd hoped, only made her feel more aroused. In the morning before she got out of bed, she thought about Jeff and touched herself, probed herself, plunged into the swollen ecstasy of her orgasms. She showered; she tried to come down to earth. Still, she went to work in a swoon, finding it hard to concentrate on her students, the tasks at hand, her fellow teachers. It was worse than when she'd been sixteen and had met Jeff Palmer in the first place.

In the early evenings after school, she came in the back door and hurried up to the bedroom. Sometimes she didn't make it that far. She'd drop everything, yank the drapes closed and toss herself down on the couch in the living room. Her fingers were barely inside her panties when the orgasm would rip through her.

How could this be happening to her after all these years? She wondered if Jeff might be going through the same thing. Late at night, she toyed with the idea of calling him to find out, but she always lost her nerve. Soon enough she'd know the answer, she told herself. Soon enough she could ask him anything and he'd be right there next to her, on top of her, under her, inside her – devouring her. There'd be plenty of time to learn his answer then.

CHAPTER SIX

S he was too timid to drive. It was bad enough she was finally facing the wilds of New York, her nerves couldn't take the added stress of trying to maneuver through Manhattan's infamous crazy traffic jams. At the last minute, she decided to take the bus in and Jeff would meet her at the Port Authority.

'Now don't talk to any strangers and if for some reason your bus is early, just wait there for me at the gate.'

It sounded as if Jeff were giving instructions to someone as young and vulnerable as Penny. 'Jeff, I'm thirty-two years old. I think I can handle a bus ride by myself.'

'All right, all right,' he said, backing off. But it was a mute issue because he was at the bus station waiting for her long before her bus arrived.

'Hello, Paige,' he said, startling her. He was practically on top of her, reaching for her baggage when she came through the door.

'Jeff, hi!'

'You look like you've weathered the trip so far. Come on let's get up to the street. I have a car waiting.'

She followed him through the mad crush of the Port Authority, up the escalator to the street, barely cognizant of the fact that this was Jeff – this was the man she'd been obsessed with for three months. He was here, in the flesh now.

The trip to Jeff's loft was a jolting, stop and go terror ride downtown, the driver cursing loudly at every intersection and jarring Paige's equilibrium. When they finally reached Jeff's building, she was more than ready for a cocktail – anything to sooth her jangled nerves.

'So this is a loft,' she declared when they got inside. She'd never been in one before. It was a cavernous place, with towering ceilings and enormous windows. One room seemed to flow into the next, in a way that made her feel lost, or in some kind of maze. The place had an industrial feel, it was sleek and contemporary, with unusual furnishings that seemed to Paige to be very expensive. 'And you live in this huge space all by yourself?'

'Yes, I do,' he said, showing her to the bar area at the far end of the living room. 'Now what can I fix you?'

'Whatever you're having, Jeff, I'm game to try everything new while I'm here.'

'I'm feeling encouraged. Should I be?'

She watched him mix the cocktails and didn't answer.

He studied her from the corner of his eye. 'Are you glad you came?'

'Yes,' she said. 'Very. I've really been looking forward to this, to seeing you again, to visiting New York, finally.'

He handed her a drink. 'Try this,' he said. It was bright blue and icy with a maraschino cherry sinking seductively to its depths. 'It packs a wallop if you're not careful, so go slow.'

She took a tentative sip. It was potent and unusual but it tasted good.

'Well, here we are, Paige, to us.'

'To us.'

She took another sip in honor of his toast and then he pulled her close to him and kissed her on the mouth. 'It tastes even better on you,' he said.

Paige smiled self-consciously, thinking that it sounded like a line. But she didn't really care. It was good to finally be kissed.

He held her close to him, barely giving her room enough to hold her glass. 'Who needs all this space now?' he said quietly. 'I feel like I can't get you close enough.'

Having him this near to her again after such a long time made her feel at a loss for words. Her head was reeling, and it couldn't possibly be from the cocktail, not yet. It was the anticipation – three months' worth – now finally coming to a head. It was years of keeping her lust at bay feeling that life was safer when love was quieter. Now it was coming back to her with a vengeance, what passion could feel like when it was given free rein. Lust was surging through her, bursting the dam, as if trying to surmount her, the prudish gatekeeper all these years, the little schoolteacher mouse responding to Jeff's kiss, to the closeness of him, with a true unbridled will of her own.

George Allen could not have been further from her mind. Not that she had any complaints, she'd been happy in her cozy marriage to him, but now she was ready to leave the nest, to really fly, maybe for the first time, ever.

'Am I crowding you?' he asked, searching the unusual expression on her face.

'No,' she said. 'But I'm feeling a little encumbered by this cocktail glass.'

'Point taken,' he replied, taking both their glasses and setting them on the bar.

Her arms were around him then in a mere heartbeat. Her lips on his, their mouths opening, their ravenous tongues pushing in. It was not at all like old times. The force of their bodies mashing together was much more intense, like nothing Paige could remember experiencing. She couldn't kiss him deep enough, hold him close enough. When she felt the hard mound of his erection pushing against her through his trousers, she felt delirious.

I know what I'm doing, she told herself gleefully. I remember how to do this.

Jeff was urging her backward, toward the couch, practically tumbling her over. She sank deep into the soft sofa cushions and before she knew it, his hands were up under her skirt, yanking down her panties. Down to her ankles they fell and then he tugged them all the way off.

This is happening fast, she thought.

He was on his knees in front of her, shoving her skirt up out of the way. The lacy tops of her white stockings hugged her pale thighs but everything else down there was naked, exposed. He pushed her thighs apart, held them open. 'I just want to look,' he said. 'I just need to see if my fantasies all these years came even close to capturing how incredible it always looked between your legs, Paige.'

She gasped when her vulva, with the lips swelling and her hole already slick, was spread wide before him, nothing shielding her obvious arousal from his ravenous gaze. This was truly being on display and Paige relished the full, aching thrill of it. She spread her thighs wider.

'Oh, God,' he groaned, and slid one finger up her. 'You're already soaking wet, you know that?'

She nodded her head, savoring the sudden intrusion up her swollen hole. She couldn't speak, too much of her concentration was glued to Jeff, to what he might do next. She wanted to experience all of it, whatever his body fancied from her, and she wanted to experience it now.

She hiked her thighs up higher, giving him better access to her hole. She watched his finger move into her deep and pull out slick and glistening. He slid in two fingers then, and the increased pressure opened her up, her swollen hole accepted them eagerly.' Oh, God,' she murmured softly, earnestly, feeling the steady, pushing, probing motion of his fingers beginning to fuck her. Her eyes drank in the site of her body's squirming pleasure. Penetration is a gorgeous thing to watch, she thought hypnotically.

Her clitoris was thick and stiff and needing attention. It was like he read her mind then. In a moment, his mouth was on her clit, his tongue sliding wet and warm over the tender aching hood. She whimpered; low moaning cries issuing from her as his tongue tormented her and his fingers probed her, pushed her, shoved her ever closer to ecstasy. 'God…' she was chanting, unable to believe that this tidal wave of passion had swelled up and overtook her so quickly. She as going to come, she knew it. She could feel the delirious pressure of it cresting in the tip of her clitoris. His tongue urged her on, in rhythm to her cries, and his steady fingers worked into her very deep now, finding that spot in her, that trigger, that switch. He rubbed her hard in there and that was it; she reached the peak, the very top. The orgasm crashed through her as if it had been held at bay an entire lifetime. She jerked and squirmed and spasmed and opened her legs completely to the force of his fingers.

'Oh, my God,' she sputtered, when the urgency subsided, every muscle in her body collapsing into a sudden dead weight.

Jeff smiled up at her, proud of his achievement. 'And you've only been here twenty minutes,' he said. 'I told you those cocktails packed a wallop!'

* * *

Less than an hour later, they were in his master bedroom, going at it again full-throttle, as it were, naked, their clothes strewn all over the floor. It was clear that the thick veil of heady lust had fallen equally over both of them and they couldn't get enough of each other. At last the thing Paige had most desired, the thing that pushed her to near insatiability in her fantasies, was happening for real. Jeff was mounting her, taking her from behind. Her soft, full ass was raised to him, her thighs spread, her knees planted firmly on the bed, ready to take the full measure of his weight, his cock, his pleasure.

She clutched the pillows and cried out, remembering now just how intrusive it had always been to get fucked by Jeff Palmer – but in the best possible way. His cock was huge.

He held tight to her hips, guiding himself into her, finding his rhythm quickly and pushing into her deep.

His grunting, groaning, urgent noises excited her even more. She spread herself wider, opened her hole more for him, pushing herself back against him, riding his relentless cock.

They were like some carnal, living poetry; their cadences of lust, and then more lust on top of lust, were a perfect match. Funny, that they had found each other so early in life, only to be so quickly repelled and now drawn back again. Was it love, lust, or a combination of both under the guise of destiny? Who could say? The thrill of their bodies coupling overwhelmed each of them; rational thought had been discarded somewhere in the other room. They were 'fucking machines' now, moving on to the missionary position, a favorite of lovers everywhere, the full frontal assault of their delirium clutching each to the other. Her legs were hiked up over his shoulders and his cock had an easy unhindered passage into the very depths of her slick, swollen hole.

'Oh, oh, oh!' Her cries came out of her in quick, stabbing sounds, matching his repeated plunges, over and over, clear to her cervix. She clung to his neck, panting, breathless, too enchanted by her own ecstasy to think straight. Her thoughts tumbled around her brain in a chaotic, disjointed train. This is nothing like sex with George had been, her mind was chanting. This is actually sex. This is the real deal, the way my body should always feel. This feels so good.

'This feels so good,' she heard herself saying out loud. And right then, Jeff's rhythm increased, the intensity went up a notch. He was coming, she was certain of it. His body tightened, he cried out, he shoved himself deep into her and his body seemed suspended, if only for the merest of moments. And then he collapsed, his dead weight falling on top of her.

'Wow,' he said, grinning, breathing hard. 'I think I needed that!'

She couldn't have said it better.

* * *

Paige swiveled lightly back and forth on a tall stool at Jeff's breakfast bar and watched him prepare dinner. He was a man who knew his way around a kitchen, she realized. Not the same man he'd been back when they were married, that's for sure.

She had no idea what he was preparing. It was some kind of Asian dish – Thai food. It required a mound of rice, several kinds of shellfish, and a myriad of vegetables that Paige had never seen in any supermarket in Pennsylvania.

'I'm going to go easy on you,' he kidded her. 'I'll tone down the heat. Thai food, for the uninitiated, can be unbearably hot.'

'I don't want to stay uninitiated,' she said. 'Not in anything. I'm ready to try it all.'

'I'm not exactly sure what you mean by that, honey, but you make it sound irresistible. Anything you want to try while you're here, I'm happy to be the initiator. In fact, it doesn't have to be only while you're here. There are plenty of other places all over the world for the 'uninitiated' to start exploring.'

'You've been all over, haven't you, Jeff? It's kind of intimidating.'

'Why? Look on it as having a private guide, or something – a talking tour book.'

'But I earn a teacher's salary, don't forget. It took me a very long time, not to mention a two income household, to even afford that trip to Mexico.'

'But I've got plenty of money, Paige. If you want to travel, let's travel.'

'I feel more comfortable paying my own way.'

'Paige, it's just money.'

'It's easy for you to say, it's your money. You might not feel that way if I were the one with all the money.'

'All right – whoa. Let's just talk about it some other time, okay?'

'Okay,' she relented. And then she smiled.

'What? What's the grin for?'

'We'll never change, will we?'

He came over to her and kissed her forehead, then looked her in the eye. 'I disagree. We've already changed in all kinds of ways. And who knows, maybe one day you'll surprise yourself and finally start seeing things *my* way. You'll see I was right all along and we won't have anymore of this bickering.'

She wanted to shoot back a clever reply, even though she knew he was teasing her. But the truth was that so far, he'd been right about an awful lot of things. Still, it had been important to Paige to follow her own path and tackle her own goals, her own dreams, the way she had. Their marriage might have lasted a little longer, had she followed Jeff to New York fourteen years ago, but she knew it would have ended eventually. She simply wasn't the kind of person who could ignore her own drives or instincts.

Maybe it wasn't so exciting anymore, but overall, teaching had been very rewarding for her. And her marriage to George had suited her to a tee while it had lasted.

'Life's funny, isn't it, Jeff?'

'Yes indeed.'

'I mean, for so long, my home, my little nest was so important to me. Now, here I am feeling like I want to spread my wings a little and here you are, ready to fly. You practically have a license to fly, compared to me, that is.'

'Oh the places we'll go and the things we'll see, my dear…Now let me get back to the food. Timing is everything.'

It sure was, she realized. Timing was the crux of everything between heaven and earth; life and death, love and marriage, and even sex.

I love you, she wanted to say, more than ever before, I love you. But that would have to come later, she knew, when the timing was right.

HER GUY FRIDAY

Catherine Lundoff

T he worst part about moving to a new town, Susan thought, was that there would be no one to share this with later. It was one of those moments that she always loved to share with her friends or with Todd. She grimaced at the memory and went on watching the drama at the counter over the edge of her newspaper. The customer who was arguing with the barista seemed to be one of those perfect 'mocha latte with just seventeen sprinkles and a touch of skim milk' coffee drinkers. Susan rolled her eyes behind the shelter of the paper. I mean who cared if it was seventeen sprinkles or sixteen or none at all. She wrinkled her nose at the thought.

Obviously this woman cared deeply, and she was going to bring everything around her to a screeching halt until she got that perfect coffee. The kid behind the counter looked frantic and the next few customers were checking their watches and fidgeting. Finally, the guy behind the woman ended the big drama. He leaned forward in the middle of the sprinkle debate and said in a voice that resonated everywhere in the shop, 'Why don't I just pay for this... no, really my treat. Go ahead and finish that up and when you're done, I'll take a regular with cream, to go. Thanks.' He flashed a bewitching smile at both the barista and the Sprinkles Woman. Susan bit back a giggle as they swooned.

And he was well worth swooning over she decided when she put her paper down for a better look. He was tall, broad shouldered and muscular, with sandy hair starting to go a little gray at the temples. He had nice bones, she decided, and looked to be in his late thirties, maybe ten years older than her, maybe less. It was hard to tell, given the rest of his looks: high cheekbones, square jaw and striking light-blue eyes. But it was his smile that put his looks into perspective, she thought. It was mischievous and open, everything the smile on a guy who looked like that should be.

Susan decided she didn't trust him at all. A guy with a grin like that was too used to getting what he wanted. It reminded her of Todd's grin. A smile that reminded her of Todd had to be nothing but trouble. That, of course, was the moment when he looked around and saw her watching him. He didn't smile exactly but a corner of his lip turned up and he arched an eyebrow just a little bit. Then he looked away, stuck a lid on his coffee and strolled out, the eyes of every woman in the place fixed on his broad back.

Great, now Mr. Ego had seen her gawking at him and was headed down the block filled with the imaginary praise of her stare, along with everyone else's. It was hard to decide if she was annoyed or amused but after a glance at her watch, she decided that she was likely to be late and that trumped either emotion.

She grabbed her things and headed out the door, coffee in hand; couldn't be late to the new job. She'd only been hired as a project manager at Byte Technologies a month ago so she still needed to wow them with her promptness. Or so she thought until she got there. When she stepped off the crowded elevator, she remembered why they hired her. The receptionist smiled politely, but Susan soon found that she was only a small island of calm amid an ocean of chaos.

Apparently the main server had gone down and their most important client had stopped by for a surprise visit right after the crash. No one seemed to know why the server had crashed and, of course, no one really understood the back up system. She'd have to get this turned around soon, Susan decided or she'd go as nuts as everyone else seemed to be. She stopped by her desk to drop off her stuff and check her email. She was still getting caught up when Sanjeev stopped by. 'Hi, Susan,' he said, 'big panic upstairs today. We're meeting in Room 810 in five minutes. Tom decided that you're facilitating. See you there.'

He smiled sympathetically as she groaned and said, 'Okay. I'll be right there.' She grabbed her PDA and coffee and rushed out of her cubicle only to collide with a broad chest in a gray suit. A strong hand caught her shoulder but it was too late. She looked up into Mr. Ego's light blue eyes and felt an electric shock go through her. In a distant part of her mind, she could feel something warm splash down the front of her, but it was like it was happening to someone else. The suddenness of the sensation made her gasp. Then she noticed that those eyes were looking down at her coffee stained skirt in dismay.

'Damn!' he said. 'I'm really sorry! I didn't see you coming. Are you okay? Did you get burned?'

Why yes. But not the way you mean it Susan thought, fighting the urge to smooth her hair. It was going to be one of those days. 'No, I'm okay. But it's a good thing this skirt is black.' She made herself step back into the cubicle to grab some tissues to wipe off the coffee. He made her feel even more self-conscious just standing there watching her, and it sent a slow pink blush over her cheeks.

'I'm Mark, by the way. I don't think we've met. I'm new in Marketing. Look, is there anything I can do? Pay for your dry cleaning? Buy you a new coffee?'

'No, no, it's fine really. It's partially my fault too. I'm just in a hurry to get to my 9:00.'

'Oh yeah, I heard about the server crisis. I'm headed there myself since my department will have to deal with some of the fallout. Susan, right?' he said, looking at her nameplate, 'the new project manager? I'm guessing that you'll be working through lunch but I would really like to make this up to you. Let me take you out for dinner after work.'

'Oh that's okay, really. You don't have to do that.' She finally looked up to meet his eyes and found herself shivering. He was even hotter up close than across the coffee shop. *Stop it, girl. Get a grip. You can't just go panting after every pretty face. And body.* She decided she liked him a lot better when he looked contrite than when he was looking full of himself. But there was no way she was going to dinner with him, dimples and nice body or no dimples and nice body. She just wasn't ready to date and that was that, especially not someone from work.

He must have seen her decision in her face before she said anything because he launched into his sales pitch. 'Really, I just want to make this up to you. I need to make this up to you. It's only my first week here and

I'm a new contractor. I have to make a good impression.' He clasped his hands together in a mock begging expression and despite herself, she giggled. 'I promise you I'm the perfect gentleman. Do you need to get home right after to work to tend to any little Susan's or anyone else? No? Good. I'll leave you my cell phone number and you can call me when you're done. I'll be here working on the new campaign tonight anyway. See you in 810.'

He whipped a card out of his wallet and put it on the desk next to her, then disappeared before she had a chance to say anything more. She managed not stand there gaping after him, but only just. He was fast, she had to give him that. He'd taken all of two seconds to figure out that she didn't have children and that she probably wasn't married. She tried to remember if she'd seen a wedding ring on his finger but she wasn't sure. *This is just crazy.* But she didn't have time to think about that now. She glanced at her watch and started off to her meeting with seconds to spare.

The day didn't get any better. The first meeting was a zoo and she almost didn't notice Mark taking notes and watching her, almost. But there wasn't really much time to pay as much attention to him as she would have liked. He wasn't at any of her other morning meetings, which she thought was just as well. Her department got chewed out by their division vice-president at the second meeting of the morning. She had three more meetings scheduled for that afternoon, she realized with a groan as she inhaled her sandwich back at her desk. *Why, oh why didn't I marry a nice future neurosurgeon back in college? What was I thinking?*

She noticed Mark's card still sitting where he left it on the desk and picked it up to read it in between emails. 'Mark Harrington' it said in a nice tasteful font over his cell number and company name. *Harrington* she thought. *I wonder if he's any relation to the Harrington Investment Company Harrington's.* They were big in town – all over the Society pages and the Business section. Not that she paid much attention to the former; besides, it was a pretty common name. But he was wearing a really nice suit. Maybe she should go to dinner with him after all. She grinned and waded back into the chaos, forcibly putting Mark Harrington to the back of her mind until later.

It was harder than she thought. He had a way of creeping back into her imagination. Mostly he was still wearing his gray suit, but sometimes not. By mid afternoon, she surprised herself by imagining him without the jacket, shirt and tie. He'd be trim and muscular, with a nicely defined chest but not the kind of definition that said that he had too much time to spend in the gym. She never thought much of real hard bodies.

With very little effort, she imagined running her hand over his naked chest. It would be a bit furry, but not too furry, just a patch or two of masculine hair. It would be soft under her fingertips, and his lips… his lips… 'Susan, do you have anything more to add? We have to be able to talk about this new process at the meeting tomorrow morning and we need to demonstrate that we're on top of things.' *His lips would definitely not be saying that.*

She looked up to find that her boss, Tom, was standing anxiously by the white board waiting for her answer. *I've got to stop daydreaming* she told herself sternly. She said something sensible, or at least she hoped it sounded sensible in comparison to what she had really been thinking about. After that, the afternoon blurred into a series of meetings and phone calls. By 6:30, she was still at her desk doing damage control and the sound of a man's voice made her jump in her chair. 'Hey there, how's it going?'

She whipped around to find Mark leaning against her cubicle doorway. 'About as well as you'd expect,' she said, trying to sound nonchalant instead of exhausted. It wasn't working, but she didn't have time for flirting anyway. And he was flirting, she was sure of it. Or at least she hoped she was sure. It would be pretty tragic if she was too out of practice to tell.

The blue eyes twinkled and his lips quirked up in a smile. 'Any chance of being done by seven?'

'Done? I'm not sure I'll know what done looks like.' She smiled in spite of herself. 'But I think I might have given up by seven. Does that count?' Great, now she was flirting back, kind of. The butterflies in her stomach gave a brief turn around the floor and she could feel some sensations stirring just below them that she hadn't felt for awhile. *You don't have time for a crush* she told herself sternly.

He gave a slow, lazy smile, showing off dimples and nearly perfect teeth. 'Great. I'll be back in a half-hour and we can head out. See you then.' And he was gone again, just like that.

Damn it. What was he, bionic? She looked like crap, she was wiped out and there was coffee on her skirt. There was no way she was going out with this guy. He was probably married anyway.

In response, her imagination began obligingly replaying her fantasy of that afternoon. She'd been touching, then kissing his naked chest, exploring it with her tongue when he leaned down and kissed her. It was a slow kiss, one that promised great things. First the touch of his slightly moist lips, followed by the gradual parting of her lips with his tongue and the slow exploration of her mouth. It was done carefully and leisurely, his... arms closing around her, pulling her in to him, molding her body to his. She could almost feel his...

'Hey, Susan, good work today. I know it's been really rough but we're getting a handle on this and it'll just get better from now on. Have a good night.' Tom nearly bounced with his words, nervousness and uncertainty coming off him in waves. She dragged a cheerful smile up from somewhere and gave him a 'thumbs up'. Fortunately, it was all the response he needed before trotting off with a happy wave.

Why did she always get bosses like this? Why not a grumpy but competent one for a change? With a sigh, she fired off a couple of emails then sat back to raise her arms above her head in a long stretch. She could feel her elbows and shoulders loosen reluctantly with the effort. Maybe she'd take a nice hot bath when she got home.

'Looks like it's the end of the day,' Mark said from the doorway.

She gave him a sidelong glance as she lowered her arms. *Ah yes, the obstacle between me and a hot tub.* She couldn't help but notice that this time it didn't look like it was just her face he was checking out. Well fine, let him look. He wasn't getting any closer than that. 'I'm really beat,' she began but he stopped her with a shrug and a small grin.

'You've got to eat, right? Did you have any other plans for tonight?' He read her response on her face before she could say anything. 'Then let's get going, if you're ready.'

She hesitated a moment, torn between yielding and telling this guy off. But she was hungry, and there wasn't anything to eat at home. She turned back to the computer to log out. Besides, if she was afraid, what was she so afraid of? That he'd be a complete psycho? Or that he'd be like Todd? Of course, if she'd taken it slower with Todd, maybe she would have seen what he was all about. Or not, she reminded herself. Hindsight wasn't always twenty-twenty. She rubbed her eyes. *Aaargh! Smeared eyeliner!* 'I just need to run to the restroom,' she muttered as she made a hasty escape, purse in hand.

She managed not to run down the hall but it was a relief to get a door between them. *Okay, Susan, get a grip. Remember, 'whole new start in a new city'?* A part of that new start was standing by her cubicle, waiting for her. He might be a psycho, though he didn't read that way. But he definitely wasn't Todd and she wasn't in love with him. Besides, she and Todd had broken up over a year ago; she deserved some fun. She needed some fun. *Now if only I could remember what that looked like.*

She tugged her makeup out of her bag. A little gel, some lipstick and eyeliner and at least she wouldn't embarrass herself. She surveyed her face critically in the mirror and tousled her short brown hair a little to bring out the best in the new cut. Viewed in profile, she was curvy but not extremely so. *Especially not after I suck in my stomach.* Her full lips quirked up in a grin. On the down side, the lipstick was a new dark-red and she wasn't sure she liked it. Then there was the coffee stain on her skirt. She made a futile attempt to sponge it out before giving up. This could go on all night, enough already. She dragged her reluctant feet from the sanctuary of the ladies room. *Here goes.*

Almost to her surprise, he was still waiting for her. He took her coat from its hanger and held it open for her with a flourish. She couldn't help smiling; it was a nice touch. 'So I take it the perfect gentleman part has already kicked in?'

'You bet. I have hot coffee on a certain black skirt on my conscience, so much to atone for.' He looked rueful. 'So what brings you to our fair city?' He ushered her ahead of him into the elevator and she could feel the tingle of an electric attraction warm her belly. *No more blushing, no more blushing! This is not high school!* For a moment, she thought she'd blurted the thought out loud. But no, he was still waiting for a response.

'Not too many jobs back home right now. Plus this is a part of the country that I always wanted to check out. Are you from here?' She could feel her nerves launch her into chatter mode. But a wary glance at him suggested that he didn't mind. He smiled down at her as they got off the elevator and it felt like time stood still. The air practically glowed with sparks for several moments. Then the phone at the security desk rang and a taxi horn honked outside and the moment passed.

He still hadn't answered her question before they walked outside. 'Pick a place, any place.' His sweeping gesture took in several blocks of downtown clubs and restaurants, ranging from the Malaysian cuisine of the *Singapore* to the high-end steaks of *Reba and Sam's*.

'*Mickey D's?* No, seriously, I have no idea. I haven't checked out any of these places yet. You pick.'

They ended up at *Singapore*, sitting in a dark quiet booth surrounded by couples who were clearly on dates. 'Well, it's certainly soothing,' Susan commented, looking around at the silken wallpaper and dark furniture. And pricey, she noted when the silk-clad hostess dropped off the menus. There was a dazzling array of choices and she could feel her eyes widen as she read the descriptions. Twenty-five kinds of spices, eight types of curry, spicy and tangy, spicy and super hot. How was she supposed to tell what was 'super hot' and what was only 'tangy'?

'Want some help?' He leaned over at her nod, and began pointing out dishes that he had ordered before. The gesture brought him much closer to her side of the table, his knee brushing hers and the warm scent of his skin washing over her until her head spun. She fixed her eyes on the menu and managed, but only just, to not pull back. *Just act casual. Breathe. In. Out. Everything's fine.* The voice of her common sense clamored in her head until it drowned out most of what he was saying.

The waitress showed up just then and she found herself ordering the last dish she could remember him mentioning, 'And a glass of the house white.' She'd feel less goofy if she calmed down. She hoped. Mark drew back a bit as he ordered, the pressure of his knee withdrawing to leave an aching warmth that spread through her like a wave. She bit her lip in an effort to sit still, to hold in a gasp at the suddenness of the sensation. A quick glance showed him still watching her, eyes wary in shadowed uncertainty. The momentary silence threatened to grow awkward until he seemed to catch himself.

'So… to answer the question you asked earlier, yes, I am from around here. I just moved back after living on the Coast for a couple of years, west, not east.' He added to her unspoken question. His features managed to look businesslike rather than sensual in the dim light and she tried not to sigh with disappointment. Clearly, this wasn't a date and she needed to get all that wishful thinking under control.

'Were you doing marketing out there too?' She caught herself watching his hands on the table, noted the absence of a ring, and then forced her eyes up to meet his.

'More or less. I was involved in a start up, one of those dot.coms we've all heard so much about.' His lips twisted into an expression that was not quite a smile and he looked away. 'Things started out well then went belly up last year.'

She nodded sympathetically. 'It's been a fun couple of years. I got laid off a few months back myself.'

'I wasn't exactly laid off but it doesn't matter. If that's what brought you here, I'm guessing that it's Byte's gain and your former employer's loss, at least from what I saw of you this morning.' He tilted his glass toward her in a toast, and she blushed. The far away look and the near grimace vanished in a moment and he was the man from the coffee shop all over again. 'What do you do for fun?'

Pick up men at the office. Stop it, stop it. I do not. 'You mean in what passes for my free time? Oh the usual things-read, go dancing, swimming, go to the movies.'

'Dancing? What kind of dancing do you do?'

'Just about any kind that's available, from ballroom to square. Mostly the older kinds, especially the kind where you get to dress-up Victorian Society balls, Jane Austen dances-that sort of thing. You seem surprised.' Susan smiled with the words, watching him study her before he replied. She remembered her reflection in the office bathroom – severe black skirt and plain green blouse, gold hoop earrings, short, practical hair – nothing that would advertise her fondness for the romance of whirling around a dance floor. *I wonder if he dances. Probably got two left feet. Anything more would be too much to hope for.*

'Well, I am a little. You don't seem like a romantic, not that it's a bad thing. Wearing your heart on your sleeve just gets it bruised.' There was that expression, the one he'd worn when he talked about his old job. It was cynical, speaking at once of pain and disappointment. She was startled to find that she longed to sooth it away with a kiss on the corner of those quirked lips, a stroke of the hair. Perhaps that would be enough.

Instead, she pulled back and weariness got the better of her. 'Divorced recently?' The moment the words were out of her mouth she wanted to call them back. But it was too late. His mask had locked firmly back in place.

'Something like that, but I don't want to burden you with it all. Tell me more about the dancing or swimming. Have you ever been sailing?' He sat back and looked polite and expectant as their dinner arrived. Susan drank her glass of wine and sampled some delightfully spiced seafood and vegetables while he plied her with questions. By the time they were ready to leave, she thought he knew far more about her than she did about him.

'Where are you parked? I'll walk you to your car.' Once again, he read her next words on her face before she said anything. 'Really, it's not all that safe in some of these ramps. I'd feel better if I knew you were okay.' Since she couldn't find a polite way to say no, she just nodded and they walked a block to her ramp in a companionable silence. His nearness was distracting: an accidental brush of the arm, the lightest of touches as he swung his arm forward sent shivers through her.

For a wild moment, she wished this had been a date, a real one. Then she'd have an excuse to invite him home for a nightcap, but it wasn't. Instead, the unfamiliar sensation made her chatter giddily. 'I'm just up here on the second floor. Thank you so much for doing this, and for the dinner. You really didn't have to.' They arrived at her car a moment later and stood awkwardly, neither speaking for a moment.

He wished her a good night, with none of the flirtatious quality that had shone through at the beginning of the evening. As he turned away, an impulse seized her and she caught his arm, turning him to face her. 'Look, I'm sorry about my comment earlier. I didn't mean to upset you.' She looked up at him, searching for the glow of shared attraction that she'd seen before.

His lips softened and he stepped closer to her, making her heart race. 'The only thing that distresses me is making a fool of myself. I hope I didn't do too much of that.' He smiled at her mute nod. 'Good. Look… I'd like to spend time with you again, maybe lunch or something if you're free.' His eyes sparkled again and she could see the laugh lines around them as the strained look melted away.

Susan nodded again, not trusting herself to say anything just then. He took her hand from his arm and raised it gently to his lips with a courtliness that made her lips part in a gasp. She nearly panted, trying to catch her breath, to recover her lost composure. 'Or perhaps I should do better than this,' he murmured, watching her response. He stepped closer, slipping one arm around her waist and tilting her face upward to meet his. 'Since I think I've gone too far to stop now.' He leaned down and kissed her.

Oh, my God. I can't believe I'm doing this. The voice of her common sense wailed in the back of her mind. She squelched it in a wave of pure desire. *Oh shut up and lecture me later.* She wrapped her arms around his neck and kissed him back. It was a kiss that melted her inside, as if a piece of ice she hadn't known was there welcomed the coming of the sun. His lips were sure and warm against hers and she could feel him harden against her thighs, just below the vast yawning ache that filled her. His chest was broad and muscular under her hands, his heart racing against her palms.

When they finally broke apart to catch their breath, she thought her knees would collapse under her. Instead, she forced words from her lips to give herself something else to concentrate on. 'Somehow, I wasn't expecting this. I'll have to let strange men spill coffee on me more often.' She smiled up at him, trying to feel less vulnerable.

'Oh I hope not. I think I'd like to keep the coffee-spilling role. You have the most beautiful eyes. I love the way they shift from green to gold and brown when the light hits them.' His fingers stroked her cheek as he spoke, their slightly rough texture making her tingle. He smiled down at her and leaned over to kiss her forehead. She closed her eyes and took a deep breath. He smelled of mint and the outdoors, a masculine scent that filled her lungs until she thought she never wanted to breathe any other air.

'Susan…' She opened her eyes again to find him looking troubled and withdrawn. 'I want this to continue. I mean I want to see you again but…' He paused as if he had no words to express what he wanted to say.

She pulled back, bracing herself for whatever would come next. 'I'm not sure I'm ready for a romantic relationship.' His blue eyes were steady on her face, blonde brows wrinkling in apology and something approaching dismay.

Susan stepped back out of his arms. 'Do I seem that desperate?'

'No! This is just me. I think you're someone I want to get to know better but I need to ease into it.' He reached out to catch her hands in his own. 'Can we do that?'

She didn't trust herself to speak over the tide of disappointed desire that filled her. *Who the hell did he think he was? First he kisses me like that, then it's 'I just want to be friends.'* She forced a shaky breath to fill her lungs and pulled her hands from his. But then again, she wasn't really desperate. She could take her time. *He isn't that special* she told herself fiercely. She made herself sound polite and understanding, forcing the disappointment down until she could scarcely feel it. 'I guess. We'll just have to see how it goes.'

He flashed a smile full of naked relief. 'I'm sorry I got carried away just now, but I meant it when I said that I want to get to know you better. Can I see you this weekend or maybe dinner next week? I don't want to have to spill coffee on you all the time.'

She waited a moment before responding. Was this all she wanted from him? But then what did she have to lose after all? At least he was a good kisser. 'Maybe next week; I have a lot of unpacking to do still.' The words didn't even catch in her throat as she schooled her face into careful nonchalance. *She was hip Susan Mathews, the gal who made out with guys from work in parking garages from time to time. No big. Yeah, right.* Well, there was no point in letting him see how confused she really felt. She stuck her keys in the lock of her car. 'I'll let you know. Thanks for the evening.'

He held the door open for her and shut it after her. Once she was inside, he gestured for her to roll the window down. He reached inside and stroked her cheek. 'I'm not playing around with you, you know. You just seem like you have enough messes to clean up during the day without adding me to them. I'll see you tomorrow.' He withdrew his hand and gave her that smile, dimples and all that she'd seen him give the coffee shop only that morning. He was still looking after her as she pulled out of the ramp.

And she was still aching a bit inside when she got home. But now it had lessened to a small but solid weight somewhere around her stomach. She sure could pick them. The thought made her smile ruefully as she got on the elevator. At this rate, she'd be picking guys who were allergic to commitment when she got to the old folk's home. *I know I've only got three months to live but I want to be friends first, terrific.*

She unlocked her door and shed her clothes until she was ready to stomp into the bathroom. After she dropped her skirt in the sink to soak, she studied herself in the mirror for several long minutes. Nope, nothing had changed since she had fixed her makeup at the office. Still the same short brown hair, the same hazel eyes, same straight nose. The dark red lipstick was pretty smudged, though. She wiped it off with a sigh of frustration and finished getting ready for bed.

Not that laying down to sleep did her any good. Mark Harrington hovered before her closed lids. She could still feel his arms around her and his fingers against her jaw, his lips against hers. She sat up cursing and reached into her nightstand for her vibrator. *Gonna wash that man right out of my hair.* The remembered song crossed her mind as she slipped off her panties and rubbed a finger against her already moist lips. *And I will.*

But that orgasm didn't do it. Neither did the next three days at work. She'd seen him across the office a few times but always just in time to duck out of sight behind a cubicle wall or into the supply room. Not that it mattered. Most of the time, it was as if he were sitting right next to her, his hands sliding up her stocking-clad thighs at meetings, his eyes undressing her as she stood at the white boards or next to the laptop changing slides. By lunch, he was galloping up on horseback in a torn shirt and sweeping her off her feet, just like a novel cover. She was so wet from thinking about him every day that she wore out one set of batteries and had to go out for more.

Not that it was the same, but it would have to do, she thought grimly. At least she'd found somewhere to go dancing that weekend. She'd go out and meet more people. Once she had a social life here, he'd be history. It was just that she was so new in town and phone calls and emails to friends back home weren't enough. That was why she agreed to go to happy hour on Friday with the gang from the office. She wasn't lonely, exactly, but it was an alternative to obsessing.

Or so she told herself Friday afternoon before she left the office. Now the bar boomed all around her with bad pop music and loud conversation, the glow of neon and occasional clouds of smoke. She nursed a gin and tonic and listened politely as Sanjeev regaled her end of the table with anecdotes about the project. The alcohol burned its way down her throat, relaxing her so she momentarily forgot about Mark. Forgot the empty seat next to her, too, at least until he slipped in beside her. 'Hi there, I thought you might be here.' He smiled down at her, dimples bewitching in the bar's glowing lights.

Susan managed not to gasp, but only just barely. His attention was drawn away momentarily by Tom and then one of his coworkers across the table. It gave her time to recover and she thanked her guardian angel when Tom began telling some long and pointless story. Maybe she could just get up like she was headed for the ladies room and duck out. No one else would notice if she ran for it, right?

'Overjoyed to see me, I take it.' His voice purred at her ear, resonating against her bones until she thought they'd split apart.

'I just didn't expect you to be here, that's all.' She dragged her gaze up from the table to meet his eyes.

His eyes twinkled a bit but he didn't say anything more for a few moments. Susan forced herself to laugh at a feeble joke or two from the other side of the table. She ordered a second drink, trying not to notice as Mark's knee brushed against hers under the table. He was too close, making her breath catch, and his light, seemingly accidental touches sent shocks through her until she chewed her lower lip in a futile effort to regain self-control. *Chill out. He's just a cute guy. Why are you acting like you've never seen one before? Friends, remember?* She reminded herself sternly. It helped a little.

'You had dinner yet?'

She hesitated before she looked up to meet his eyes. 'I just figured I'd eat dinner here, then head home.'

'Can I make you a better offer? At least my stories are funny.' He nodded at Tom who was holding forth about the joys of midsummer motor boating. 'Come on. I'll even meet you outside so no one notices us leaving at the same time.' His lips quirked in a wry smile as her lips parted in astonishment. 'Don't stand me up. It's so hard on my fragile ego.'

What was he, psychic? He was certainly quick on his feet. He nodded to Tom and the others around them then stopped off to talk to someone else. In less than twenty minutes, he had vanished, presumably out the front door to wait for her. What was she supposed to do now? She didn't think she could face another dinner like last time without making a fool of herself. But he'd be back in to get her if she didn't go out. She knew that with complete certainty. *C'mon Suze. Just tell the guy to take a hike and get it over with already.*

That seemed easier said than done. Tom chose that moment to get up and stretch. 'Well, time for me to head home.' It was apparently a signal for almost everyone else to do the same. Susan glanced around. If she didn't go now, she'd be the only one sitting at her end of the table and she didn't know anyone else. All right, maybe he wouldn't be waiting and she could head out to her car without running into him. She was a big girl, she could handle this guy. She stood up and grabbed her coat as she walked out with Tom and Sanjeev.

He wasn't outside when they came out onto the street and Susan sighed with relief. But no sooner had she turned the corner to walk toward the ramp than a car pulled up beside her. 'Hop in.' He craned his neck to look up at her. 'That is unless you've changed your mind. Which I hope is not the case.' The blue eyes twinkled in earnest now. She wondered if he'd ever been turned down. She wondered if she had it in her to be the first. 'Just food, I promise.' He looked more somber now and despite herself she walked over and joined him in the car.

The car was one of the new sports car hybrids, the electric and gas-fueled cars whose dashboards were filled with mysterious glowing dials and gages. 'I figured you more for the BMW or Lexus type, somehow.' Susan remarked dryly.

'Once upon a time I was. But I like these better. Would I be more appealing in a Lexus SUV?' He gave her a sidelong glance as he turned a corner and headed into a part of the city that she hadn't explored yet.

'Where are we going?' Susan decided to avoid the question of his appeal for the moment. The streets around them looked grimier and the lights were dimmer than downtown, but the neighborhood had a village like quality. People walked together or shouted across the street to neighbors and friends. Little cafes and coffee shops spilled their light out onto the sidewalks, making her smile. 'Where's this?'

'Well, it used to be our version of Little Italy. Now it's Little Everything. You like Russian? I know a great place.' His eyebrows rose with the question, giving his features an earnest quality that they had lacked before. Uncertainty made him more appealing and she made herself look out the window like she was trying to see restaurant names instead of looking at him.

'I don't know I never had it. Do they serve anything except borscht?'

'Yep, they have their own version of pirogues, too.' He smiled and drove a few more blocks before turning into a postage stamp-sized parking lot. He parked, then came around and opened her door for her before she'd had a chance to get out. He held her arm like a knight escorting his lady, fingertips resting on her sleeve as if she were too fragile to clutch. They entered through the back door, emerging into a cozy, candlelit restaurant.

'Mark!' A round man in his fifties greeted them across the room full of plush chairs and dark wood tables. 'Good to see you again! And you, too, Miss.' He gave Susan a quick glance before he bustled over and ushered them to a warm and secluded corner table.

Mark chatted with him about his family and the business for a few moments before introducing Susan. 'This is Piotr. Piotr, my friend Susan.' Piotr smiled so enthusiastically that she thought his round face would split in two.

'Any friend of Mark's is always welcome here.' He winked with the heavily accented words as if to suggest that she would be welcome even without him.

That's a relief Susan thought. *I'd hate to think my eating out was limited to dates with my new 'friend.'* She winced at her own cynicism and Mark looked up in alarm.

'Something wrong?'

'Just the burden of my own thoughts. So what's good here?' She forced herself not to look at him, not to reach for the softness of the hair at his temples, to smooth the tiny wrinkles at the edge of his eyes. *What was it about this guy, anyway?* She wondered, impatient with the depth of her desire.

'I bring you a sample of the special appetizer,' Piotr's voice summoned her back from the edge of the imaginary precipice. She tried not to sigh with relief as he put a plateful of odd little dumplings and savory sauces in front of them.

'How do you know him anyway?' She asked as he bustled off into the kitchen, nearly bowling over a waitress.

'I gave him some help when he starting this place up. Listen, I hope I haven't been too pushy tonight.' He studied her across the lit candle and the small dumplings. She tried not to groan with frustration as her thighs burned and her stomach twisted. Couldn't he tell how much she wanted him? Didn't he feel anything at all? She settled for shaking her head in response, not trusting her lips to obey her mind.

Piotr reappeared to take their order and she stammered out the name of the first thing she vaguely recognized on the menu. It took a moment to realize that Mark was asking her a question. 'Shall I order wine?' Unthinking she nodded and then wished she hadn't. A glass or two of wine and she wasn't sure she could trust herself with this man. *On the other hand, it couldn't be worse. Maybe a futile attempt at seducing him will get him out of my mind.*

The suggestion made her straighten in her chair. Maybe she was just lonely, not obsessive or falling in love or anything crazy like that. She looked across the table to find him watching her and tried not to blush. She wondered how many of her thoughts were written on her face for him to read. He gave a slow, hesitant smile that sent a warm jolt through her. *Time to turn the tables.* 'So what do you do for fun?' She tried to slow the words down, nearly purring to give them a vaguely suggestive quality. She gave him a sidelong glance under her lashes to lend a flirtatious edge to the words.

His smile deepened and the look that went with it made the breath catch in her throat. 'Oh, lots of things. What's the line? Long walks on the beach in the moonlight, excruciatingly long talks about my relationships, romantic films...' He stopped as she burst out laughing and laughed with her. He had a deep, masculine chuckle that reminded her of an underground river.

When she recovered, she gave him a genuine smile and scrapped the 'come hither' look she'd been trying to cultivate. 'No, I'm serious. Hobbies? I know you said you liked to sail. Where do you go around here? I've always wanted to go out on a sailboat.'

Piotr appeared with the wine then the waitress showed up with their food. The conversation wandered to work and back again. He told her about sailing and they talked about books, movies, plays they'd seen, things they had in common. There turned out to be quite a few of those, to Susan's surprise, though conversation wasn't the only thing connecting them.

Once she threw her head back when she laughed and looked up to find his eyes tracing the line of her throat, the round curve of her breast. She watched his hands on the table and the curve of his lips, both smiling and not. She could feel herself moisten in anticipation, in longing, and no amount of internal lecturing could make it stop.

Finally, she bolted for the ladies room in an effort to recover her composure. She splashed cold water on her face and redid her makeup, then unbuttoned the top button on her blouse. Then she re-buttoned it and combed her hair. *This is ridiculous.* It was. She unbuttoned it again and walked back out, determined to act like there was nothing out of the ordinary going on. His eyes rested on her newly exposed skin for an instant before flicking up to meet hers. His grin reminded her of a sleepy tiger and she gnawed her lip, uncertain what to do next.

No bill appeared even after their plates were cleared. She finished her wine and looked around for Piotr. 'I just run a standing tab here, like you would at a bar.' He said in answer to her unspoken question. 'Shall I take you home or back to your car?' His tone suggested that 'home' was the one to pick. She was warm and sleepy and a little buzzed. She could always take the bus in on Monday. Besides, this way there was always the possibility of a nightcap.

Oh yeah, like that's a good idea. What happens if he says yes? Then what? What'll that make life like at the office? After a moment, she realized she hadn't answered his question. He had gotten up and was standing behind her and sliding her chair out. He held her jacket out for her and slipped it on, leaning close to pull it up on her shoulders. She could feel his hands, the heat of his legs and chest through his suit. He leaned in to whisper in her ear. 'Why don't we get out of here?'

To her horror, Susan could feel her eyes half close and her lips part as her body responded to his voice, his closeness. It was if she had lost all control and he spoke to some inner animal instinct that slept inside her, awakening only to the sound of his voice or a whiff of his scent. He turned her in his arms before releasing her and guiding her to the door on his arm, waving his farewell to Piotr on the way out. 'I think I better just take you home. That okay?' He had an odd sound to his voice, as if there was something else he wanted to say but he was fighting the impulse even as she gave into hers.

She turned to face him as they got to the car, her heart pounding until she couldn't hear any of the city noises around them. He looked puzzled as she tilted her face upward with parted lips and kissed him. He recovered quickly, she noticed in some distant part of her mind. His arms pulled her close and his lips burned against her own. If his first kiss had been gentle and exploratory, this one was hot and fierce. She welcomed his tongue into her mouth and pulled him closer, tightening her arms around his neck, molding herself to him. Her blood was on fire and she surrendered herself to the whims of the aching void inside her.

It was only the grating sound of gravel under car tires that brought her back to the present. She pulled away from his lips as he leaned down to shower kisses over her ears, her neck. A tiny groan tore itself from her lips as she made herself speak. 'Umm... the parking lot may not be the best place for this.' He pulled his face away to give the new party getting out of their car a baffled glare as if he wondered what they were doing there. Then he nodded and stepped away to open her door. She caught her breath with an effort and sat down, waiting for him to open the other side and come back to where she could touch him.

Once inside, his eyes seemed to burn in the dim streetlights and he raised one hand to run his fingers lightly along her jaw, then down over her collarbone and below to the upper edge of her bra. This time, she made no effort to control the moan that worked its way up from deep inside her. He raised her hand to his lips, palm up. His lips were hot and moist against her skin and he slowly turned up each of her fingers one after the other and slid them into his mouth. Blue eyes fixed on her as her back arched a little, letting her head fall backward. 'Please...' The word startled her; she hadn't meant to say that. She had wanted to say something sensible, something that would stop this before it went too far.

'Please what?' He growled, his words thrumming through her like a big cat's purr as he planted a kiss on her palm and closed her fingers around it.

'Can we please go somewhere a little less public before I make a complete fool of myself?' Fixing her eyes on the car that had just pulled in next to them, with its exiting occupants sending amused glances their way certainly made it easier to talk. But the words that would get her away from this man and back to the safety and calm of her own apartment, alone, those wouldn't rise to her lips. He followed her gaze and nodded, releasing her hand reluctantly.

'Home?' he asked, not specifying which one he meant. He looked at her for a long moment as if he were considering the consequences of his next question. She could see him catching his breath and she thought she knew what he would say next before he said it. She braced herself for the 'let's be friends' speech, but his words took her breath away. 'Is mine okay?' She nodded, too far gone for caution, for good sense to prevail.

He drove quickly and competently down the narrow streets, his hand coming to rest on her leg between turns. She traced his fingers with her own and he began sliding his hand higher, stroking upwards until her thighs parted to permit him to slide up her skirt. She reached out to rest one hand behind his head, playing with the stiff curls of his short hair. His hand rested lightly on her inner thigh, just inches away from where her flesh begged to welcome him. She managed not to squirm, to bring herself closer to those tantalizing fingers, but only just.

Between watching his hand and studying his profile, Susan realized that she had no idea where they were. Glancing around, she saw that they were in yet another neighborhood she'd never been in. Upscale restaurants and hotels with doormen zipped by, as did the bright lights of converted warehouse condos, large bay windows with curtains open to display expensively decorated apartments. She scarcely had time to notice this before he was turning into a secure parking garage.

He slipped his hand away to enter his code and to park and she tugged her skirt down regretfully. The warmth of his hand on her skin felt almost like a mild burn and it took all of her remaining self-control to not respond overtly to his every touch, every gesture. Bad enough that every inch of her body screamed 'Take me!' until she thought it must be audible to him and even to the couple they passed going out to their car.

The elevator had its own security code and a camera, which made her eyebrows soar a bit. He grinned down at her. 'Yeah, I know it's a bit much. My dad picked the place out for me when I moved back here from the Coast. His taste is a tad more security-oriented than mine.' He leaned down and kissed her again, lightly this time, his careful arm wrapped around her waist as if the security camera was the equivalent of a cold shower.

If it is, I wish it was working on me, Susan thought ruefully. Instead, her heart was racing and she could feel her nipples harden, quivering sensitively under her shirt's silky fabric. His hand gently brushed against her breast as if by accident, sending shivers through her entire body as he escorted her out into a hallway. The floor was done in tasteful shades of brown and beige, carpet and wallpaper all clearly of very good quality and well maintained. Susan almost regretted her considerably funkier dwelling, but only for a moment. This place was a little too unreal, too perfect and spotless for her to really appreciate it. It looked like people only visited here briefly, never long enough to make their mark on their surroundings.

He stopped before a tan door and unlocked it before ushering her in and turning on the lights. She paused in the doorway, stunned. His apartment was one of the ones she'd been admiring from the car window, complete with a fireplace, a large painting of sailing ships hanging above the mantle, an inviting couch, two armchairs and bookcase-lined walls. There was a wall-hanging by the front door and several carved statues from different countries on various tables and bookcases. It was remarkably clean for a man who lived alone.

What was she getting herself into? She took in her surroundings for a moment before he spoke, his voice strained. 'Listen, I know I'm rushing things. Is that okay with you?' She turned around to face him and tugged his hand from the door so it shut behind him. His eyes darkened with desire and she could see his erection straining against his pants even in the dim light. 'Or maybe it's too late to ask that.'

'Yes, we are rushing it and I'm not completely sure how I'll feel about that tomorrow. But I don't think I mind it so much right now.' She slipped into his arms and kissed him again. He held her tight with one arm around her waist while the other stroked its way along her ribs, grazing her hip but staying just below her breasts. He deftly tugged her jacket off and tossed it behind her into a convenient chair. Then he began kissing her neck, teeth tugging gently on her earlobe, tongue caressing her skin until it ran with shivers of gooseflesh. He worked his way slowly and sensuously down to the V of her buttoned shirt.

There he paused until a small moan tore its way from Susan's lips. He unbuttoned the first button and his lips worked their way down to the upper edge of her lacy bra. He worked his tongue into her cleavage, darting swift and snakelike against her aroused flesh. She wrapped her hands into his hair and lowered her face to nip gently at his ear and shower kisses on his forehead. Her blood raced and she could scarcely catch her breath as he undid the next button, then the next, and pulled away her shirt to expose her breast. His lips engulfed her already hardened nipple through the lacy fabric of her bra and a startled 'Oh!' burst from her lips.

His lips were gentle but persistent, sucking and exploring until she could hardly stand. When he unbuttoned the last of the buttons and shifted his voracious mouth to her other breast, she pulled his face away for a moment. 'Maybe we could lay down for this?' She murmured between gasps.

He gave her an impish grin. 'Certainly.' He gathered her into his arms and scooped her up despite her murmured objections. Instead of putting her down, he leaned down to kiss her again, distracting her from anything but him until he deposited her gently on a soft surface. She found his jacket buttons and tugged his tie off as he knelt beside her on the large bed. He leaned down to kiss her once more, stretching out beside her as he kicked his shoes off. The gesture reminded her that she was still wearing her heels and she sat up and tugged them off. She turned back to him, and climbed up to kneel over him as she unbuttoned his shirt. His hands slid up her thighs and under her skirt as she leaned down to kiss his chest.

He groaned as his thumbs pressed against the moist fabric of her stockings, the rocking of her hips against his hands speaking to her desire. She kissed him ferociously now, her mouth exploring him, now devouring his nipple, now caressing his neck, his shoulders. She scarcely felt him tug off her blouse and unfasten her bra until he sat up abruptly and took her bare breast into his mouth. His fingers found the zipper on her skirt and slid it slowly down as her back arched against him and she watched him through half closed eyes. He pulled her off him and down to his side on the bed while he slid her skirt and stockings off, pausing to nibble her calves, to slowly caress the skin of her inner thighs.

With a swift movement, he pulled himself up to kiss her, his thighs resting between her own, the muscles of his bare chest hovering lightly against her breasts. She could feel his hardened flesh rise against her thin panties and met his mouth hungrily while her hands tugged his belt free and unzipped his pants. Together they slipped his pants and socks off and he leaned her back against the pillows, his lips once more finding her own. His hand caressed the elastic band of her panties before diving beneath it to bury itself in the moist folds of her skin. His fingers found her clit and her thighs parted to welcome them.

He shifted so that his thumb rested on her clit while several of his fingers worked their way inside her. The sensation scorched its way through her, even as she fumbled her way down to stroke his erection through his boxers. 'No,' he murmured, 'not yet, you first.' She could feel her juices pour from her, soaking his fingers until he tugged her panties off before driving his fingers back inside. Moans and gasps rolled from her lips, sounds that he was clearly using to gage her pleasure. He shifted his fingers as they got louder until the pressure against her clit, the movement inside her took her away. She came, her back arching to press her body against his, her hips thrusting against his fingers, her hands in his hair.

He stroked her until her body stopped shivering, her next orgasm held at bay with a shift of his fingers. But it kept her ready, begging with her hips for more. He kissed her again, this time letting her tug off his boxers so she could feel the hard muscular length of his body press against hers. Her flesh sang, cried out again and again for his touch, pleaded to be filled with him until he reached into a bedside drawer. He pulled away, a condom in his hand. 'You're sure?'

Susan stared at him in disbelief but tried to acknowledge the concern in his face. 'Umm… yeah, but thanks for asking. You?' She pulled her hand away from his crotch to hear his answer. *Play fair* she sternly told herself, trying to ignore the demands of her body for an instant.

He pressed one hand to her cheek and she kissed it without thinking. 'Oh, yeah, I think so. Promise me something, though?'

Anything you want. And I do mean anything. But she didn't say it. It would be too much, somehow. Instead, she reached out to run her fingers lightly across his chest, watching him catch his breath, quivering a little at her touch. 'That you'll have dinner with me on Monday and we'll talk about this. There are some things I think you should know about me.' She nodded and tugged the condom package from his fingers. Monday was miles away; she could worry about it then. He let her take the package and open it, gasping as she slid it down over the solid length of his hardened penis.

'Now, where were we?' She nearly whispered the words as he pulled her toward him and rolled her on her back. He hovered just above her, his fingers once more buried inside her, intensifying her desire until she wrapped her legs around his thighs, trying to pull him into her. They kissed passionately, their tongues entwined as he entered her. He stopped at her slight cry and rocked his hips gently until she could take him all in. Even then, he rested his weight on one elbow, the fingers of his free hand finding the burning circle of her clit as he thrust slowly into her.

He felt right, gloriously right inside her and her nerves sang to his touch as she rose and fell against him, meeting his thrusts until neither could stand it anymore and they both came almost at once. Their moans mingled together until they dropped off into gasps and quiet, intense kisses. He lay beside her, his eyes serious now as he studied her face in the dim light from the living room. 'You're beautiful.' His grave expression nearly made the words less cliché, less unbelievable. Susan smiled and ran a finger over the sweat-moistened skin of his chest. He was still inside her and she could feel him twitch a little at her touch.

She leaned over and kissed him as he pulled out of her. It was an after sex kiss, one that said 'Thanks for a lovely time,' but it soon turned more serious, more intense. One thing led to another and soon they were making love again, practice making them more skilled, the sensations more sensual, more erotic. It was well after midnight when they drifted off into exhausted sleep, wrapped in each other's arms.

Sunshine woke Susan the next morning, lighting the room around her with a golden glow despite the thick curtains. It took her a few moments to remember where she was and to ease into wakefulness in a new place. She rolled over to watch Mark sleep for a few moments. He looked peaceful, blonde eyelashes resting lightly over closed eyes, his chest rising and falling gently with each breath.

She felt a shiver run through her as she watched him. *I hate mornings after*, she thought. *Now what?* Would he wake up and freak out because she was still here? Even worse, what if he was just like Todd? She didn't think she could stand dating any more charming losers who cheated on her. Still, she could feel something stirring in her as she watched him sleep and she tried sternly to quell it. He was certainly a marvelous lover. But what did she really know about him? She forced her gaze away from him and looked around the room for clues.

The bed was old fashioned, with an oak headboard with carvings that suggested that it was an antique. Apart from it, bedroom furnishings were pretty sparse. A bed stand with a clock and a lamp on it, a bureau on the other side of the room, a plush carpet that looked like it might be Turkish. There was a painting on the far wall, a landscape of a beach with waves crashing on the rocks. It made her feel lonely looking at it. She eased slowly out of the bed and looked for something to throw on for a trip to the bathroom.

In fact, why stop there? If she bolted for it now, claimed a morning appointment or errands, it might make this easier, whatever 'this' was. She didn't have much experience with one night stands. If that's what this was, then she realized that she had no idea how to handle it. Well, first things first. Getting dressed would help. She hoped. She found her bra and panties and pulled them on. Her shirt was lying in a crumpled pile at the foot of the bed. Her skirt had wrinkles in it that probably wouldn't come out at the dry cleaners. She sighed.

'I'm good for breakfast, you know. Unless you've got somewhere else you need to be.' He was still lying back against the pillow but the blue eyes were open now, sparkling in the morning light. 'And I have an iron if you really want to use it.' He gestured to the ball of skirt in her hand and smiled a slow, bewitching grin that turned her insides to jelly and stopped her refusal before it could get out of her mouth. She tried to force it out anyway as she watched him swing out of the bed and walk toward her. He leaned over and kissed her before she could manage more than a slight gurgle.

That was slick. Hiya. I'm Suze. Not only am I easy, I'm incoherent. Go you. She kissed him back anyway, dropping the skirt to wrap her arms around him once again, holding him tight. His body felt warm against hers, the slight salty smell of his sweat and the caress of his hands sending a jolt through her. Then his stomach growled, breaking the mood, and they pulled apart laughing. 'Probably just as well, for the moment at least.

Have to keep our strength up.' He grinned at her, the glint in his eyes brought a hot blush to her cheeks and she looked away.

'Allow me to show you the bathroom, madam, or at least the guest version of same.' He held his arm out toward the open bedroom door and bowed with a flourish. Susan smiled in spite of herself and bit back the urge to invite him to shower with her, settling instead for letting him kiss her at the bathroom door. The guest bathroom was an okay consolation prize, clean and well equipped, complete with a bathtub with water jets, a shower and clean towels, even a hair dryer.

It made her wonder how often he had 'guests' who required it, though. The thought sobered her a little, making her reconsider taking off before breakfast, using errands to run, places to be as an excuse. Once she was clean and had finished blow drying her hair, she pulled on her underwear and her shirt, only to realize that she had once again left her skirt in his bedroom. Well, there was nothing to be done about it now. She emerged warily to the scent of frying bacon and eggs.

He was in the kitchen standing over the stove frowning at a couple of frying pans, wearing clean boxers but nothing more. The sight almost took her breath away. He was a lot handsomer than she had let herself realize. No wonder all those women in the coffee shop wanted him. 'You drink coffee? Of course you do. I remember you were at the coffee shop the other day. Cream and sugar? It's the best I can do, no mocha lattes with sprinkles to be had here, unfortunately.' He pulled two coffee cups out of a cabinet and handed them to her with a wry grin and a nod toward the full coffeepot.

'You remember me from the coffee shop? I'm amazed. You had your hands full that morning as I recall.' She poured coffee into both cups before looking up.

He stepped up behind her and wrapped his arms around her, pulling her close. 'How could I not notice you?' He murmured against her damp hair. She put the cups down and leaned her head back on his shoulder, resting her hand lightly on his. He rocked her gently from side to side for a moment, kissing her hair, then her ear, then leaning lower to taste the sensitive skin below it. One hand rose to cup her breast, stroking her nipple until her breath caught in her throat. His thigh parted hers and she stretched her hands back to run them along his legs, over his hips. She could feel him harden, feel her heart race and her breath come in gasps as his skilled fingers slipped between her legs and pulled down her underwear.

Only the smell of burning bacon forced them apart. 'Shit!' he muttered as he turned off the burner. 'Now where were we?' He held her close once again, his fingers thrusting inside her until she writhed against him, sounds of pure animal need torn from her throat until she didn't recognize her own voice. When she came, her knees buckled and only his arms held her up.

'Um…' she leaned her head back on his shoulder as he pulled his fingers gently out of her, 'much better than bacon, but I think I'm going to need sustenance soon.' She turned in his arms and kissed him, her hand still caressing his leg. She reached for his erection but he caught her hand in his and kissed it before she could go any further.

'I think we can arrange that.' He pressed kisses on her closed eyes before pulling back reluctantly and letting her pull her panties back on. The bacon was pretty singed but Susan grabbed a piece anyway and pushed down the lever on the toaster while he poured new cups of coffee for them both. 'Scrambled okay?' At her nod, he threw some eggs and ingredients into a bowl and twirled them with a fork.

'All this and you can cook too?' Susan tried to keep the astonishment out of her voice but it lingered there despite her best efforts.

'I've had a lot of practice and even I get tired of eating out. Now let's just hope you think it's edible when I'm done. I think I like it when I surprise you.' He grinned at her before pulling plates from the cupboard.

Susan watched him as she sipped her coffee. Part of her wondered if he had any more surprises up his sleeve. She didn't know whether to hope he did or not. *Live in the moment, girlfriend,* she told herself sternly. He made it easy to do. She sat across from him at the kitchen counter eating bacon, eggs and toast and trying not to look too amazed. He looked up, catching her gaze, and his eyes twinkled down into hers. 'I'd like to spend the rest of the day like this…' he began. The phone rang behind him and he gave it a strange look.

'Do you need to get that?'

'Probably.' He didn't sound very happy about it, so she took her coffee and food into the other room to give him some privacy. She made herself take a book from one of the shelves so she could ignore what he was saying, but his angry tone got through loud and clear. Finally, he got off the phone and joined her, frustration and worry written all over his face. 'I'm so sorry. It's a kind of a family crisis and I'll need to go take care of it. Nothing serious, I hope, but it'll probably eat up the rest of the weekend.' His eyes were dark now with some emotion she couldn't identify and he scowled, almost as if he didn't know he was doing it.

'I can just call a cab,' she began, trying to sound understanding, to ignore the little surge of disappointment that filled her. It came with a burning desire to know what was going on but she didn't want to ask. They weren't ready for that. Not yet. She got up to bring her dishes into the kitchen and he caught her wrist, pulling her around to face him.

'I'll take care of those.' He brushed her cheek with his free hand. The scowl was gone and his eyes had gone all soft and blue again. 'I also think I'll be clearing out my schedule for next weekend, if that's okay with you.' He tilted her face up and studied her as if he could read her thoughts. Whatever he saw there must have satisfied him. 'Why don't I take you back to your car? I have to head back downtown anyway, unless it would be easier to go straight home?'

'No, I'll need the car for the stuff I need to do.' *Sure, but we couldn't remember that last night.* She wrinkled her nose in response to her inner voice before walking toward the bedroom, trying not to feel him watching her move. Despite every piece of sensible advice she could give herself, something didn't feel right and the disappointment stung. Her skirt was lying on the floor where she'd left it and she began pulling it on. She took a few raw breaths and looked up to find him in the doorway watching her. She forced a grin to her lips and gave a jaunty tug to her zipper after pulling her skirt back up. He gave her a lazy smile in return, one that quivered through her and melted her determination to keep her distance, before walking over to the closet.

A few minutes later, they were out in the parking garage and the warm curve of his arm around her waist made any fears she had seem foolish. He stopped by the car to lean down and kiss her again before opening the door for her. He held her hand in the car as he maneuvered through Saturday morning traffic back to the garage where she had left her car. Everything was fine. In fact, it was terrific. What was she so worried about? He insisted on driving into the ramp and dropping her off right at her car, despite having to pay an extra fee. His goodbye kiss made her toes curl in her pumps and her stomach flutter with a cloud of butterflies.

True, she watched him drive off with a sigh of regret but they had exchanged cell numbers and they had a dinner date for Monday. What had he said about needing to tell her something? She couldn't quite remember it right now, but it could wait. Anticipation would make their next date that much sweeter. She smiled to herself as she headed home, dismissing her concerns with an airy wave. Clearly, she was overreacting. Nothing he had said or done suggested that anything was wrong so why should she worry?

The rest of Saturday passed in a blur. She went folk dancing in a church basement and enjoyed herself immensely but couldn't remember anyone she met after she left. The one thing that stood out was that there would be a Victorian ball in a couple of weeks; maybe she could get Mark into breeches and a tailcoat. But she'd have to find out if he liked to dance first. The thought made her smile as she ran her errands in a happy fog, nearly oblivious to her surroundings. But she didn't call Mom or any of her friends back home. Not yet. It seemed too new and fragile for that. She could do that later, maybe in a couple of days.

Instead she basked in a warmth she had never known before. It lasted right up until she went to the coffee shop around the corner after her jog on Sunday morning. Her favorite couch was free so she curled up and tucked her feet up beside her to enjoy her cinnamon roll and her cup of coffee. She opened the newspaper on the table in front of her, took a big whiff of fresh roll and sighed with contentment. Some time soon she'd have to get her apartment unpacked and set up so she could do this there, but not just yet.

She flipped through sections of the paper, picking and choosing what to read at random. It was hard to read when all she wanted to do was daydream about Mark. She looked up and rested her chin in her hand while she stared into her coffee and smiled. It reminded her of him, but right now everything did. *First stage infatuation soon to be followed by falling head-over-heels if I don't watch myself.* She smiled more and nibbled at her cinnamon roll. After all, what was wrong with having a crush? Or even falling in love?

She glanced again at the paper and this time something in the gossip column caught her eye. She froze and picked up the paper in trembling hands. This couldn't be happening. It was a lie, it had to be. The snippet read: 'Reconciliation ahead? Mark Harrington, the Harrington heir, was spotted dining out at *Chez Les Amis* with his estranged wife, Fiona. The two filed for divorce last month but maybe a romantic dinner will prove the cure.'

Afterward, she couldn't have said when she started breathing again. She put the paper down in front of her, shut her eyes and took a gulp of her hot coffee. Then she leaned forward and read it again and again. It couldn't be her Mark, it just couldn't. It wasn't that uncommon a name. Surely he would have mentioned a not so 'estranged' wife, right? *Oh shit, it's Todd all over again.*

But it wasn't. It was much, much worse. Todd was always too charming for his own good, even when she wanted to believe in him. It was easy enough to not trust him completely, or so she told herself now. But Mark seemed real, like someone she could really fall in love with. *Okay, Suze, let's be honest, breaking up with Todd really hurt. Why deny it?* The little voice in her head made her want to scream and she pressed her hands against her face as if pure pressure could drown it out. All right, so dumping Todd had been excruciating. Even worse was thinking that she'd learned to recognize the signs; that it wouldn't happen to her again.

Okay, Suze, time to calm down, she told herself sternly. She'd made a mistake and had a fling with a married man. It happened to a lot of women. Particularly when the guy was lying scum like this one. How dare he not tell her this? Who did he think he was? Pure anger burned through her until her hands shook when she picked up her coffee mug. *Bastard.*

She took another gulp of her coffee then tossed the cup back to finish the rest. The fresh cinnamon roll that had seemed so savory only ten minutes ago had lost all its appeal and she tossed it out as she got up to go. She left most of the paper on the table, taking only the gossip column with her. Some mistakes you needed to be reminded of, she thought. Otherwise, you might find yourself repeating them over and over again.

She made herself walk out the door, nodding to the counter staff on her way out. Well, she wouldn't let it ruin the coffee shop for her. In fact, she wouldn't even let it ruin her day. She went home and showered and threw on clean clothes. Then she made herself shop for her new apartment and unpack. She was able to keep herself busy, if unable to ignore the sinking pit inside her, right up until she went to bed. Then the tears she'd held back all day welled up, spilling down her cheeks until she sobbed into her pillow. She was still sobbing a little when she finally fell asleep.

Dragging herself to work on Monday morning was the hardest thing she'd ever done, harder even than moving to a strange city. Her mood hung around her neck like a weight until she could barely get out of her car to go into the building. She found herself hoping that Mark had reconciled his way back to the Harrington Corp and out of her life forever.

An instant later, she was dying to tell him off, waving the paper under his nose so he'd know he couldn't get away with this kind of thing. Then maybe slash his tires. The thought brought the ghost of a smile to her lips and she stood a little straighter while she waited for the elevator. *All right, I've lived through worse. I can make it through this,* she told herself bravely. It didn't really help, but it was a start. Just to be on the safe side, she turned off her cell. She'd talk to him when she was good and ready and not a moment sooner.

Tom pounced on her when she got upstairs and dragged her off to a seemingly endless series of meetings that filled the morning. Then Sanjeev asked her to go to lunch with the rest of the team when noon finally crawled around. She went along like a sleepwalker, trying not to think about last weekend and hoping she wasn't going to fall apart. But judging by her co-workers' acceptance of her performance, she thought her stiff upper lip routine was going over well, at least for the morning.

The flowers waiting for her at her desk when she got back from lunch dented her hard-won composure for a few moments. Susan found her teeth grinding together involuntarily when she saw the bouquet. It was perfect: big, beautiful, nothing too heavy duty like a dozen roses, just narcissus and baby's breath and tiger lilies in a tasteful green vase. *Damn him.* 'Wow! Those are gorgeous!' A woman from down the hall volunteered. 'Anniversary?' She smiled at Susan.

'In a manner of speaking,' Susan replied, forcing the words out from behind a fixed smile. *Yeah, what anniversary would that be, the don't get fooled again newspaper one?* She tugged the little white card free with trembling fingers. 'Until we meet again,' it read, and nothing else, no initials, no signature, no reference to a wife. She crumpled the note savagely in one hand before tossing it into the trash.

She glared at the flowers, only just resisting the urge to hurl them to the floor and dance on them; it would be fun, but there'd be too many explanations required afterward. Even now, several people were standing in the aisle cooing about them. Susan wondered if she was developing a large pulsing vein in her forehead from the strain of trying to look pleased. *That'd be attractive, sort of Hulk- like.* She imagined herself turning green and trashing the place. *Tempting…*

What did he mean by the note? What had happened to the whole 'must see you Monday' thing? As if she didn't know. The message light on her phone flashed bright red at her until she forced herself to sit down. His message was the third one in. 'Susan, I'm so sorry I missed you. I've been called out of town for a couple of days and I need to reschedule. Please let me make it up to you next weekend.' *Gee, what a surprise, all that reconciling really should be done out of town, makes it easier to hit on women at work.*

He left his cell number so she could call him back. Her finger hovered over the redial button. She'd call him back and…but no, this wasn't the place or time. Susan sighed. Being a comparatively good girl was such a nuisance some times. She erased the message and the number with it.

'Hey Susan, nice flowers. Can you come over to the conference room for a minute? We've just got a quick question.' Tom herded her out of her cube and back into yet another meeting, and then another. By the time the afternoon was over, she didn't have the energy to hurl the flowers or even have a tiny tantrum. Instead, she whipped through drafts of several documents and a whole series of emails before finally dragging herself out the door for home.

Once back in her cozy little apartment, her mother called while she ate a quick dinner, then her friend Melodie called, and then a phone solicitor. She finally collapsed into bed, too tired to read but wired enough to have troubled dreams about Mark. She found her body retained a perfect memory of the touch of his hands, the pressure of him inside her. She'd wake wet and panting only to slide back into nightmares where Mark left her repeatedly for other women, women who threw themselves in his path in every scene that she could dream up. She couldn't help noticing that he never seemed to mind too much.

She greeted the alarm with an aching head and puffy eyes. It took two cups of coffee to get her feeling almost human again, and three the next morning after yet another nearly sleepless night. She tried chamomile and hot baths and masturbating and even a fruitless call to a dating service before Friday finally rolled around again. The sharp pang was subsiding to a dull ache by the time she got in that morning, only to be greeted by a fresh bouquet. This time the note just said: 'See you tonight.'

Was this a threat? She wondered wearily, biting back a groan as she heard Tom's voice heading toward her cube. It was going to be another happy twelve hour day, this time with a encounter she was not looking forward to at the end of it. Still, she could feel her breath quicken when she looked at the bouquet, all daisies and wildflowers this time. Maybe one quickie wouldn't be so bad. She could always tell him off after that. The emotions that filled her at the thought made her blush and chew her lower lip. But she'd never respect herself for doing that, mores the pity.

'Hey Susan, how ya doin'? I'm afraid it's time for the usual quarterly pep talk. It's Room 516 and some VP from headquarters this time. But at least today we've got coffee and donuts.' Tom gave her an apologetic grin as he darted off, missing her sigh and the roll of her eyes. Well, maybe coffee would help. She dropped her stuff off and headed for the conference room.

But the feelings that filled her when she saw the flowers stayed with her even in the conference room, making her skin tingle with warmth. They pulled her out of the meeting and back to last weekend despite her best intentions. If she closed her eyes, she could very nearly feel the brush of his lips on her neck, hear his throaty whisper. Hear him saying her name. 'Hi there… Susan, I know it's dull but try and stay with us.' Her lids shot open to find that Mark had joined the meeting late and was now sitting next to her.

'What are…?' She began the question in a normal tone of voice which subsided immediately under the warning gaze of several of her co-workers. She settled for scowling briefly at Mark before turning her attention back to the meeting. After that, there was nothing to do but try to ignore him. The vice-president droned on and Mark brushed his knee against hers under the table. She pulled away despite the lightning flash that warmed her entire body at even that accidental contact. The instant message icon flashed on her PDA and she made herself ignore that too. *I am not going to give him the satisfaction, I'm not,* she told herself fiercely.

It made a very frail shield. She could feel every shift in his body as though they were bound together, his glance burning against her cheek until she thought she'd go up in flames. She could feel herself moisten and her breath catch just a little and gave him a sidelong glance, just to make sure he hadn't noticed. He gave her a ghost of a smile in return, one that barely curled the corners of his mouth. His eyes looked worried, though and that made her happier than she expected. *Let him worry. Do him some good to sweat.* She didn't smile back.

Eventually even the torment of an early morning meeting had to come to an end and the VP ground to a mumbled halt. Several people asked enthusiastic questions to indicate that they cared, deeply, and then they were dismissed. Mark was right on her heels as she walked out. 'I've been trying to call you but I couldn't get through on your cell,' he began.

'Susan… oh, sorry to interrupt, Mark, we need to do a quick recap to make sure we're all on the same page,' Tom interjected and Susan tried not to sigh with relief.

'We'll have to touch base later.' She gave Mark a brittle smile that overflowed with insincerity and walked off, leaving him to stare after her.

Her team huddled together in one of the small conference rooms while Tom went over how the policy changes would affect them. She heard maybe a third of what he said. Her mind roiled in doubt and anger. When Tom was done answering questions, she reached into her pocket and pulled out her cell just to see if he had really tried to call her. She scrolled through her messages, noting several phone calls from a number back home that she didn't recognize as well as several from Mark.

Out of curiosity, once she was back at her desk she dialed the number she didn't recognize. 'You have reached the voicemail of Todd Graham. Please leave a–' She hung up like she'd been stung. *Great, just great. The day couldn't get any better than this.* An instant message popped up on her screen. Mark again and this time he sounded angry. 'Can we at least discuss this tonight?' *Wow, am I the luckiest girl in the whole wide world or what?* She began typing a response, but then erased it. Her desk phone rang and she got three more emails while she debated how to respond. He had to be dealt with and the sooner she got this over with, the less it would hurt. *Right.*

She responded with a terse message that informed him that she'd meet him at his cube at 5 and to let her know if that wouldn't work. Then she sat back and rubbed her temples. *Okay, now what the hell did Todd want? Things didn't work out with Tammy? Well, too damn bad.* Her lips thinned into an almost straight line. Last she'd heard her former friend and her ex were talking about tying the knot, which was good in the sense that they would stop inflicting themselves on the unwary. But if they were together why call her? None of the reasons that she could think of were very pleasant.

The memory of Mark's face in the Thai restaurant during their first dinner, when she asked if he was recently divorced chose that moment to resurface and her anger began to fade a little. Someone had hurt him pretty bad, too; bad enough that he sure didn't seem like he wanted that person back just then. Odds were good it was the ex, but maybe not. And he seemed hesitant to do more than kiss her that night. What if he wasn't a villain after all? What if something had happened after that? The realization that she might be misjudging him as Todd's spiritual twin came with an unexpectedly deep pang.

She hadn't seen any photos of kids in his apartment but then she'd been otherwise engaged. What if he took his ex back for the sake of their family, if they had one? What chance did she have then? It had just seemed so perfect that night, like it had so much potential. She scrubbed away a tear and forced down a sip of cold coffee while she glanced at her unanswered emails. But all this drama needed to wait for a few hours or she'd be out of a job on top of everything else.

She made herself knuckle down and work, despite her growing misery. Five o'clock rolled around way too quickly and she gathered up some work to take home. With any luck, she'd be done by Saturday afternoon. But first, she had one more unpleasant task to take care of. She moved slowly toward Mark's end of the floor, her shoulders slumped under the weight of her thoughts. He was typing on the computer when she got there and glanced up warily when he felt her watching him.

'Hi. Let me just finish this and we can go.'

She closed her eyes and made herself take a deep breath. *Let's get this over with.* 'Look, no need to rush. I know about you and your wife getting back together. There was something in the paper.' She opened her eyes to find him flushed red with anger.

'Damn them! Can't we ever have a minute's privacy?' He ran a hand through his hair and glared at the desk. She jumped at the movement. It has a tightly controlled, intense quality that reminded her of the way he had made love to her. He suddenly seemed to remember that she was standing there.

'Look, I told you that it was complicated. That's why I wanted to meet on Monday and why I kept calling to talk to you about it. Just give me ten minutes to finish up and calm down. I'd like to take you to dinner and explain what's going on, if you're willing to give me a chance to do that.' He looked her in the eye, with none of the shiftiness she expected, no suggestion that he was lying. 'I know I'm making a mess of this but please let me explain before you decide.' The blue eyes were still stormy and there was no hint of pleading to be found in them. He would accept her decision to listen to him or not and that would be the end of it... or the beginning.

She frowned back at him, weighing her options and deciding before answering. 'All right, though the taking me to dinner part isn't necessary. I'll be at my cube when you're ready.' She turned away, still wondering whether it was worth it to put herself through this. Maybe it would be better to get it over with now.

His hand touched her elbow lightly, interrupting her thoughts and making her start. The butterflies in her stomach began a kind of fluttery rumba and the heat of his hand scorched the skin under her silky shirt, sending a wave of pure desire outward from his touch. Without thinking, she reached out and touched his lips with her fingertips, then jerked her hand away from his kiss as though she'd been stung. His eyes blazed and he reached for her but she pulled away, not daring to speak, terrified at what she might say or do.

'I'll be in my cube,' she mumbled, and fled. Once in the safety of her own cubicle, she dropped into her chair and groaned. *Really slick there, Suze, looking good on the whole mature adult thing.* She fought the urge to bury her fingers in her hair and scream. Damn him. There had to be some way to get this out of her system before she met with him. Otherwise, she'd be alternating between breaking it off and jumping him. She drew a slow, shivery breath, trying to ignore the tingle of her fingers where they had touched his lips. The movement made her cell phone click against the arm of the chair, reminding her of something.

There had been something she was going to do. She pulled the phone out and scrolled through her recent messages. Todd. She had forgotten Todd. How had she managed to do that? *Oh yeah, I remember now, twelve-hour days, flings gone awry, all that good stuff.* Todd had to be good for something to get her out of this. Maybe she should tell Mark that she was getting back together with her ex. Yeah that might do it. Her stomach sank at the thought and she grimaced. It seemed like a cowardly way out and she hated lying.

A warm hand dropped gently onto her shoulder, interrupting her thoughts, and she flinched. 'Hey, I didn't mean to startle you. Are you about ready to go?' Mark was leaning over the back of her chair, his hand reluctantly withdrawing. She nodded and stood up slowly. He was too close and standing put her almost in his arms. She tried stepping back but only succeeded in bumping into her chair. 'Would you believe me if I said I missed you this week?' He murmured the words to her downcast face then reached one hand out to tilt her face upward.

The action made her gasp and shove his hand away. Who did he think he was? 'Listen, I've already said that I get the whole reconciling thing. Stop treating me like – '

'Like my lover?' He held her eyes steadily but she could see his lips thin as though he was biting back something else.

Okay, time to play the Todd card. 'Look, I've got some reconciling of my own going on.' She stopped to hunt for words. He was inches away, his eyes piercing through her until she had trouble breathing. She looked at his hairline, unable to meet those eyes that would see right through any lie she told. 'My ex called when you were out of town and he wants us to give it another shot.' Hell, it was probably even true. It would be very like Todd to try something like that.

'Really? How nice. Why did you and your ex break up anyway?' He stayed right where he was, not giving her any ground to recover. She looked away now, desperate to avoid his scrutiny.

'Umm… it wasn't working out.' It sounded like the lie that it was when she said it like that. 'Oh what difference does it make? You've got your relationship and I've got mine, so no harm no foul. Let's just go our separate ways.' She glared up at him now. Was he laughing at her?

'Do you really want that? I'm thinking that you don't seem like a woman who'd take back an ex who 'wasn't working out.' But even if you are, I'd like the chance for one more date with you. No strings attached. We just talk. Come on, what have you got to lose? I take it your ex hasn't moved here in the last week?' She looked up to find that he was the man from the coffee shop, the one used to getting his own way. To having women fall over him.

'I don't think that's a good idea.'

'No? And I think you'll always wonder. I know I will.' This time, she could see the hurt in the back of his eyes and see some of the effort that this cost him. Her cell chose that moment to burst into song. 'Going to get that? I'll wait outside.' He stepped out into the aisle leaving her to glare after him.

She switched on the phone with a snarled greeting, remembering too late that it might be someone she wanted to talk to. It wasn't. 'Hey there, how's life in the big city?' Todd's smooth voice purred into her ear. This was the last straw. Her eyes narrowed and she vented all her fury into the tiny speaker, keeping her voice low in hopes that Mark couldn't hear what she said. Not that she really cared right now.

'I'm fine. What the hell do you want? No, don't tell me. Yes, this is a bad time. You know, I don't care why you're calling. I can guess. Haul your ass back to Tammy and apologize for whatever you screwed up this time and don't you dare call me again!' The problem with cell phones versus the old fashioned telephone is that they lack a satisfying slam. She managed to not beat it against the desk, but only just. She took a deep shaky breath and switched her phone back off. It'd be just like Todd to decide that she was playing hard to get.

She could feel Mark standing behind her before she turned around.

'We still on for dinner?' He was holding her jacket out for her and waiting like he had known all along what her answer would be. As she lunged out of her chair, ready to tell him off, too, he continued smoothly, 'Maybe we can fix up your ex with my soon-to-be. They seem like they'd be quite a pair. I didn't mean to listen but the last part got a little loud.'

Susan froze. Did that mean that there'd be no reconciling after all? He gave a wry smile, one that looked more sympathetic than sexy. He wrapped her jacket around her shoulders and handed her her handbag. 'Ready? I think we have some talking to do.' She let him steer her out to the elevator.

'Why didn't you just tell me what was going on?' she finally demanded.

'Oh, I haven't even gotten to the full glorious picture of what's going on, unfortunately. It's not so easy to talk about it when you feel like you've been a fool and fallen for someone who isn't worth it.' His eyes had that cynical look to them now, the one that clashed with the laugh lines surrounding them. 'For starters, I didn't plan on last weekend at all. I thought we'd date for a while and see how things went. I knew I wasn't ready to deal with a new relationship but you do have a certain effect on me.' He smiled down at her with an intensity that made her knees sway under her and she leaned against the elevator wall for support. *When did we get on the elevator? Oh, no.*

'Low blood sugar? You're giving me the weirdest look. Not that I mind.' He smiled at her and gave her a slightly puzzled glance. 'Anywhere in particular you'd like to go? If not, I've got someplace in mind.'

Of course he did. He must know every restaurant in the city, possibly in a five state radius. 'Wherever, your choices have been pretty interesting so far.'

'I suppose I deserved that.' He grimaced and guided her across the street, his hand on her arm. She thought about saying that she hadn't meant it that way, then changed her mind. No point in lying about how she felt. He didn't say anything as he guided her around the corner to a quiet, expensive-looking place at the end of the block. 'I think this place will work. They'll kick us out if you start screaming at me.' He gave her a rueful grin. 'Not that I don't deserve it, I suppose.'

The maitre d' acted like Mark owned the place. No pesky questions about reservations or anything like that. They were ushered past a line of people and into a quiet corner table before Susan could do more than raise her eyebrows. Once they were seated and had menus in hand, Susan growled, 'Hey, spill the beans. You've put me through hell this week and I want to know if you're worth having dinner with. Then you can me tell whether or not you own this place.'

'Half share. You want to order a drink first? It may help.' He looked grim and rubbed a hand over his eyes. A waiter appeared as if by magic and they ordered while Susan tried not to bounce with impatience. 'All right, I'm going to level with you. You have probably guessed that I'm one of the Harrington's of Harrington Investment and Harrington Realty, and too many other things to be worth going into. In fact, I'm my father's heir.'

Susan's eyebrows shot up. Better than a neurosurgeon, maybe. 'Then why are you at Byte? Not that it isn't an interesting place to spend forty-plus hours a week.'

'Every now and then I like to take a look at the world outside of Harrington Corporation. The limo drops me at the edge of town and I hitch back in.' He grimaced, and began again in a calmer tone. 'You know how weird family dynamics can get? Mine are worse than most. I took the job at Byte to get some perspective while I got things sorted out.' He paused like he expected her to say something. She forced herself to sip at her drink and to wait for more, biting back several clever comments with an effort.

He continued, 'You already know about Fiona. What you don't know is that I started a dot.com out on the Coast with one of my best friends from college. She had an affair with him, and then he got caught embezzling funds and went to jail. So she tried to get me back by telling my father that she was carrying my child. That's the short version of how we got to last Saturday's phone call.'

Susan stared at him in disbelief. 'No offence, but this is all a little hard to believe.'

'Gee, I never realized that before.' He glared back at her, only to be interrupted by the waiter. They both picked from the menu at random to get him to leave, and then sat a moment in silence. Finally, he leaned back against the leather side of the booth and asked a question that made Susan gape. 'So what happened to you?'

'What do you mean, what happened to me? I have trouble believing a story even you admit is far-fetched and there must be something wrong with me?' Her voice rose with the words and the couples at the surrounding tables gave them worried glances. She took a deep breath and dropped her voice. 'You're the one whose life is a soap opera!'

'Are you done? Good. Now answer the question.' His eyes were steely in the dim light. She started to get up and he caught her wrist in a light grip. 'Running away from me won't help.'

'I'm not running away. I'm… I'm… what am I doing? You are infuriating.' She sat back and glared at him. He responded by raising her hand to his lips and kissing it. She tugged it free and he let go and smiled. 'If you're asking what happened with Todd,' she began reluctantly, 'We were engaged right after college but I wanted to wait before we got married. So we tried living together for a year before the wedding. It was pretty rocky.' She finished abruptly. He didn't need to know any more than that.

But he was much closer now, his arm around her shoulders, his face inches from her own. 'Just say it, Susan.'

She found that her voice quivered with the effort it took to continue. 'I came home early one day to find him in bed with one of my best friends.'

He gave her a searching glance. 'And you thought that I was stringing you along while I had a wife stashed someplace else?' She was hypnotized, her head nodding before she could stop it. 'Listen very carefully: I have no kids and a divorce in progress. I want nothing more right now than to go dancing with you then take you out sailing with me. Well, all right, I do want something else but it can wait.' He leaned down and kissed her, then pulled back slowly. 'That will be in the gossip column in about two days, by the way.' He reached for her free hand and met her wide-eyed look.

She caught her breath and pulled away a little so she could face him. 'So why me? I'm betting you can have any woman you want. I'm not putting myself down but I don't see how I can compete in high society.'

'Do you have any idea how hard it is for me to meet a woman who doesn't know or care who I am? You seem generally interested in me, not the family vaults. Am I wrong? Good, I didn't think so. And to find such a woman who's also beautiful, smart and funny? I've already had the society bride and all that goes with her and I'm sick of it. So, have I convinced you yet?'

Susan looked up at him, her reaction still wary but beginning to soften. 'Maybe. Thank you for the complements, by the way. I am flattered.' She sipped at her wine while she hunted for words.

He reached into his pocket and pulled out two tickets. 'What are you doing next Saturday night?'

'Hmm, spending it with you, perhaps?' She realized that she liked the idea. In fact, the more she thought about it, the more she liked it. 'What are those?' She took the tickets from his hand and her eyes widened as she read them. 'Tickets to the Victorian Society's Ball? I can't believe you remembered!'

'How could I forget something like that? I suppose I have to wear a top hat.'

'Even better than that,' she responded mischievously. 'You get to wear a coat with tails, breeches and riding boots.'

'And what will you be wearing?' He traced a finger over her cheek and smiled.

'Layers of dresses and petticoats that unhook very slowly.' She blushed a little as she spoke and reached up to lose herself in his kiss.

BIMINI BLUE

Kathleen Kulig

CHAPTER ONE

I need to keep a close eye on Adam York,' Melinda told Rick, as they strolled along King Street on the tiny island of Bimini. Along the road, palm trees offered little shade, and sun-bleached stucco houses radiated heat from the sweltering tropical day. 'He could be trouble. He has that reckless, macho attitude.'

The sea-salted air was stifling; it felt as heavy as warm syrup. Melinda lifted her face toward the sea breeze. It cooled and dried the droplets of perspiration on her face.

'Do you have the hots for Adam York?' Rick asked.

Melinda smiled, and then slapped him playfully with the back of her hand. 'No, it's not that. Although, I admit, he is nice to look at.'

'So what's the deal?'

'I don't trust him,' Melinda said flatly. 'That no fear, carefree mentality is dangerous on a dive boat – and I can't handle another diving accident.'

Rick slipped his arm around Melinda's shoulders and gave her a reassuring squeeze against his barrel chest. 'Adam was okay during his advanced class, a bit over anxious at times, but he learned the techniques. Stop worrying.'

Along King Street, Melinda and Rick passed an outdoor market. Hand woven straw baskets were hung on hooks or stacked on the ground; tee-shirts and brightly colored sarongs swayed and flapped in the breeze. Despite the tranquil, laid-back scene, Melinda's forehead was creased in a worried frown.

'I need these charter trips if I'm going to stay in business,' she said. 'And I can't have some daredevil causing trouble.'

'Part of the hazards of having this type of business is that you have to cater to a few jerks. But you set the rules. If a diver doesn't follow them, he doesn't dive. If he causes trouble, I can take care of him.' Fortunately, few people would challenge Rick. His size alone was intimidating.

'You're playing my big brother again.'

'Just watching out for you. I know this has been a tough year.'

Melinda nodded then pushed away the sad thoughts that threatened the beautiful day and gave him a devilish smile. 'No guy will ever come up and ask me to dance with you standing by me. You look like my bodyguard.'

'If you see someone interesting, just let me know, and I'll persuade him to ask you to dance.'

Melinda chuckled. 'Don't you think I'm charming enough on my own to get a man to ask me to dance?'

'I think you could attract any guy you wanted, if you gave him a chance.'

She sighed. 'I'm ready for a Goombay Smash.'

After the four hour boat ride over choppy, white-capped seas from Pompano Beach, Florida to the island of Bimini, Melinda's legs felt like rubber walking on solid ground. I need to retrain my sea legs, she thought.

'Those Goombays are loaded with rum, you know.' Rick opened the warped screen door for Melinda and they went inside the dimly lit bar, *The Compleat Angler.* 'They'll catch up to you if you're not careful. Then you'll be feeding the fish on our dive tomorrow.'

'I never get seasick.' She went straight for the bar and ordered.

Melinda sipped her frozen fruit concoction; the sweet tangy mixture laced generously with dark rum felt cool sliding down her throat, and the alcohol soon made her feel deliciously woozy. The breeze from the ceiling fans lightly blew the strands of hair that were sticking to her sweaty neck.

Their drinks in hand, she and Rick wandered around the rustic old house that had been converted into a hotel and bar. Hardwood floors creaked with each step. Pictures of fishermen with their huge trophy catches covered the dark wood paneling. She especially liked a picture of Ernest Hemingway standing next to a giant blue marlin. Hemingway had stayed there while on his big game fishing trips. *The Compleat Angler* was now a popular hot spot for scuba divers and fishermen.

'Awesome,' Melinda said. 'I just love these old pictures of Hemingway. He was such an adventurer.'

'These remind me of his book, *The Old Man of the Sea*.' Rick pointed to several photos of Hemingway proudly posing with large fish.

A deep voice behind Melinda cut into their conversation. 'And some say he got the idea to write that book while he stayed in Bimini.'

Melinda spun around, almost spilling her slushy red drink. 'Adam! When did you get in?'

'I've been here since noon.' Adam raised his beer bottle to his lips, took a swallow. 'Bit of a wild ride over, huh?'

'Yeah, we hit rough seas this afternoon. Where are you docked?' Rick asked.

'Weeches Marina.'

Out of the corner of her eye, Melinda noticed Adam eying her up and down. A chill shot through her, going straight to her nipples.

'Cold?' Adam gave her a sly smile.

Melinda held up her frozen drink. 'A little; drank this too fast.' But she knew he'd glimpsed her nipples poking through her thin blue tank top and wickedly realized that she didn't mind him looking. A fluttery sensation sprang up in her stomach. Those deep brown eyes and dark, thick eyebrows were an intriguing contrast to his surfer-blond hair. He must be in his early thirties, she decided, but he could pass for ten years younger.

She hadn't seen Adam since the scuba class. Although she'd been crazy in love with Dan at the time, she'd still admired Adam's good looks – any woman would.

'How long did it take you to make the crossing?' she asked.

'About three hours.'

Rick was skeptical. 'You had to be *flying*.'

Adam shrugged. 'It was a little bumpy, but I like going fast. Besides, my boat can handle rough seas.'

Melinda gave Rick a quick *see what I mean* look.

The metallic tones of a steel drum from calypso music echoed from the next room. 'Should we find a seat?' Adam asked. His hand rested on the small of Melinda's back as he steered her toward a table. Rick followed and they sat down. Scantily clad vacationers and locals, many barefooted, danced to the music.

'What time do we leave tomorrow?'

'Eight-thirty, but be at the boat by eight,' Rick said.

Adam nodded and took a long swallow, finishing his *Dos Equis*. He stood up and put his hand out toward Melinda. 'Dance?'

'I think I'll pass.'

'Oh, go on, Melinda, you love to dance.' Rick winked at her.

She shot him a look that said *I'll get you later.* Then she took Adam's proffered hand and followed him to the dance floor.

He pressed his body hard against hers, slipping his arms around her back.

'So, are you and Rick related or just business partners?'

'He thinks he's my big brother sometimes, but we're just friends, have been for a long time. And we're business partners. He owns the dive boat and I own the store.'

Adam pulled her closer. Their hips rocked together to the music, and Melinda's breasts crushed against his hard chest. It did feel nice to be held again; it had been a while. The arousing island music and the rum-laced drink melted away all her tension and resistance. Her body felt deliciously relaxed and sensual. A sudden urge for some playful flirting dissolved any remaining inhibitions.

Her hands gently squeezed the muscles in his arms and shoulders. He had a nice build. Hard muscles stretched his tee-shirt that displayed a scene of dolphins leaping over curling aqua waves. She slid a hand over his shoulders and felt the firmness of his back. When she rested her other hand behind his neck, combing her fingers through the hair at the nape of his neck, Adam closed his eyes and tilted his head back.

'Feels nice,' he whispered.

Adam wasn't much taller than Melinda's five foot, nine inch frame. Their bodies molded together like warm sculpting clay. The stiff denim of his cut-offs rubbed her lower belly and she wondered how long he could dance like this without getting a hard on. Tilting her hips against him, she imagined him moving against her like this while naked, and felt a certain heat throb between her thighs.

His hands glided up and down her back to the beat of the music, almost hypnotizing her.

Her mind wandered to other wicked thoughts. She closed her eyes and fantasized him sliding his hands under her tank top and cupping her breasts, squeezing them, and rubbing and pinching her nipples with his fingertips until they were hard like pebbles. Her breasts ached for his mouth. In her fantasy, she slid her hand down, took hold of his cock and glided her fist up and down. She knew that would make him moan.

She wanted him.

At the thought of him guiding his engorged shaft down between her legs, parting her sex lips and thrusting his cock deep inside her slit, she felt her pussy getting wet. A groan almost escaped her lips.

'He really enjoys playing,' Adam said softly in her ear.

'What?' Melinda was jolted out of her sexy daydream.

'The drummer, check him out.' Adam tilted his head towards the three musicians on the cramped stage. The steel drummer had his eyes closed as he banged the bowl-shaped drum, and his dreadlocks swayed to the beat. Fishing nets draped with shells, starfish and plastic tropical fish surrounded the stage on three sides. Behind the drummer, bass guitar player and singer, a hand painted mural of a beach scene hung on the wall.

'He certainly does. They're pretty good.' She slurred over her words. Oh, this rum drink was going to her head. The drumming matched the pounding of her heart.

As the song finished, Adam stepped back from Melinda, took her hand and led her back to the table. 'Thanks for the dance.'

'No problem.' Melinda hoped that she was walking straight. Sitting next to Rick, she wrapped her hands around her frosty cup and tried to keep them from shaking. She silently scolded herself for being nervous. Yes, it has been along time since she had a man's arms around her, and it felt good. Was she ready to get involved with someone again? The warm tingling sensations she was feeling now were a good sign that she was. Although handsome and sexy as hell, Adam was not a good choice. She didn't need a carefree, irresponsible, 'perpetual Spring Break' kind of man in her life. She downed the rest of her slushy drink.

'So what dives are we doing tomorrow?' Adam asked.

'Probably a reef dive at about sixty or seventy feet, and then we'll dive the concrete barge; it's a shallow wreck,' Rick answered.

Adam nodded, and then fidgeted in his chair like a nervous airline passenger. He shifted his attention to Melinda clutching her empty cup. 'Can I get either of you another drink?'

'I'm fine, thanks,' Melinda said.

Rick shook his head.

'Where's the rest of our group?' Adam asked.

'We have four other divers. They decided to take the seaplane over instead of tackling a four hour boat ride,' Melinda said.

'I watched the Chalks plane land about an hour ago; they're probably at the hotel by now,' Rick added.

Adam finished the last of his beer, then grasped Melinda's left hand. 'When I took the advanced class last year, you were engaged. I notice you aren't wearing an engagement ring.' He stroked her fingers with his thumb. 'Did you finally dump the bum?' Adam grinned.

Adam instantly regretted his words. Melinda yanked her hand away; her face and neck blossomed red, and a steely look of anger shot out from her stormy gray-green eyes.

Oh no, I hit a sore spot, he thought.

She rose from her chair slowly while continuing to glare at him.

'I'm sorry, Melinda. That was a stupid thing to say.' Adam reached out and took her hand. 'Please sit.'

She jerked her hand back and strode out of the bar, slamming the screen door behind her.

'Great job, Einstein,' Rick said with heavy sarcasm.

Adam let out a long breath. 'Damn! Stupid, very stupid. Did the guy break up with her?'

'In a way,' Rick said. 'He died.'

'Oh, God, when?'

'Almost a year ago, right after you finished your class.'

Adam shook his head in disbelief. 'During that class, I always teased her to break up with him and marry me.' He stood up and threw a few bucks on the table. 'I need to go apologize.'

CHAPTER TWO

Adam ran down King Street, his leather boat shoes kicking up crushed shells and dirt. He scanned each side road as he passed them. At the top of one road, he glimpsed Melinda's short reddish-brown hair blowing before she disappeared over a hill. She was heading for the north side of the island, the beach side. He jogged up the road and stepped onto the powdery white sand beach.

There she was, marching along the beach, flip-flops swinging from one hand. Then she crossed her arms tightly around her waist as if she were in pain.

He caught up to her and grasped her arm. 'Melinda, I'm so sorry. I didn't know.' She jerked her arm out of his grip and strode down the beach. Foamy swirls of aqua waves splashed their feet, and each step left wet footprints in the sand.

'Melinda, please stop and talk to me. Yell at me… something…' Adam could see trails of tears down her cheeks.

She ignored him and walked faster.

'If you don't let me apologize, your bouncer-size partner is going to beat the crap out of me.'

'Well, you'd deserve it,' she said, then stopped and looked up at him. The pain he saw in her eyes crushed his heart.

'Come on, let's sit down,' he said.

She acquiesced with an audible sigh then followed him to a cluster of leaning palm trees that cast long shadows from the setting sun. A light breeze rustled the green palm fronds and tossed strands of hair across her eyes. Melinda didn't look at him. Instead, she gazed at several sandpipers with toothpick sized legs, racing along the water's edge, leaving star-shaped footprints, and quickly stabbing their tiny beaks into the wet sand searching for food.

'Please, tell me what happened.' His soothing tone emanated his concern.

They sat beneath the trees and Adam took her hand between his. This time Melinda didn't pull away.

She took a deep breath and let it out slowly. 'I really don't want to talk about it.' Restlessly, she started to dig a hole in the sand with her toes, then moved her feet aside to pick up a frosted green object about the size of a silver dollar and examined it. 'Sea glass,' she stated, 'I'll add it to my collection.' She held it out to show Adam.

He rolled it over in his hand. It was smooth and rounded and looked like an emerald stone dusted with fine sugar. 'It probably was once a broken beer bottle.' Over time, the ocean ground pieces of glass against the sand, polishing them into jewels from the sea.

Melinda snatched it out of his hand and slipped it into her pocket. 'Are you making fun of me?'

'No, not at all, I have a ton of the stuff at home. Do you collect shells too?'

She smiled. 'Yes, an enormous collection.'

'We'll have to go to Honeymoon Harbor. It's the best place to collect conch shells.'

It peaked her interest. 'I've heard of it, but haven't been there.'

'How many times have you been to Bimini?' he asked.

'This is my fourth trip, but I just dive. I don't go exploring.'

'I could show you sometime. It's not too far from here.'

'Maybe.' She wouldn't commit to anything.

Melinda was as beautiful as Adam remembered her from the dive class a year ago. Her skin was golden brown, smooth and inviting to touch. As were her breasts, they looked just the right size to fit in his hands. Those white shorts showed off her nicely rounded hips and long, athletic legs.

So much fire burned inside him, a savage desire to make love to her shuddered through him. But the memory of that guy still pained her, so he'd have to give her time. How much time? He was sitting close enough to lean forward and kiss her. Should he?

Adam combed his fingers through her brown hair; the sun reflected her burgundy red highlights. Large expressive eyes exposed her inner feelings. Within those gray-green depths, he saw sadness, but also loneliness and he wanted to wipe that all away and comfort her.

A titillating sensation fluttered inside his gut as he gazed at her plump, moist lips. Trailing his fingers along her jaw, then under her chin, he tilted his head down and brushed his lips lightly over hers. He searched for signs of protest in her eyes, and when he found none, he kissed her again, more intensely this time.

A slight moan from her encouraged him further as he opened his mouth, and with his tongue, parted her lips and delved into her mouth. Their tongues met, and her panting breath matched the rhythm of the blood pumping through his body. Adam felt his cock throbbing, swelling and pressing against his cut-offs. He shifted position to allow a little room for the painful pressure within his pants, and Melinda wrapped her arms around his neck, slowly rocking her body against his.

With the softness of her breasts flattening against his chest, his breath caught; he wanted naked skin, their slick bodies touching. Adam reached over and hooked his arm underneath Melinda's legs and pulled her onto his lap.

She was breathing hard, her mouth open, and his desire mounted as she squirmed against him; her thigh massaging his cock. That worked him up. A low groan rattled deep within his throat. He slid one hand under her arm and roamed his fingers along the outer swell of her breast.

'Yes, Adam, touch me.' She whispered against his ear.

He shuddered from the sensation of her warm breath. 'Here?' He moved his hand onto her breast and gently squeezed.

'Oh, yes, harder…' She rocked in his lap, rubbing his erection.

Cupping her breast, he grabbed and fondled and used the flat of his thumb to tease her hard nipple. 'You feel so good; you're driving me insane.' He tugged her tank top out of her shorts and slid his hand underneath and captured her breast.

Immediately, her body trembled; she gasped quick breaths as she kissed him, her tongue probing deep and possessive. She yanked his shirt from his pants and ran her hand up across his chest and then down toward his belly.

A wild urge to take her now nearly overpowered him. He wanted her, wanted to feel her naked beside him, to pleasure her with his mouth, his fingers, and his cock.

Melinda yanked her shirt down and shoved Adam away. 'Stop, Adam, stop,' she whispered, 'someone's watching us.'

He nuzzled her neck, his tongue darting at her pulse. 'Let them watch.'

'No! I mean it. Let me up.' She pulled away from him and stood up, brushing the sand off and adjusting her tank top.

Adams heart was racing and the bulge in his pants was evident, so he remained seated on the sand and wrapped his arms around his knees. On the edge of the beach, a man stood facing the ocean and occasionally glanced over at the couple.

Although Adam didn't mind if someone watched, he didn't want to be interrupted by a local or vacationer taking a stroll on the beach. But she was so hot, and apparently so ready for him, and he had worked himself up to some serious wood. How he ached to fuck her now, here on this beach, in the soft sand.

Melinda had her back to the man, and stared at the setting sun. The distant look on her face told Adam that the heated moment was slipping away, as quickly as the sun was descending into the ocean.

Adam finally mustered the strength to stand up. He moved behind her and slid his arms around her waist, but Melinda stiffened. His cock was still hard, but he resisted the urge to rub it against her ass. 'Don't worry about him; he probably came out to watch the sunset.'

Melinda settled into Adam's embrace. Time seemed to stand still as twilight drifted over the tiny island. Pink and orange streaks radiated across the sky like the spokes of a wheel, and a florescent blue line marked the division between ocean and horizon. After the golden sliver of sun disappeared beneath the distant waves, a few stars appeared in the eastern sky, and the crystal aqua blue color of the water darkened to a gray-green shade.

'Maybe we should move inside.' The husky, sensual tone still quivered in his voice.

'I need to get back to Weeches and make sure everything is ready for tomorrow.' Melinda stepped away from him. 'See you later.' She sprinted toward the road.

Adam chased after her, and reached out to grasp her arm. 'Hey, wait up.'

Her lips looked rosy and swollen, her eyes glazed and sultry. He took her into his arms again and kissed her hard and fervently. But she pushed him away. Dropping her flip flops on the ground, she brushed sand off her feet and slipped on her sandals. 'I really have to check the dive boat, and I need a shower. I have sand everywhere.'

'Great idea. Your place or mine?' Adam asked in a teasing tone, but he wasn't teasing, only testing the waters. The look on her face told him it wasn't happening tonight.

'I should track down the other divers in our group and remind them what time we're leaving.' She crossed her arms over her chest and continued walking, the emotional gap between them suddenly widened into a canyon.

Adam's shoulders sagged and he swore silently. 'Come on, I'll walk you back.'

* * *

After a few more beers at *The Compleat Angler*, Adam staggered out of the bar onto the dimly lit road and headed toward Weeches Motel. An eerie silence descended over the sleepy tropical island. During the early hours after midnight, the wind had picked up; it howled through the palm trees, and rocked the boats in the harbor. Rigging lines on sailboats clanged against the tall swaying masts, and ropes creaked as boats tugged at their moorings. It was a peaceful sound, but Adam knew that a storm was coming and that the seas would be rough tomorrow.

He didn't mind the boat ride in rough seas – he'd been around boats all his life, but diving would be a challenge. His fists tightened and bile churned in his stomach as he told himself he could handle the dives if he stayed cool. If he was going to hide the truth from Melinda, he would have to tough it out.

The small, two story motel was dark and quiet. Fishermen usually turned in early since their day began long before the sun came up. Smart divers didn't over indulge, if they were diving the next morning, nothing like a rocking boat to aggravate a hangover.

Guess I wasn't too smart tonight, he thought. He'd spent the evening trying to figure out how to pursue Melinda with the ghost of her fiancé hanging around. He didn't want her mourning the guy forever; he wanted her in his life. As he passed Melinda's room, he noticed her lights were out, and he checked his watch. Almost two, not a good idea to try to talk to her again tonight, it'll have to wait until after the dives – if he survived them.

He quietly shut the door to his small room. Two twin-sized beds, an old wood laminated dresser and matching nightstand filled most of the floor space, and two dollar-store pictures of beach scenes decorated the walls. Climbing over his dive gear and duffle bag, he squeezed into the tiny bathroom. He yanked off his tee-shirt, stepped out of his shorts and briefs, dropping them in a heap on the tile floor.

Adam stood in the shower and let the tepid water wash away sweat and sand. His heavy necking session with Melinda replayed over and over in his mind and his cock swelled and hardened.

He wrapped his hand around his shaft and started to stroke. Leaning one hand against the shower wall to support himself, he jerked his sex faster, with quickening strokes. He imagined her naked, standing by the palm trees. He watched her touch her breasts and slide her hand down between her legs. Then she had his cock in her hands, her tongue gliding along his shaft and over the swollen head. With the thought of her taking him completely into her mouth, his ass muscles tightened. A deep groan escaped his parted lips as he ejaculated his seed in warm spurts that mixed with the water in the tub and swirled down the drain. Intense spasms wracked his body and his knees threatened to buckle.

CHAPTER THREE

The next morning, Melinda greeted the divers as they stepped on board the thirty-five foot dive boat. She helped them stow their dive equipment under bench seats and doubled checked that bungee cords secured the scuba tanks. Not wanting to alarm the divers, Melinda tilted her head close to Rick and whispered, 'It looks like it might be a little rough today. What's the weather update?'

Rick loaded up the coolers with cans of soda and bottled water. 'Seas should stay around two to four feet and we shouldn't get any rain until late this afternoon.'

Melinda nodded. 'This is our first dive on this trip; I want everyone to have a great time and get their money's worth.'

'They will,' Rick said.

Melinda glanced at Adam. He seemed quiet today. When he arrived at the boat, he had smiled and said, 'Good morning,' but hadn't said anything since then. Now, he focused his attention on connecting his scuba equipment to his air tank.

Maybe he feels awkward around me after what happened on the beach yesterday, she thought. Why hadn't she just gone to his room last night?

She'd thought about it – all night, she'd thought about it! What was wrong with her?

Earlier she had told Rick about her passionate encounter with Adam on the beach, and then her reluctance to get involved with him. Rick suggested she let go of her past – meaning Dan – and move on with her life. If she wasn't ready for a committed relationship, she should just have some fun.

Rick was probably right, but could she have a casual fling? Lord knew she could use some physical attention. Maybe getting laid is just what she needed. She smiled to herself as she thought about seducing Adam. He certainly knew how to use his mouth. Thinking about him on the beach yesterday, made her heart race.

She loved the feel of his mouth pressing on hers, his tongue probing and teasing. His kisses stirred the most wonderful sensations and the thought of him using that mouth on other sensitive places made her stomach flutter and that spot between her legs throb. Besides his mouth, she wanted his hands, large and strong and rough, caressing, stroking, setting her skin on fire with every touch, reaching and exploring every secret place.

'It's nice to finally see you smile,' Adam said. 'You've seemed preoccupied this morning. Are you okay?'

'What?' Melinda was startled and heat rose to her face. 'Oh, I'm fine, just making sure everything is set for our dives today.'

Adam nodded and walked back to his equipment, and checked that the strap of his buoyancy compensator vest was securely attached to his scuba tank. Then he tested and scrutinized the connections of his regulator hoses and gauges again.

That's the third time he's examined his scuba gear, she thought. It was always good to double check your equipment, but Adam seemed to be overdoing it.

She wondered if Adam was aware that two of the other divers, both young women, were totally enthralled with every move he made. Barb and Colleen were experienced divers and both very attractive. With Barb's short red hair, sultry dark eyes and athletic figure, and Colleen's bewitching personality, long black hair and huge breasts, both women easily caught the attention of any man. They continued to hover around Adam like two hawks ready to swoop in on fresh prey. A twinge of jealously stung Melinda and the idea of her being jealous surprised her.

The two remaining divers seated on the bench, Mike and Cassidy, were in their forties and newlyweds. Melinda admired the starry-eyed look they gave each other as Mike slung an arm around his wife, and Cassidy rested a hand on his thigh.

The boat engines of the *Sea Venture* stirred the crystal blue water around the dock and gray puffs of diesel fumes swirled up from the stern.

Adam approached Rick. 'Would you like me to untie the bow line?'

'Thanks Adam.'

Adam reached over to the dock, untied the rope from the metal cleat, and wrapped the loose line into a tight bundle. Rick turned the wheel and slowly maneuvered the boat away from the slip and directed it toward the narrow inlet between North Bimini and South Bimini islands.

Outside the inlet, they rode parallel to the shoreline. Beyond the narrow strip of white sand beach, dense vegetation of short palmettos with fan-shaped leaves, banana plants and flowering cacti dominated this part of the island. The boat then turned sharply and headed straight toward the open ocean.

Melinda overheard Colleen ask Adam if he wanted to be dive buddies with her and Barb. Good safety practices recommended that all divers never dive alone. And it was a requirement on her charters.

Adam glanced up at Melinda then answered Colleen. 'Well, if Melinda is diving, she'll need a buddy, and since I'm the odd man out....'

Colleen shrugged and sat down next to Barb.

* * *

The *Sea Venture* rocked and four foot waves crashed against the hull as Rick struggled to set the anchor at the dive site called Moray Alley Reef. The divers prepared to suit up and hung onto the railings or planted their feet in a wide stance to keep from falling.

A little rough, Melinda thought as she glanced over the ocean, but they'll be fine. The sky was clear, with only a couple puffy white clouds. Sunlight glittered silver over the blue-green waves and penetrated into the depths below.

After Adam pulled off his shirt, Melinda tried not to stare while she admired his broad shoulders, muscular chest and arms. He was ripped. A nest of dark hair stretched across his chest, narrowing down toward his flat abdomen, and the yellow and black swim suit showed off his sinewy thighs.

Melinda turned to the other divers. 'Everyone ready to go?'

They all gave her a thumbs up or nod.

'The deepest part of the reef is around seventy-five feet. Watch you bottom time and return to the boat with at least five hundred pounds of air left in your tank.'

The divers moved to the dive platform. Mike and Cassidy were the first to take a giant stride into the water, and Barb and Colleen followed. Adam adjusted the strap on his mask, then tested the buckles of his buoyancy compensator vest.

'Are you ready Adam?' Melinda asked, getting impatient.

He nodded and moved onto the platform then stopped and adjusted his mask and checked his gauges again.

'Is everything all right?' Melinda thought he looked like he was stalling.

'Fine,' he said sharply. 'I'm ready, let's go.'

'You go first and I'll be right behind you,' Melinda said. Whatever happened to that macho, reckless attitude? She thought he looked more like a nervous novice diver, but she knew he was advanced certified.

Adam slid his mask over his face and placed the regulator into his mouth, gave a shaky okay signal with his fingers and jumped in. Melinda followed after him.

Melinda descended behind the stream of air bubbles from Adam's tank, and easily discerned the intricate patterns of coral and sponges from the reef sixty or seventy feet below. Great visibility today, Melinda thought. Shafts of sunlight flickered through the crystal blue water and reflected rippled shadows on the patches of coral.

Once she and Adam reached the bottom, they slowly kicked their fins and glided over the length of the massive reef. Huge sea fans swayed in the current among the crowded shapes of coral and sponges. Melinda reached out and grabbed Adam's hand and pointed to schools of multi-colored fish darting among the jagged formations giving a spectral show.

While Adam explored the treasures of the sea, Melinda observed him. The volume of bubbles from his regulator showed that he was breathing hard and rapid. They weren't swimming fast, why would he be out of breath? Nervous divers sometimes breathe rapidly, she thought, but Adam didn't seem to be the nervous type. His eyes were wide with excitement when he glanced at her and pointed to a coral formation, a lobster, or a spotted eel. She loved the thrill of scuba diving and was pleased that Adam did too. The ocean was another world, a peaceful escape, an underwater paradise, and she enjoyed seeing the look of delight in another diver's eyes – especially Adam's.

Watching his body move, sent waves of desire to every nerve, and Melinda's thoughts drifted. She craved to wrap her arms and legs around him and float through the warm, turquoise water, their bodies joined and writhing in an intimate spiral dance, like a mated merman and mermaid lost in ecstasy.

Adam followed a large sting ray that soared above the reef, its black triangular fins slowly flapping like wings. Melinda was so mesmerized by the graceful creature that she didn't notice the schools of fish frantically swimming out of sight or darting into hidden holes in the coral. At first, Melinda wondered why all the fish had disappeared. Then a malevolent shadow darkened the deserted reef, and an eerie chill radiated straight through her; she knew what was circling overhead.

Melinda looked up and let out a short shriek through her mouth piece creating a burst of air bubbles. Grabbing Adam's arm, she urgently gestured at a large reef shark hovering above them. The shark swam down to their level, circling around the two divers. Melinda froze in place. Most sharks wouldn't bother a diver as long as the diver didn't appear threatening, and didn't possess bloody fish caught during spear fishing. Slowly swimming in the opposite direction was usually the best way to deal with a shark. If the shark realized it wasn't in danger, it would go on its way.

Melinda's heart pounded in her chest; she could hear her blood throbbing in her ears as the shark moved closer. Her eyes widened in horror, and her breath caught in her throat when Adam turned and swam toward the shark.

CHAPTER FOUR

The shark moved closer and continued to circle around Melinda and Adam; the shark's back arched in a defensive pose. Not a good sign, Melinda thought. She knew that if the shark felt threatened, it would attack. Adam continued to swim away from her, aiming for the shark. Anger mounted inside her at his reckless behavior. She frantically swam toward him, knowing that her sudden movement could aggravate the shark. As she reached Adam, she grabbed his arm and jerked him to stop. The playful, unconcerned look in his eyes irritated her even more. He has no idea the danger he was putting them into, Melinda realized.

She signaled for him to stay in place, hopefully demonstrating to the shark that they weren't a threat. Slowly the shark made one more pass and then swam off, disappearing into the dark, indigo depths beyond the reef.

Melinda twirled her finger in a circular motion – a signal to turn around and return to the boat. Adam scrambled up the anchor line, and Melinda had to grab his ankle to slow his ascent. If Melinda hadn't stopped him, he would've shot up to the boat, risking a life threatening condition like the bends or an embolism. Another rule Adam had ignored.

The current was stronger now. They gripped the anchor line tightly as the rush of water dragged at their bodies, and they flapped on their tether like flags on a flagpole. When Melinda examined Adam's air gauge and saw that it read only fifty pounds per square inch, she felt the heat of anger rise in her face. Before the dive, she had told all the divers to return to the boat with five hundred pounds of air. She was going to read Adam the riot act when they got back on board. Another reckless diver she did not need on her boat. Besides being a risk to himself and other divers, that carelessness could worsen her already floundering reputation. Her business had been on the edge of bankruptcy since the last accident, and that incident was due to a thrill seeking macho diver.

The memory of that day came back to her in a rush. Tears burned her eyes behind her scuba mask. The pain of the loss still haunted her, and the nightmares still plagued her sleep. She couldn't bear to go through that again; her heart couldn't endure it and her dive shop wouldn't survive financially.

Melinda climbed on the boat and yanked off her mask and dive gear, then strode up to Adam. 'I need to speak with you.' Her voice trembled with anger. Fortunately, the other divers were busy setting up their equipment for the next dive and didn't seem to notice. Walking toward the bow, she passed Rick standing at the wheel and gave him a sharp look. Rick's eyebrows raised in a question. 'Problem?'

Melinda didn't answer and continued past him.

'Sounds like I'm in trouble,' Adam said with that bad boy smirk.

The wind had gained strength and the boat rocked and pitched over four foot waves, the salty spray whipping in her face. Melinda had to hang onto the railing to the upper deck in order to keep her footing. She took in a deep breath and let it out slowly, trying to calm herself and keep from loosing her temper. 'Rules are made for a reason – for your safety and for the safety of other divers. If you can't follow the rules, you don't dive on my boat.'

That bad boy smirk slid from Adam's face, but his eyes held hers in a serious, fiery gaze. 'And what rules are we talking about?'

'Keeping your buddy in sight and not swimming off to chase sharks. Returning to the boat with five hundred pounds of air, not fifty – I checked your gauge. And doing a slow, controlled ascent.' She glared at him and then checked the divers in the back of the boat, hoping they wouldn't hear their conversation.

'I guess I was excited about seeing my first shark and just forgot.' His eyes pierced hers; he didn't look away, as if he were challenging her to see who would break eye contact first. 'Relax, it's no big deal.'

Melinda glared at him. If it wasn't for the other divers, she'd forget about preserving her professional appearance and tell him, with every foul word she could conjure, exactly what she thought. 'Yes, it is a big deal. I'm liable for every diver on my boat. Consider this a warning. Next time you forget the rules, you're off my boat.'

Melinda strode over to the cooler, grabbed a bottle of water and took a long swallow. Barb, Colleen, Mike and Cassidy were sitting on the bench seats, quietly discussing their dives. From what she could hear, they had seen the shark, too.

Rick maneuvered the boat over the waves and drove the boat toward their next dive. He looked at Melinda and smiled. 'Everything okay with your boyfriend?' he teased.

She glared at him. 'He's not my boyfriend. I just had to remind him of some basic diving rules.'

'You want me to throw him overboard?' Rick's smile and teasing diffused her anger.

'Not at the moment, but I'll keep that in mind.'

She tried to look pleasant and forced a smile when she questioned the other divers. 'So how were your dives?' Melinda's heart sank with their unenthusiastic answers. The sullen look on their faces told her that they had heard the heated conversation with Adam after all.

* * *

After the dive boat returned to the dock, Melinda went back to her room and flopped down on her bed. How could she perk up the mood of this trip when the other divers looked at her like she was the bitch of the Bahamas? Maybe Dan was right after all. Maybe she wasn't cut out for owning her own business and running dive charters. He'd never thought she'd be successful. Even after his death, she was still trying to prove him wrong. Before the accident, things hadn't been going well in their relationship, and she wondered if they would have worked out their problems if he had lived.

She needed to get Dan out of her mind and move on with her life. If Adam followed her diving rules, and she didn't have to kick him off the boat, a summer fling with him might help her find fun, enjoyment and a little gratification in her life again. He was good looking, had a great body and could be very charming at times, yet he did have a way of irritating her.

Her tense muscles ached and her skin felt dry and sticky with salt. A long bath would help relax and reenergize her. After that, she'd search out her other divers and do some socializing – public relations work – and flirt with Adam. The idea of seducing Adam made her heart skip a few beats. It was a small island, and it wouldn't take long to find him. The bitch of the Bahamas was about to be transformed into a tropical hedonist.

Dragging herself off the bed, she stripped out of her one-piece bathing suit, retrieved a packet of lavender bath crystals from her duffle bag, and wandered into the bathroom to start her bath.

Melinda slid into the pale violet water and inhaled the spicy flowery scent. The water was warm, but not steaming, and the surface lapped at her rosy nipples. She slipped down into the bath and tilted her head back to soak her hair, when she sat up, trickles of lavender water streamed down her chest. Except for her tan lines, her skin was a bronzed olive shade. She always tanned easily. Pressing her palms to her face, she could feel warmth from a slight sunburn or windburn from the day on the boat.

While gazing into the water, she fantasized about a lavender colored ocean. In her daydream, she and Adam swam naked underwater, not needing the use of scuba gear, weightlessly floating while exploring each others bodies. By rubbing against the bristly dark hairs on his hard chest, she imagined her nipples becoming raw, sensitive and taut. The warm purple water caressed their skin and supported their bodies. He slid his hands across her silky wet skin, along the sides of her breasts, past her waist, down along her hips and finally between her thighs. Each touch, each stroke electrified every nerve. She lifted her hips and spread her legs to encourage more of his touch.

Her heart thrummed in her chest, matching the throbbing in her pussy. With the rough heel of his hand he rubbed her swollen clitoris, then with his fingers, parted her inner lips slick from the lavender sea and her own honeyed juices, and burrowed one finger deep into her hole. Moans and cries escaped her in a trickle of bubbles.

Gazing down between their bodies, she saw his engorged cock bobbing in the crystal water. The fluttering delight of desire rose within her to wild heights, like turbulent seas. His need shone in his sultry brown eyes. Quickly he freed his hand from between her legs and guided his hard cock to her slit. He grasped her hips with both hands, and pulled her down onto his hard shaft. With his thrusting, and her writhing against his body, their intertwined bodies glided and spiraled through the water into the welcoming depths the deep purple sea....

Opening her eyes, Melinda's body was a convulsion of pleasure. The water in the bathtub had cooled, but her skin was hot. Her hand moved between her legs, her fingers rubbing her clit. Melinda groaned aloud to the intense sensations. Her vagina clenched, aching to be filled. The throbbing of her clitoris reached the pinnacle of her orgasm, and then the quaking slowly dissipated.

CHAPTER FIVE

Melinda entered *The Compleat Angler*, walked straight to the bar and ordered a Goombay Smash. Her short sundress of orange, magenta, and rose, the colors of an island sunset, clung to her body showing off all her curves. The back was open almost to her waist and the front scoped down to expose the mounds of her breasts. She didn't miss the looks from fishermen and divers who had stopped telling their adventure stories to watch her.

While leaning against the bar, Melinda scanned the rustic room and sipped her frozen drink. Barb and Colleen were watching Adam swing a ring on the end of a string, trying to catch a hook on the wall. Melinda crossed the creaking wood floor. 'Who's winning?'

Startled, Adam swung around and eyed her with a quick up and down look, his eyes sparkling with playfulness. 'Nice dress.'

'Thanks.' Melinda loved the way his blond hair hung over one eye. The loose fitting tee-shirt didn't hide the muscles of his chest and shoulders.

Barb grabbed the ring out of Adam's hand and started to swing it toward the hook.

Colleen flipped her long dark hair over one shoulder and flashed her seductive mistress eyes at Adam and ran her hand down his arm. 'Are we going soon?'

A pang of jealousy and defeat struck Melinda in the gut.

'Melinda would you like to join us?' Adam asked. 'I've been coaxed into taking an evening cruise around the island.'

'Coaxed?' Melinda laughed. 'Hard to believe you needed coaxing to take out two beautiful women on your boat?' She enjoyed Adam's panicked look that seemed to say, *don't leave me alone with them.*

Colleen smiled at the beautiful women comment, but her downcast gaze said she wasn't keen on Melinda joining them. Should Melinda pursue him if the other two women were doing the same? Why not? She always had a competitive spirit, but competing with her customers may not be the best plan.

'Come with us, Melinda.' His eyes held her gaze, almost pleading.

* * *

When Melinda reached Weeches Marina, Colleen and Barb were already aboard Adam's boat. Melinda untied the bow line, and hopped on as Adam pushed the boat away from the dock. 'Rick's not coming; he's trying to call his girlfriend in Fort Lauderdale, and not having much luck with the antiquated phone service.'

'Damn.' Adam said under his breath. He had hoped Rick would've joined them to help entertain Barb and Colleen so he'd have a chance to talk to Melinda. She had a wall around her and he wasn't sure why. Was she still angry about the dive earlier? Was she still mourning her late fiancé? Did she have second thoughts about mixing business with pleasure, or maybe she just didn't like him?

It was obvious that she loved her work and scuba diving, but he wanted to get to know more about the real woman and not the serious business professional who was always on stage. Tonight he could show her how adept he was at boating, maybe then she'd overlook his lack of scuba diving skills.

Adam guided the boat through the narrow inlet and skimmed across placid seas. Glowing streaks of clouds emblazoned the sky in colors of orange, pink, and violet – a surrealistic painting. A warm, humid breeze flapped the blue canvas top above the steering wheel and two swivel chairs. The twenty-three foot open design vessel also had a cushioned bench seat behind the chairs, facing the stern. Colleen had claimed the swivel seat next to Adam. A light mist sprayed over the bow, and Adam licked his lips and tasted salt.

'There's beer, soda and water in the cooler,' Adam said. 'Help yourself.'

Barb opened the cooler, digging through the ice for a soda.

'Hand me a beer,' Colleen called to Barb.

Colleen wasn't about to give up her place, Adam thought. She'd been aggressively pursuing him since he arrived, but he wasn't interested.

'Wind's kicking up; it's getting choppy out here.' Melinda pointed to white-capped waves ahead. She wrapped her hands around the aluminum pole attached to the canvas top and spread her feet on the deck for balance as the boat rocked and plunged over the swells.

She's quite at home on a boat, Adam mused.

'We'll be fine,' he said. That dress looked so hot on her; it showed off her body and slim legs. Although they weren't practical to wear on a boat, he'd love to see her in four inch heels instead of the flat sandals she wore now – better yet, her feet in four inch heels hooked over his shoulders while he thrust inside her wet pussy. He grinned to himself; the thought threatened to spur another hard on.

'What are you smiling at?' Melinda asked. Her prankish smirk and sultry gaze made him wonder if she read minds. 'Think you're hot stuff escorting three beautiful women on your boat?'

'Absolutely.' He should have figured out a way to get Melinda alone without the two darling divers, Barb and Colleen.

That day on the beach, when Melinda had been so passionate and aggressive; it turned him on every time he thought about it. He thought something had clicked between them, that it was more than a physical attraction.

'Those thunderheads are building up; we need to keep an eye on them,' Melinda told him.

'Oh, they're way out over the ocean, not a problem.' He leaned toward Melinda and lowered his voice. 'I'm sorry about the dive today. I was a jerk. I got so excited about the shark….'

Scuba diving was helping him to overcome his fear of the water, but he would get so distracted trying to stay calm, he'd forget to check on important things like his bottom time and air supply. How could a boat dealer be afraid of swimming in deep water? It's something that had haunted him his whole life, but he was trying to work it out. If he told Melinda about his phobia, she'd think he was a coward and probably wouldn't let him dive.

'I remember how excited I was when I saw my first shark.' She smiled reassuringly. Melinda glanced out over the ocean. 'I love this time of day; it's so peaceful. Right after the sun goes down, there's a glow from the ocean, like blue candlelight, and time seems to stand still.'

'Twilight on the sea; it has its own magic,' Adam said.

'Where are you taking us?' Colleen interrupted.

'Just a short cruise to check out a few small islands around Bimini.'

'Great! Let's go exploring.' Barb clapped her hands. 'We can have a beach party.'

'It's too dangerous beaching a boat in the dark,' Adam said, 'too many shallow reefs.'

'Too bad,' Colleen said with a pout. 'Barb hand me another beer.'

'What am I, your maid? Let me sit up front for a change.'

Colleen reluctantly gave up her seat to Barb and grabbed another beer out of the cooler. She then stood next to Adam, holding onto his seat back.

It was getting dark, and several stars glimmered in the sky. He aimed the boat toward a small island. Black silhouettes of palm trees bordered the white sand beach.

'There's a ship wreck on that beach.' Melinda pointed to the rotting hull of a boat resting on its side.

'A sailboat,' Adam said. 'It wrecked on Honeymoon Harbor during a hurricane. It's been there for years.'

'No one lives on the island?' Melinda asked.

'It's uninhabited. Sailboats frequently anchor offshore, because it's a safe harbor. The island blocks most of the ocean currents and wind.'

'Not very safe during a hurricane,' Colleen contradicted.

'No, but it's a mini tropical paradise, a great spot to spend a day.'

Melinda's eyes had a wicked glint, and her mouth twitched into a slight smile. Adam wanted to ravish those luscious lips. A knot of excitement twisted in his chest. 'So what are you smiling about?'

'Oh, just daydreaming.' She held his gaze with a sultry look.

'Hmm... maybe you'll tell me later.'

Clouds stretched across the night sky, blocking out the stars. A cool wind blasted them and the black clouds flickered with flashes of lightning. 'Looks like that squall will hit us sooner than I thought,' Adam said. 'We should head back.' He hoped they could out run the storm.

After a jolting half hour ride, the island of Bimini was coming into view – at least he hoped it was Bimini; he had forgotten how dark the ocean was at night. Only the tiny lights from houses illuminated the outline of the island. He aimed the boat north, with the island to their starboard side. The inlet should be along this stretch, but he couldn't find it.

Adam propelled the boat through the turbulent seas. The wind assaulted the boat, and waves splashed a briny spray over the bow. Lightning flashed and outlined sinister roiling thunderheads towering like a celestial mountain range. Then a gray curtain of rain appeared and advanced toward the boat, blocking Adam's view of the island. All for trying to make a good impression on Melinda, he thought.

'Looks like we're going to get wet, Ladies.'

Barb and Colleen huddled under the cover of the canvas top.

Melinda laughed as she looked up at the flapping canvas over their heads. 'That's not going to keep you very dry. In this storm, it'll be about as useless as one of those paper parasols in a Piña Colada.'

The wall of rain hit their boat. Adam shivered as large raindrops pelted his skin, and the wind, thunder and lightning intensified.

Melinda met his eyes and held his gaze. 'The sooner we get through the channel and into the harbor the better, Adam.'

He read her silent message of concern and nodded that he understood. They were in trouble and Adam didn't want to panic Barb or Colleen, but he knew that Melinda recognized the danger.

Finally, Adam decided to ask Melinda for help. 'I can't find the inlet; we should've past it by now. Can you see it?'

Melinda shook her head. 'I'll watch for it. You keep us off the reef.'

Adam slowed the boat down and strained to see through the rain and darkness. 'I don't recognize any landmarks.'

'Are we lost?' Colleen asked.

'Not exactly, just can't see the entrance to the inlet. Maybe I should turn around.'

Melinda checked the gauges. 'We're low on fuel; we better find it quick.' Then she looked at the compass and her mouth dropped open. 'That can't be....'

'What's wrong?' Adam asked, and then looked at the compass himself. 'We were heading North with Bimini on our starboard side, but the compass says South.'

'But we didn't turn around, and the island is still on our right,' Melinda said.

'Uh oh, aren't we in the Bermuda Triangle?' Barb asked, humming the *Twilight Zone* tune.

'Don't start, Barb,' Colleen said. 'Maybe the compass is broken.'

'It's not broken, and we're not victims of the Bermuda Triangle,' Adam said. 'Just relax.'

'There's got to be a reason,' Melinda said as she stared down into the water. Then she reached out and gripped his arm. 'Oh my, God, Adam, turn the boat around, now!'

CHAPTER SIX

Adam swung the boat around, and headed north again. 'What is it?' He asked. 'I can see the bottom,' Melinda said, pointing in the water. 'I know why were heading South instead of North.'

Barb and Colleen ran over to the side and stared into the dark water. 'We're over a reef,' Barb said. 'It's shallow.'

'Oh shit,' Adam said. 'We're on the eastern side of the island aren't we?'

Melinda nodded rapidly, and her eyes widened. 'Get us out of here before we run aground.'

'What's wrong? Where are we?' Colleen shouted over the thunder and pounding rain, her voice edged with panic.

'We rode all the way to the other side of the island.' Melinda said. 'It's all shallow reefs on this side – not safe for power boats.'

'Melinda, watch for exposed coral,' Adam ordered.

She ran up to the bow, hung over the railing. 'Take it slow.'

Adam's heart thundered in his chest. If his boat runs up on the coral, it'll damage the hull and they'll be stranded several hundred yards off shore in the dark. How could he be so stupid? While he was so busy trying to impress Melinda, he put them all in this dangerous situation.

'I think we're off the reef,' Melinda said. 'I can't see the bottom anymore.'

Adam checked his compass. 'We're at the tip of the island and heading to the western side.'

'Thank God,' Colleen said. 'Now where is the inlet?'

'I'm watching for it,' Melinda answered. 'The rain has slowed so I can see landmarks now.'

Finally, Adam safely reached the inlet. When he docked at Weeches Marina, Barb and Colleen quickly climbed off the boat.

'A little too much excitement for me,' Barb said. 'Thanks for the ride anyway.'

'Dry clothes are all I want right now,' Colleen said as she and Barb hurried in the direction of their motel room.

'Nothing like a little excitement to get your adrenalin pumping.' Adam tied rubber bumpers between his boat and the dock.

Melinda shook her head. 'You were very lucky tonight. You had no business taking us out on your boat if you knew a storm was coming.'

Adam stepped on the dock next to her, crossing his arms over his chest. He could see the storm brewing in her eyes. 'I *did* check the weather report, and a storm wasn't expected to hit us until late tonight. A rogue storm isn't my fault.'

'Well you shouldn't take your boat out at night if you don't know where you're going.'

He tried to stay calm and not shout back at her. It wouldn't solve anything. 'I do know these waters. I've been here several times, but no one can see landmarks when the visibility is ten feet.'

'I hate that reckless, macho *attitude*.'

'I would never put anyone in danger on purpose, Melinda.' He ran a hand though his wet blond hair. 'Reckless? Macho? Maybe you don't know me as well at you think.'

'Well, you can't deny that you were trying to show off.'

'You're right. I was trying to show off a little.'

'I figured as much.' Her anger seemed to abate slightly.

'But not to Barb or Colleen,' he added. 'I've been attracted to you since we first met.' And not just your good looks, he told himself. He also admired her adventurous nature and her professionalism.

Finally, she smiled. 'Why didn't you say something before?'

'Well, I've started to a couple times, but with the giggle sisters following me around, I haven't had the chance to get you alone.'

Melinda laughed. 'Yeah, I'd say they both have the hots for you.'

'Nice ladies, but not my type.'

Melinda looked up at the sky and changed the subject. 'We'll probably get another storm tonight. I should check out Rick's boat and see if it took on any water after all that rain. Want to keep me company?'

The full moon's milky glow appeared between parting clouds, illuminating their short walk to Rick's boat.

Melinda jumped on board. 'Looks like the Sea Venture weathered the storm.' She lifted the hatch to check the engine. 'Bilge pump is working fine.'

Adam stepped onto the boat. He liked the way her wet hair was slicked back away from her face and hooked behind her ears. He eyed her earlobes and thought about nibbling them. 'I owe you an evening cruise on a better night.'

'I'll take you up on it. I just hope Barb and Colleen won't have bad memories of this trip. I need to keep good customers. Mike and Cassidy seem to be enjoying the trip, but they're from Pennsylvania, so there's no telling if I'll get return business from them.'

Adam moved close to Melinda. 'You seem overly concerned about your business. Are you having problems?'

Melinda turned away from Adam and glanced across the harbor. 'There was so much bad publicity in the newspapers after Dan's accident, business has tapered off.'

He moved up behind her and touched her shoulder. 'Do you want to tell me what happened?'

She was silent for a moment, and then sighed deeply. 'We were having problems anchoring the boat in thirty feet of water. Dan always bragged about how long he could hold his breath and how deep he could free dive, so he said he would dive down and secure the anchor. I told him not to. We got into a fight, and I told him I was tired of his daredevil stunts. He just laughed and said, 'watch me.' After he dove underwater and didn't come up for a long time Rick went in after him.' She hesitated, then took a breath and swallowed hard. 'Dan had passed out underwater. We pulled him on board, tried to resuscitate him and called for rescue, but he didn't make it.'

Adam came up behind Melinda, wrapping his arms around her. 'I'm so sorry, Sweetheart. That's horrible; a real tragedy.'

Adam felt Melinda lean into his embrace. She rested her hands on his arms.

'It's been almost a year and I'm recovering, but my business hasn't snapped back yet.' She sighed heavily. 'I must sound pretty shallow.'

Adam whispered in her ear. 'Of course not, that's how you make a living, pay your bills, and put food on the table. That's not shallow.'

'Thanks for saying that.' Melinda turned to face him, backing away slightly, but staying close enough to keep within his light embrace. She studied his eyes and her lips parted.

Adam's heart leaped in his chest. He was dying to kiss her, to draw her against his body, but he didn't want to rush her. 'So, when would you like another island cruise?' His voice sounded unexpectedly hoarse, full of building passion.

'Soon.' She smiled wickedly. 'We'll take off and cruise the islands, escape the world, live on coconuts and fish, sunbathe nude, eliminate our tan lines…'

Adam felt her words in his groin. 'I like the way you think. How 'bout we take a cruise early in the morning? I can have you back in time to do the night dive.'

'Sounds like a plan, although I guess I'll have to forget about the 'escape the world' idea.'

Adam took her face earnestly in his hands. 'No, don't give up on that dream. We could take an extended vacation some day and cruise the Bahamas or the Caribbean.'

There was no mistaking the emotion in her eyes now. His cock stirred, threatening to swell. He tilted her face toward his and at last, lowered his mouth on hers.

His tongue thrust between her lips, blindly searching for her tongue. She opened her mouth for him, returning his kiss with fevered intensity. Then he pulled her impossibly close, crushing her soft breasts against his chest. A slight moan escaped her lips and the sound of it sent a throbbing heat straight to his cock. The hard bulge now strained painfully inside his jeans.

They kissed deeper, ignited in passion. Melinda dug her fingers into his hair and ground her hips against his erection. Adam's mind reeled, like he was drunk on one too many beers.

He devoured her neck then, licking her fiery skin, running the tip of his tongue to her ear, nibbling her tender earlobe.

Melinda shivered in his arms. 'It feels so good.'

'It certainly does,' he whispered back.

She ran her hands over his chest, down his hips, over his ass.

He caught his breath. 'Melinda.'

'Yes.' She breathed hot against his neck.

'Maybe we should go inside.'

'Yes.'

Adam relaxed his hold on her. He looked into her eyes. 'Are you okay with this?'

She nodded; a provocative gleam sparkling in her eyes.

'Your room or mine?'

'Here.'

'Here?' He looked around at the hard, wet deck, then up at the sky. Clouds gathered overhead, and the wind rustled the palm trees. Another storm was coming. 'A bed would be a lot more comfortable, and we wouldn't have to worry about getting drenched, or be seen by someone wandering by.'

'Where's your sense of adventure?'

He gave it some serious thought. 'Well, why not?' he decided, pulling her back into his arms.

Melinda pushed him away and laughed. 'No, I meant there, in the cabin!' She pointed to a small door next to the steering wheel.

'Ah, there is good.' Adam took her hand and led her down the steps into the cabin.

CHAPTER SEVEN

Moonlight filtered through four tiny portholes, illuminating the small cabin with a surreal glow. Melinda felt like she was walking in slow motion within a dream. The boat rocked and creaked, and the wind howled outside.

Adam came up behind her. He glided his rough hands along her shoulders; his warm breath tickled the back of her neck. He folded her into his arms and nuzzled her ear. 'Cozy in here, I like it.'

Along one side of the cabin was a built-in twin-sized bed, and along the other side, a table with a built-in bench. At the end of the cabin, a sink, mini stove and compact refrigerator completed a small galley. Another door led into a cramped head with a shower and toilet.

'It's small, but comfortable.' Her hands shook now in anticipation. How long had she needed this? Heat throbbed between her legs. She faced him, pulled him to her, sought his mouth again, liquid fire pulsing in her veins.

He was more than willing. 'You're sure this is what you want?'

Her voice came out in a sensuous whisper. 'Definitely… oh, God, wait, we should get some protection first.'

He smiled. 'Have it.' He retrieved his wallet from his back pocket, lifted out a couple foil packs and waved them in the air. 'I came prepared.'

'Were you planning to get lucky with all three of us tonight?'

'Hmm, interesting thought, but no. Besides, you should never question a guy about keeping condoms in his wallet. Be grateful that he's prepared.'

'Come here.' Melinda seized Adam's arm and drew him close again.

He took her mouth with bruising force, shoving his tongue in. A soft moan of approval purred in her throat. His hands, however, approached her tentatively, roaming up around her ribs.

Too slow; she couldn't wait anymore. She grabbed his hands and placed them squarely on her tits. He took her hint, squeezing and kneading them. He pinched her nipples until they stiffened into hard nubs. Slipping his fingers under the straps of her dress, he yanked the top down, exposing her. When he slid is tongue over the nipple and sucked it into his mouth, her gasp filled the room.

She reached out and tugged his shirt out of his pants. 'Take this off.'

While he pulled the shirt over his head, Melinda stroked the bulge inside his jeans. With excited hands, she unbuttoned his pants and slid his zipper down.

'Let me help.' His voice was urgent with passion. He shoved the jeans down his hips. Melinda smiled; he wasn't wearing any underwear. His cock was thick and hard; a drop of semen glistened at the tip.

He turned his urgent attentions to Melinda. He tugged her dress down over her hips, letting it drop to her feet; a filmy pile of tropical colors.

Naked except for a red, silk thong, she slid her hands up seductively to her breasts and squeezed them while he stood back for a moment, admiring her body with a mesmerized gaze. 'Nice,' he managed to say. He moved closer, his fingers sliding along the string waist band of her thong. 'Oh, I like these.' He reached behind her, grabbed her ass and then pulled her against him.

His stiff erection pressing against her thigh made her moan, and she ground her thigh against the hard shaft. She was soaking wet now; her thong was drenched.

Through the thin silky fabric, Adam found her sensitive nub and rubbed it. She caught her breath, rocking her mound into his touch.

He then hooked his thumbs into the front of her thong, and slid the red triangle of material down to her ankles. When he knelt to help the thong over her feet, he grabbed her ass and pressed his mouth on her pussy, lightly sucking and licking.

She groaned low in her throat, her breaths quick and panting; her knees quivering.

Between the exquisite sensations she was feeling and the rocking motion of the boat, she had to spread her feet apart to steady herself. She gripped his hair to keep from tumbling over.

Adam pushed open her labia, teasing her raw, throbbing clitoris with the tip of his tongue. Her head was spinning. She was propelled into a whirlwind of ecstasy. 'Oh, you so know how to use you mouth,' she gasped. The pent-up desire was about to explode inside her. 'Adam if you don't stop, I'm going to come.'

But he wouldn't stop. While he drove her mad with his mouth, he suddenly thrust a finger into her hole. Her sharp cry echoed within the walls of the small cabin as the orgasm rocketed through her body and the pulsing contractions rippled through every muscle.

Slowly, very slowly, the aftershocks died down and her moans quieted.

Adam stood and pulled her into his arms. 'Did I do okay?'

Melinda's body was still quivering. 'So so,' she teased him. 'You'll have to practice some more.'

'Oh, you are a wicked one,' he said as he swung her up off the floor, carried her to the narrow bed and dropped her onto the cushion. Then he lay down beside her, the full length of his muscular body resting against her hot skin.

Melinda sat up then, and knelt between Adam's knees. 'My turn,' she said. She seized his cock in her hand and glided her fist up and down. Squeezing slightly, a pearly drop slipped out of his slit. When he groaned, she moved her hand faster, then dropped her head to run her tongue over the head, lapping the salty drop. She opened her mouth wide and slid his engorged cock in. The musky male scent made her wet and droplets from her pussy trickled down her sensitive skin.

Adam stretched his arms behind his head, showing off the muscles in his shoulders and chest. Melinda groaned at the sight, and slid her mouth down to his sack. Adam's body shuddered. 'Yes,' he said, his voice a throaty groan, 'that's incredible.'

Melinda heard the sound of a foil wrapper being torn, then felt Adam's hands lift her up to him. 'I can't wait. I want you now.' With shaky hands, he slid on the condom. He gripped her around her waist as she straddled him and positioned herself over his cock. In one motion he raised his hips and pushed her down, thrusting his thick cock inside her. They both cried out.

She rode him until her legs ached. Her clit was swollen and throbbing, her hole wet and clenching his sex. He sat up, roughly turned her onto her back, and entered her again. Beads of sweat trickled down his face and she reveled in that massive body hovering over her, thrusting deep into her. She wrapped her legs tighter around his waist and tilted her hips up to him. A low groan escaped her as her body jerked into another orgasm.

'That's it, baby.' His breathing was hard and rapid as he continued the rhythm. He exhaled in a deep growl as violent shudders raked his body. When he finally caught his breath, he stretched out alongside her.

She ran a hand over his damp chest and felt his heart pounding. He wrapped his arms around her, sliding his fingers into her hair, and pulling her head down against his chest. Their breathing, their heartbeats slowed in synchronicity.

After a time, he untangled himself from her and hopped off the bed. Melinda couldn't take her eyes off his body as he walked to the head. Incredible body, she thought, like a God from Atlantis. Satisfied and amazed with their love making, she realized she had finally ended her year-long sequester from men. Now what?

Melinda felt a tug at her heart as Adam gently sponged a cool, damp towel over her body. Was she falling for him, or was it all just sex? Was she ready to sink herself into another relationship? And was she risking her heart on yet another carefree, reckless type like Dan?

Rick had told her to have a summer fling, not to get serious. She wasn't sure if she could do that. In the past, she jumped into relationships with a daredevil's compulsion. Maybe she was reckless, too – when it came to relationships. She would try to slow things down this time, get to know him, have a little wild sex, but not let her heart lead her blindly.

'We should drag ourselves back to our rooms,' she said. 'We can't spend the night here. Rick may decide to take the boat out early in the morning.'

'Your room or mine?'

Melinda smiled at his impromptu Groucho Marx impersonation. 'If I spend the night with you, I don't think I'll get any sleep. I haven't slept with anyone for a while...'

'You don't have to explain, Melinda. It's okay. I'll stop by in the morning and then we can go out on our private cruise. We'll be back in time for the night dive.'

He picked up her dress and thong and tossed them to her, then stepped into his jeans.

CHAPTER EIGHT

Adam's boat skimmed over the sparkling water. In the distance, an isolated cluster of palm trees and a horseshoe-shaped white beach seemed to float on water. They approached the tiny island of Honeymoon Harbor.

Easing back on the throttle, Adam slowed the boat and let it drift toward shore.

'Could you drop the anchor?'

'Sure.' Melinda ran up to the bow and grabbed the anchor line and chain in both hands, swung the metal anchor like a pendulum, and then flung it out over the water. It splashed through the surface and settled on the sandy bottom.

Adam reversed the boat, moving slowly until the anchor was set. 'Ready to go exploring? The water's probably waist deep so be careful when you jump in.'

Melinda untied her sarong and stuffed it in her beach bag. She had worn her favorite two piece suit. The metallic blue green color matched the color of the ocean.

Adam let out a long whistle. 'Wow. Nice suit. Haven't seen you wear that one diving.'

'Bikinis have a tendency to shift around under scuba gear. Once, after a dive, I found my top around my waist.'

'Wished I'd been there.' Adam hooked a ladder on the stern, then entered the water.

Melinda sat on the bow and used her hands to push herself off the boat and into the aqua water. 'The water's wonderful, so warm.'

When Adam caught up to her, he locked his fingers with hers and led her onto the powder white beach, the foamy water skimming their feet. 'Want to check out that wreck?'

They strolled over to the large sailboat hull half buried in the sand. 'Not much left of it.'

'The mast, rigging, and electronics were stripped down to the frame after it was beached here. The bow section was damaged beyond repair, so the owners salvaged any valuable parts.'

'I wonder where she sailed before her untimely end here on this beach.' Melinda thought how frightening it must have been to be on a sailboat caught in a hurricane. She pulled Adam by the hand away from the wreck. 'Give me the island tour.'

They continued up the beach, then turned inland and followed a sandy path toward the center of the island. Tall, palm trees tossed their green fronds against the breeze. Clusters of red hibiscus, palmettos with fan-shaped leaves, cactus and a few banana plants were densely packed on either side of the meandering trail, creating natural walls. The breeze was fragrant with sea spray and sweet jasmine. After a few minute's walk, they reached the center of the island. Melinda could see the ocean on both sides and hear the waves rhythmically caressing two shorelines.

The path then opened onto a small circular clearing surrounded by flowers and palm trees. 'What a beautiful spot.' Melinda leaned up against a palm tree, its bark was smooth and cool. She slid her hands behind her back. 'Perfect place for a kiss.'

The sultry gaze in Adam's eyes made her heart skip. He came up to her, grasped her wrists, pinning her arms behind her back and kissed her with such force that Melinda was soon gasping for air. He released her hands and slipped the bathing suit straps off her shoulders, then pulled her top down to her waist. A trail of hot, moist kisses glided over her tits.

Then his tongue teased each nipple until they were erect and sensitive. A string of nerves seemed to be connected to her female core. Each time he licked or sucked her nipples, her vagina clenched and her clit throbbed.

Melinda combed her fingers through his hair and pulled herself hard against his chest. The dark, coarse chest hairs tickled and electrified the skin of her breasts. His bulging erection pressed against her mound. She rocked her hips and rubbed against him. She was wet and hot with arousal. An annoying thought suddenly came to mind. 'Oh, no…'

'What?' Adam whispered into her neck.

'We forgot something.'

Adam abruptly stopped kissing her neck. 'Damn, you're right. Guess we need to make a stop at the boat.' He stepped back and stared at her breasts. 'You're beautiful; I love seeing you naked. We don't need our suits here.'

Melinda adjusted her top back into place. 'Tempting, but what if someone shows up?'

'You can see boats coming into shore; you'd have plenty of time to put your suit back on if you wanted. Though, most people wouldn't care.' Adam took her hand and followed the path back to the beach, then ran into the water. 'Hold on, I'll get them.' When he reached the boat, he placed his hands on the side and lifted himself up, giving Melinda a great view of his flexing arm and back muscles. She slowly walked up to the boat and stood waist-deep in the water.

Adam slid his yellow and black trunks over his hips and kicked them to the side, then grabbed a foil package out of a small duffle bag.

'Want me to come on board?'

'No, stay there, I have an idea.' He climbed down the ladder into the water.

She couldn't take her eyes off his naked butt, or his thick cock pointing straight up. 'Think you need to work on your tan lines,' she teased.

'Why don't you work on yours?' When she didn't answer, he clucked his tongue. 'Chicken?'

She unhooked her top and flung it onto the boat. 'Okay, but keep an eye out for boats.' She slid the bikini bottom off and tossed it next to her top. The warm water stroked her naked body and she shivered at the shear delight of it. It made her feel free, decadent, and extremely horny.

'Should we head back to our private spot?'

'No. Here, in the water.' He held up the condom package, and then placed it on the top of the ladder. 'I'm prepared this time.'

'Do condoms work under water?' She grabbed his ass and pulled his body against her.

'We'll find out.' He slipped two fingers in her hole and she cried out.

She rode his hand while his thumb rubbed her clit and the back and forth motion of the waves heightened her desire. 'That feels so good.' She half closed her eyes as she responded to his fingers probing her soft, slick vagina. The delicious pressure rose, bringing her to the edge of her control. She tried pushing his hand away. 'I want you inside of me, now.'

He resisted and shoved deeper inside her with his fingers, quickening his pace. 'I'm not done playing, baby, just enjoy it.'

She dug her fingers into his shoulders to balance herself as the pleasurable sensations built up, gathered force like a huge wave cresting, and then curled and crashed into turbulent quaking. She panted against his neck and wrapped her arms around him until the currents of rapture subsided.

'Let me sit on the ladder for a minute.' He had lifted himself out of the water, slipped the condom on, then slid back into the blue-green sea and pulled her into his arms.

She raised one leg around his hip and Adam guided his engorged shaft to her swollen sex lips and thrust his cock inside, filling her deeply. A groan caught in her throat as she wrapped her legs around his hips. Adam played to the rhythm of the waves and bounced her up and down the length of his cock. He closed his eyes as he bucked hard inside her and came in shuddering tremors. He leaned up against the rocking boat and let out a long satisfied sigh.

CHAPTER NINE

As soon as they finished their lunch of conch fritters and chicken sandwiches, Melinda checked her watch. 'Stop watching the time,' Adam said. 'We still have a couple hours before we have to leave.' He had to teach her how to focus on something other than her business. Running her own dive shop had to be demanding, and she did a great job, but she didn't need to obsess about it. She worried too much, and her life seemed totally consumed by her work. Although, today, he'd seen glimpses of the real Melinda – her intelligent, outgoing and very affectionate side – and he wanted to know more. She was so comfortable in the water, and he wished he could get over his fears so he could enjoy diving with her. Scuba diving was her life, her passion. If he told her about his fear of deep water, she wouldn't want to have anything to do with him. He was determined to get over those fears while developing his scuba diving skills.

She combed her hair while sitting on the bow, and stared at the island. He liked how she looked, so relaxed, hanging out on his boat nude. Earlier, when they'd climbed on the boat, she didn't even grab a towel to dry off; she just let the sun and light breeze whisk away the salt water on her skin.

'Feel like a little role playing?' Melinda asked with a wicked grin.

His eyes widened. 'You have my attention. What do you have in mind?'

She pointed to the wrecked sailboat. 'How about… I'm a ship wrecked castaway on this deserted island, and you're the sexy, native who captures me?'

'I'm game.'

'First we need a few supplies.'

He quickly figured out her meaning. There were a couple condoms left; maybe they could use them up before they had to leave. 'There, in my bag.'

Melinda grabbed the remaining two foil packs, then untied the line attached to one of the rubber bumpers and coiled it into a bundle.

'Rope?' He tried to look nonchalant, but felt his cock pulse and begin to get hard.

'How else are you going to tie up your captive?' She handed him the condoms and rope, and her sly smile took his breath away.

'Guess we have everything we need.' Was his voice quivering? He suddenly felt like a teenager about to get laid for the first time. She was going to drive him mad.

After they jumped into the water, he swept her up into his arms and carried her to the beach, then gently set her down on her feet. He held the condoms in his teeth as he tied a loop around the end of the rope. 'I think a bowline knot will work.' He started to tie her wrists together, but she slipped away and sprinted down the beach.

'You'll have to catch me first,' she shouted.

He chased after her, but his steps slowed in the soft sand, and were even more difficult with a raging hard on. When he reached her, he flung his arm around her waist. She squirmed playfully and cried out, but he managed to slip the rope around her wrists, then he gently tightened the loop. Her hands were tied in front of her, her arms squeezed her tits, jutting them upward, enhancing her cleavage.

'Captured,' he announced, then hesitated. 'The rope isn't too tight is it?'

'No, it's fine.' She was panting now, her breasts heaving with every breath. 'So where are you taking me, native?'

'To a place of fantasies and pleasures beyond imagining.'

'Oh, I like the sound of that.'

He gently pulled her along the sandy path, weaving through the thick growth of palmettos and cacti to the sandy clearing surrounded by palm trees and tropical flowers. Watching her breasts sway and bounce with each step turned him on, and his cock ached for that warm, moist place between her legs. He didn't know how long he could maintain control.

Looping the rope several times around a palm tree with half hitch knots, Adam tied her arms above her head. She had only enough room to sway her body slightly away from the tree.

'Touch me,' she pleaded, her eyes gleaming with desire.

He massaged her breasts with both hands while probing her mouth with his tongue. He caught her gasp of pleasure in his mouth as he squeezed her tits and rubbed her nipples until they were hard and taut.

One smooth, slim leg wrapped around his knee, attempting to pull his body toward her. Obligingly, he grabbed her buttocks with both hands and ground his engorged sex against her pubic bone, gently crushing her breasts with his hard chest. She swung side to side from the rope, rocking her body against his. He slid his body down and knelt in the powder-soft sand between her legs. Opening her labia, he lapped around her clit, her inner folds, and then slipped his tongue inside her hole.

She cried out. 'Slow down, I don't want to come yet.'

'Just hold back a little longer, baby.' With a feather touch of his tongue, he tantalized her raw, oversensitive clitoris, stopping just when he knew, by the sound of her breathing, that she was close. Her body was shaking with need and he couldn't hold back any longer. He picked up one of the condom packs he'd dropped, shook off the sand, and opened the package and slid on the condom.

Swiftly, he lifted her up and she wrapped her legs around his hips, locking her ankles. Her panting and sighs of pleasure heightened his desire. With his hands on her ass, he guided himself to her hole and thrust hard inside her. They both cried out. The corded muscles in his neck and chest strained as he struggled to hold her up and keep his balance. She pulled on the rope, using it for added support.Her dark eyelashes fluttered closed as she threw back her head, squeezed her legs tighter and shouted his name, the climax shuddering through her body.

He gripped her ass and pumped harder and faster, until the quaking rattled his body and he came.

* * *

Melinda could feel his heart pounding in his chest. Every delicious nerve in her body sparked with sensation. Still tied to the tree, she rested her head on his shoulder, enjoying the closeness. For months, she had refused to acknowledge the aching sexual tension imprisoned in her body, but Adam had managed to stir up and release the passions inside her. What had passed between them was more than just good sex. Maybe she was falling in love. Still, she wasn't going to push herself, or him, into anything. Leaning back against the palm tree, she noticed a light sheen of sweat glistening on Adam's skin. *God he was handsome.*

He uncoupled from her, eyeing her body. He smiled. 'Wow, you're beautiful.' Then he remembered the rope. 'I'm so sorry, Sweetheart. How are your arms?' He reached up and tried to loosen the knots, but with Melinda's struggling she had inadvertently pulled the knots tighter.

'I'm fine.' But then Melinda looked out at the sparkling blue water, and gasped in horror. 'Adam, quick untie me, there's a boat coming to shore.'

Adam swung around and froze. 'Shit!' He charged down the path, weaving around the spiny bushes and palmettos, leaving Melinda tied to the tree. She struggled to loosen the knots, but had no luck.

'Adam, untie me!' she shouted.

She saw him run into the water, but he stopped abruptly when he reached chest-deep water. Then the realization and horror hit her. It was Adam's boat, and it was drifting away from the island. He stood motionless in the water as the strong current carried the boat swiftly out to sea.

'Swim for it, Adam! You can reach it!'

Either he didn't hear her or he ignored her. What was he doing? Why wouldn't he go after it? She struggled and tugged on her bindings. If she could only get loose, she'd swim to the boat. She was too far away to hear his words, but Melinda figured by his gestures that his vocabulary was limited to colorful profanity. With a sinking sensation in her chest, she watched the boat drift farther out to sea. What would they do now?

Adam trudged up the path to Melinda. When he reached her, the devastation was evident in his eyes. He shook his head and without a word untied her.

She lowered her arms and shook them to ease the stiffness. 'Why didn't you swim after it?'

He shot her a strange look and didn't answer.

'I would've at least tried. It wasn't that far out,' she said.

'You don't understand, Melinda.' His voice was hollow with defeat and frustration.

'No, I do understand. We're stuck on this island with no food and no water.' Melinda's voice shook with anger. 'All we have is a piece of rope and a condom, and we're naked. I thought you secured the anchor!'

'I did. But the current changed directions and pulled it free.'

'Why does every outing with you turn into a disaster?'

'I don't have control over the weather or shifting currents or…' He shook his head in defeat.

Melinda stared at the white speck heading toward the faint indigo line dividing the blue sky from the aqua sea. Adam's boat was disappearing over the horizon. A jumble of emotions bombarded her – anger, panic, fear. Once his boat drifts into the Gulf Stream currents, it will be carried out into the open sea and lost forever.

They were stranded.

Adam pulled her into his arms and tried to soothe her. 'I'm so sorry, sweetheart.'

Tears stung her eyes, but she willed herself not to sob. 'This will put me out of business for sure. If I had my cell phone, I'd call my father at my shop and tell him to hang a 'For Sale' sign in the window.'

'A cell phone wouldn't work out here anyway,' he offered half-heartedly.

'I hope Rick at least takes the divers out on the night dive tonight. But even if he does,' she realized, 'this whole fiasco is going to make me look flighty, incompetent and unreliable – not the professional I'm trying to be!' And just when she'd thought Dan's accident would at last be forgotten in the media.

She could hear Dan saying, 'I told you so'. She collapsed on the sand, drew her knees up and hid her face in her hands.

'I think we have more to worry about than your business. We could be stuck here for days.' Adam turned and strode off toward the center of the island.

She jumped to her feet. 'Great, just great! And what are we supposed to do now?' She kicked sand, sending a cloud of white powder in his direction.

'Look for food, water, and make a shelter,' he shouted over his shoulder.

CHAPTER TEN

I t doesn't look pretty, but it'll keep the sun and rain off us.' Adam tried to sound upbeat, but the tension between them was as thick as quicksand. He secured the lean-to between two palm trees with the rope. Branches and vines tied together with smaller vines formed the rectangular frame that held several layers of woven banana leaves and palm fronds. If they were lucky, the wind wouldn't demolish it.

After dropping a small bunch of bananas next to the shelter, Melinda studied Adam's creation. 'Nice job. Looks like we're moving in.'

Adam examined his work, then attached a few more leaves. 'At least for the night. I doubt they'll be searching for us in the dark, especially with that storm moving in.' He tilted his head in the direction of several thunderheads building over the ocean. The water once sparkling blue-green had changed to a dull gray, and the wind shook the shelter. It was his fault they were stuck there. He should have checked the anchor. Fear of deep water prevented him from swimming after the boat. Now their lives were in danger. Why was a frightening childhood experience still affecting him now? He needed to tell Melinda, explain it all to her. If there was any chance for a future together, he had to be honest with her. She could decide to keep him off her dive boat, or worse, she could write him out of his life. The thought struck a pain in his gut, but it wasn't right to keep this from her.

'I found bananas, but didn't have any luck finding water.'

Adam stood up and took her in his arms. 'Don't worry, I found a few conch shells to collect the rain.' A loud crack of thunder rumbled over their heads. It's going to be a long night, he thought. 'Rick's a smart guy; it won't be long until he realizes we're missing.' He knelt down and started digging a trench around the shelter.

Melinda knelt down and used a piece of driftwood to help. 'But we didn't tell him we were coming here.'

'Boats stop here all the time; we'll just have to keep an eye out and wave a boat down.' He jumped tó his feet, snapped off a fan-shaped palm frond, several feet long, and waved it back and forth like a flag.

'Oh, sure, and who do you think will come to an island with a naked man waving a palm frond in the air?'

'Yeah, you're right, here…' He handed her the palm frond. 'You try it; someone will surely come when they see a beautiful, naked woman waving a palm frond.'

Melinda chuckled then gazed into his eyes; she was searching for something there, trying to read his mind. 'Thanks for trying to make me feel better… oh, God,' she said in horror, dropping the palm frond. 'My parents will be frantic.'

Adam tried to calm her. 'We'll be all right, and our families will get through this.'

After another crack of thunder, Melinda crawled under the lean-to.

'Cold?' Adam sat down and slid his arms around her.

She shook her head. 'I'm warm enough.' She took in a long breath. 'I can smell the ozone. It'll rain soon.'

'We need the water. Besides, a storm will be a good durability test on my shelter.' He winked at her. Large raindrops splattered on the sand. 'You would've had to cancel the night dive anyway.' 'You must think me a fool worrying about my business when our lives are at stake.' She had to raise her voice to be heard over the rain pummeling the shelter.

'It's good to take pride in your work, but you can't let it consume your life.'

Melinda nodded. 'Maybe it's time to stop letting my business and my past run my life.'

'Damn, you're beautiful *and* smart,' Adam teased. 'I don't think this ordeal will hurt your dive shop. Don't give up yet.'

'I guess I just hate failing.'

'Successes and failures both have merit. You can learn a lot about yourself during tough times. Melinda, I have to tell you something.' He reached for her hand. 'It's my fault that we're stranded here.'

'No, we both should've remembered to check the anchor.'

Adam shook his head. 'You were right; the boat wasn't that far off-shore when I reached the beach. Some people are afraid to fly – I have a fear of deep water.'

She was stunned, disbelieving. 'Then how can you scuba dive?'

'Sheer will. Having an air tank strapped to my back makes it easier. I took up diving to help me get over this fear.'

'Why?'

He let out a long sigh. 'I was six years old and deep sea fishing with my dad. The seas were rough and I got seasick. When I leaned over the boat to heave my breakfast, a huge wave crashed over the bow and washed me overboard. Even with a life preserver on, I was tossed and beaten by the waves like a piece of driftwood. After several passes in the boat, my dad managed to pluck me out of the water. That was twenty-six years ago, but I still freak out in deep water.'

Melinda was silent for a long time, then pulled her hand free of Adam's grasp. 'You should've told me. You're putting yourself and other divers at risk.'

'I'm sorry Melinda, but I have to do this. I didn't tell you before because I was afraid you wouldn't let me dive or want to have anything to do with me.'

Lightening flashed, revealing her grim expression. 'You were right,' she snapped, 'it was foolish and dangerous.' She lay in the sand, turned her back to him and curled into a ball. Soon, the heavy rain and thunder inhibited further conversation anyway. Adam touched her shoulder, but she ignored him.

* * *

When Melinda awoke, it was night. Feeling disoriented, she frantically glanced at her surroundings. The rain had stopped and the lean-to had survived the storm. Her body was nestled against Adam's; his arms encircled her and her head rested on his chest. Not wanting to wake him, she didn't move. Wrapped in his strong arms, she felt peaceful, protected and loved. Why had she rejected him just when he'd tried to be honest; had showed her a glimpse of his feelings?

Her emotions reeled in her head. She was drawn to him – maybe falling in love with him – and yet the extreme actions he took to overcome his phobia reminded her of Dan's reckless, macho attitude even though there was a big difference between the two men. Dan was a foolish daredevil; Adam was trying to conquer his fears. Still, is it worth risking your life to conquer a shortcoming?

Except for the waves rhythmically skimming the shoreline, the island was silent – no wind, no rain, and no seagulls. The moon appeared through parting clouds, reflecting a glittering silver path across the black sea. The eerie luminescent beacon shone into their shelter, but offered little comfort. The sound of Adam breathing and the feel of his warm, hard body lulled her back to sleep.

Hours later, Melinda opened her eyes to a golden and orange sky. A light breeze rustled through the palm trees and the leaves on their shelter. She smiled at the seagulls scurrying along the shoreline, calling to other birds with a squawking chatter.

'Morning Sweetheart,' Adam said after a yawn.

She liked the sound of him calling her Sweetheart.

He drew her closer, his legs entangling with hers. 'Did you sleep okay?'

'Yes.' She felt his erection thick and hard against her thigh, and felt a trickle of moisture between her legs. Her body ached for him; she wanted him deep inside her.

He kissed the top of her head, then stroked her cheek with his fingers. He lowered his mouth over hers and kissed her softly, deeply. When he raised his head, the intense look in his eyes held her spellbound. 'Melinda, I love you.'

'You hardly know me, and I'm not sure how I want to handle…'

'You had a right to be upset, but it doesn't change how I feel. I've been in love with you since we first met a year ago.'

His words sent a burst of joy through her. Still, she hesitated. It was too sudden.

'Marry me.'

'Now I know you're delirious. We barely know each other, not to mention we're shipwrecked.'

'Spending eighteen or more hours stranded on a deserted island is equivalent to at least eight months of dating. And while we're getting to know each other better, we can plan a wedding.'

She smiled. 'I'll have to think about it. In the mean time...' She slid her hand between his legs, gripped his cock and slowly stroked it. 'We still have one condom left.'

His eyes sparkled with mischief, but then Adam suddenly sat up and froze.

'What is it?'

He was silent for a moment, then scrambled to his feet. 'Boat! I hear a boat!'

CHAPTER ELEVEN

Adam raced down the beach and snatched up the long palm frond and started waving it over his head. Melinda stumbled out of the lean-to, snapped off another palmetto frond and started waving it. 'I think they see us. Oh my God, it's Rick's boat.'

'Damn! They found us.' Adam laughed when he saw Melinda duck behind the shelter to hide her nude body. 'What's the matter, you're suddenly shy?' Adam used the fan shaped palm branch to cover himself.

Melinda strained to see the other passengers on the boat. Oh, God, she thought, the rest of my divers are on board. 'Adam, ask Rick for a towel or something for me to wear.'

Rick anchored the boat, then climbed into the water and walked toward the shore with something gripped in his hand. 'Everyone okay?' Rick asked. He waved to Adam, then to Melinda crouching behind the banana leaf and jungle-vine refuge.

'We're good,' Adam said.

Melinda waved.

Rick glanced at Adam's strategically placed palm frond and grinned. 'Your idea of a fig leaf?'

'Long story.'

'Can't wait to hear it.' Rick handed Adam two swimsuits. 'I thought you might need these.'

Adam shook his head in disbelief. 'How did you…? We left them on my boat.'

'A fisherman found your boat drifting around Great Isaac's Lighthouse. He towed it to Bimini late last night. Weeches Marina notified the Coast Guard. They've been searching for you two several miles north of Bimini all night.'

Adam slipped his swim trunks on. 'I figured my boat was halfway to England by now. I owe that fisherman a beer, for starters.'

Rick chuckled. 'When I noticed the swimsuits on the deck, I had a hunch. I know all the private romantic islands around here. And Colleen said you toured this area the other night. So, I headed south and searched a couple unnamed islands and then finally came here.'

'We should notify the Coast Guard to call off the search,' Adam said.

'Already radioed them when I saw two naked natives waving palm leaves. The Coast Guard said they'd contact your families and let them know you're okay.'

'Great news,' Melinda shouted from behind the shelter. 'Now, would someone please hand me my bathing suit?'

* * *

Shortly after they returned to Bimini, Adam and Melinda strode into the luncheonette and took a small table by the window; they were ravenous. When the waitress came over, they ordered scrambled eggs and Bimini bread with honey butter.

When Melinda spied the public phone in the back of the restaurant, she got up to call her parents. Adam sipped coffee while waiting for Melinda to finish.

She shifted her weight from side to side, punched numbers on the phone, waited, and then tried again. Frowning, she hung up the phone and plopped into a wooden chair across from Adam. 'I couldn't get through. The operator said the lines are busy.'

'Phones don't always work that well here. Why don't you try later tonight or tomorrow morning?' Adam reached out and squeezed her hand. 'Don't worry. The Coast Guard notified your parents.'

'I know, but still… we'll be getting back late from the night dive. I guess I'll try tomorrow.'

'You don't have to do the dive if you're tired, the others will understand.'

'But I don't want to disappoint our group.'

The waitress brought their orders. Melinda buttered a slice of bread and devoured it, then jabbed a fork into her eggs. 'Colleen and Barb are still interested in my Mexico trip, even after they knew about us spending the night on the island together. And Mike and Cassidy said they plan to come back to Bimini next year.'

'After what I told you, will I be diving with you again?'

'As long as you're not trying to prove anything to me,' Melinda said. 'It's okay if you don't ever get over your aversion to deep water.'

'I appreciate that, but I have to try. Now, are *you* trying to prove anything to anyone?'

Melinda shook her head. 'Not anymore. I know now that even after Dan died, I was still trying to show him that I could succeed in this business.'

Adam leaned across the table and kissed her gently. 'Maybe you need to look for someone willing to share your triumphs and failures.'

'And you have someone in mind?'

He nodded. He was in love with her and he was prepared to wait until she was ready to love again. 'Don't let the past hold you back from falling in love. Please.'

She held his gaze, her eyes sparkling with emotion. 'I *am* letting go of my past, because I've fallen in love with you.'

'Damn, I love you.' The few people sitting at the luncheonette counter had politely turned away, but Adam knew they were listening to their conversation. 'Let's get out of here.'

Outside, Adam pulled Melinda into his arms and kissed her. 'I hope you don't mind, but I plan to sign up for all your dive trips.'

'Looks like I'll be keeping a close eye on you.'

Adam glanced at his watch. 'We have about eight hours before the night dive. What would you like to do until then?' He hungered for the taste of her, the delights of her mouth, her body. 'I still have one condom left.'

'I'd love a warm bath.' She stroked his palm suggestively with her fingertips.

The heat pulsed in his veins. 'Your place or mine?' His cock hardened, threatening an obscene bulge.

'Mine. I have these wonderful lavender bath crystals. The aroma is so sensuous; it'll stir up all of your sexual fantasies.'

'Too late, I'm already stirred up.'

* * *

The next day, Adam was scrubbing his boat when Melinda jumped on board. Grinning and giddy, she wrapped her arms around his neck and kissed him fervently. He struggled to keep from toppling over.

'I guess you got through to your parents?'

She nodded. 'We made the front page of the *Sun Sentinel*. My dad said that the phone at my shop has been ringing all morning. Divers are signing up for the Bimini charter and asking if the trip includes an excursion to Honeymoon Harbor.'

Adam laughed and kissed her. 'Damn, I don't want to share our secret fantasy island.'

'It's not a secret anymore.'

Adam checked his watch. 'How about one more fantasy trip before our secluded island becomes a resort?'

'Another captured castaway gets ravished by the sexy native fantasy?'

He nodded. 'I'll make sure the anchor is secure this time.'

She kissed his neck and then whispered in his ear, 'Okay, but this time I do the ravishing!'

THE FRUIT OF HER LABORS

Iris N. Schwartz

CHAPTER ONE

Gretchen Collins hated everything about herself this morning. As she pulled black jeans up her pale and shapely legs, she thought, *Ugh, I can't stand this ghost-white skin.* As she snapped the pants shut, she thought, I detest this outie navel. And as she drew her dark blue sweater over the front of her body, *I hate these huge breasts.*

Last night, Elliot had emptied his dresser drawers of every bra, sweater, and pair of panties Gretchen had ever left at his place. He had cleared his living room shelves of all the CDs she'd lent him. Last night, Gretchen's boyfriend of two years had ferreted out of his apartment both birthday cards in which she had lovingly detailed her wishes for him, each photograph taken of the two of them, even the Museum of Modern Art passes she'd wanted to use with him next weekend. Anything and everything from their time together had been dumped into a cardboard box that Elliot had kicked across his carpet until it stood flush against the inside of his front door.

Elliot had pointed to the box. He'd told Gretchen to take it all. Then he'd pointed to the door. Her boyfriend of two years said he couldn't deal with her anymore. He couldn't be what she wanted him to be. Gretchen should get used to that and get out.

This morning Gretchen made the mistake of looking in her mirror. Damn this stick-straight hair! *Why do I have such a short, wimpy nose? And look at these obnoxiously large lips. I could give Mick Jagger a run for his money.* She sighed. Hadn't her best friend Margaret told her never to look straight into a mirror until two days after a break-up?

Sure, this twenty-eight-year-old artist felt more than a little deflated, but she certainly wouldn't walk out her door looking like a slob just because Elliot told her he wanted to see other people. Gretchen would fluff up her hair and reapply her lipstick before heading for her favorite produce stand – Elliot or no Elliot.

Besides, what was this 'see other' people terminology? When breaking up, why did men always say 'see other people' when they meant 'see other women'? Why did women always say 'see other people' when they meant 'see other men'? Was saying 'people' supposed to soften the blow?

Gretchen was breathing rapidly now. She was cursing Elliot under her breath. She wished she could curse him in several languages, but the fact is she remembered little of her high school French, and even less of her one-summer-abroad Italian. At least she had been smart enough not to move in with Elliot, though that hadn't kept her from being moved by him. No one stirred her – her loins as much as her heart – like Elliot.

Gretchen needed to get Elliot off her mind. She needed a pep talk from Margaret. Or better yet, a compliment from her new neighbor, six-foot-tall, dark-blonde Frank.

Frank, a thirty-year-old photographer arrived just last month from his native Indiana, hadn't caught on to the minimalist art of apartment dweller repartee. Unlike many residents of Manhattan's multistoried dwellings, Frank did more than grunt acknowledgment on the elevator, tilt his head when passing you on the stairs or croak hello while emptying his bulging laundry bag into a basement washer. Frank looked a neighbor in the eye with his own clear aqua gaze. He'd ask you your name, unaware that some might consider this no concern of his. When next you met, he'd address you by name, inquire of your health, and wait for a response – a response he seemed eager to hear!

Gretchen thought that Frank must be a good photographer, as he really wanted to know people. He must want to understand, perhaps even inhabit, his subjects. She imagined this would be as true for him with people as it would be with urban landscapes, architecture, flora, fauna – anything he might capture with one of those 35-millimeter beauties she'd seen slung over his shoulder.

Unlike the tired phrases tossed at her by Elliot while she'd stood, awkward, hopeful, in front of him, tag still hanging from the sleeve of a new dress, unlike those half-thought-out quarter-felt words, a compliment from Frank would be sincere. She'd want to hold it in her hand like a fragrant Winesap apple. She'd want to paint it, to the finest detail, with her Kolinsky sable brush.

Gretchen needed a compliment. At the very least, she needed to turn away from the mirror. Newly single Gretchen – passionate painter of the muted still life, pale portrayer of the dark side of fruits and vegetables – this Gretchen needed to lighten up. She grabbed her coat. *Black, of course*, she thought. *Do I own anything green? Pink?* She tossed her keys and money into a pocket, then bounded out the door.

She would buy fruit for the new painting commissioned by Frank: *Still Life with Berries and Wine* Gretchen had decided on the title almost immediately. Her new neighbor had admired her work when in her apartment for the first time last week, when he had knocked on her door and asked her if she could spare an orange or an apple. He'd forgotten to purchase fruit that day, and disliked ending a meal without one. (Gretchen figured it must be the farm boy in him, or the health enthusiast or, dare she hope, the sensualist?)

She remembered that, after gaining entrance, her new neighbor had studied each painting of hers for several minutes. Gretchen had two of her oil paintings hanging in the living room, and one in the kitchen. All three were lush, almost baroque depictions of exotic fruit – casabas, Freestone peaches, Jonathon apples, greengage plums – fruit in bowls, atop draped tables or arranged on trays, all ready to rumble with a viewer, or threatening to tumble onto a floor in the painting, past the matte borders, beyond the frame, off the canvas, and into an astounded but welcoming art lover's arms.

Frank studied each un-still life close up and from afar. He said he enjoyed the sensuality in her art, but would she mind working in a lighter palette for a painting for him? Would she accept a commission to paint for his kitchen a still-life arrangement of her choice?

Gretchen hadn't received a commission in over a year. She hadn't, more importantly, painted 'lighter' in maybe two years, not since... not since the advent of Elliot! She wouldn't stop to ponder that now. Gretchen could use the money; her last show hadn't sold as well as she'd hoped. And so she agreed to brighten her tone, elevate the mood, almost without thinking. Her sepia-washed brain might make way for vermilion, cadmium, golden ochre. She would paint something sunnier for Frank. Who knew what possibilities awaited her on this canvas?

Before she was aware of where her feet took her, she was at the nearest bus stop. Margaret thought it foolish for Gretchen to travel for produce when she had perfectly good food close by, but to Gretchen, perfectly good was not good enough.

Because of this the persnickety artist took the bus twice a week to her favorite produce stand, where the vine-ripened tomatoes were the reddest, the Greenleaf lettuce the springiest, the zucchini the smallest and sweetest, the peaches and plums the plumpest and most aromatic she could find anywhere in New York. And nothing was irradiated, waxed, or sprayed with poisons. If her relationships with men couldn't be perfect, if her finished paintings couldn't be perfect, if her sex life couldn't be perfect, then at least her fruits and vegetables could be – for artistic as well as nutritional purposes.

Margaret, Gretchen thought, may know about self-esteem, but she understood squat when it came to the less grand, but nonetheless essential, things in life. Like sketching unblemished eggplant cradled in a wooden bowl on your kitchen table or playing catch-up tongue with piquantly sweet mango juice rushing down your lover's arm.

Throughout her bus ride, Gretchen imagined the ripeness awaiting her at *Fong's*, a West Village landmark and purveyor of superior produce since long before Gretchen had moved to Manhattan. The half-hour trip was over almost as quickly as it started, and Gretchen was practically swooning by the time she arrived at the store. Her neighbor Frank would be thrilled with the results of his commission. Gretchen would see to that.

Once near the entrance, the artist began eyeing almost criminally voluptuous strawberries piled one atop another in pale mint green cardboard boxes. The berries looked so succulent that she wanted to smash her face into one of the containers, suctioning up three or four crimson nubbins at a time.

Gretchen turned away from the strawberries, ashamed at her sudden lasciviousness. Then she found herself staring at India-ink-hued blackberries cushioned in similar containers. This was followed by a boundless supply of purplish-black, indecently rotund blueberries. She yearned to devour all of these, on the spot.

What was the matter with her? She wondered what Margaret would have to say about this. Or what Elliot might opine. Still, she decided to give in and buy the berries. Certainly she had seen – and experienced – worse vices than this.

Gretchen smiled to herself, or so she thought, but looked down and realized she had been squeezing a strawberry rather suggestively, probably leering while in the act! If she kept this up she'd have to abandon *Fong's* for the run-of-the-mill stand near her apartment. Gretchen stared straight ahead while on line, and exited *Fong's* as quickly and decorously as possible.

While awaiting the bus home, she peered inside the market bag. She had memorized her shopping list, but in lieu of marinated tofu, bottled water, a head of broccoli, and a judicious supply of fruit for Frank's painting, Gretchen had purchased copious amounts of strawberries, blueberries, blackberries, peaches, and heavy cream. Now what would she have for dinner?

It was Elliot's fault. If he hadn't broken up with her, Gretchen would have followed her list precisely, right down to grass-green crucifers and plastic bin of bean curd.

Gretchen shook her head and looked down the street for her bus. Elliot had said he was tired of trying to figure her out. He said whatever he did never seemed to be good enough. Gretchen bit her bottom lip. It's not that she had complained. He knew that, and had told her so, but that had only made it worse. Elliot said he'd felt dissatisfaction emanate from her like cold air from a faulty heater.

Gretchen, now settled on a bus seat, stiffened at her next thought: *Maybe Elliot was the faulty heater.* Did it really matter now? The still-life painter thought she would be crying, or wanting to punch pillows, but didn't feel the need. Instead, she felt curiously free. Perhaps she had left before they'd said goodbye.

Gretchen picked at a blackberry through clear plastic wrap. The bumps on the one under her finger were similar to yet tiny compared to the ones on the berry to its left. Gretchen lifted the wrap and touched both gingerly. They were springy and cool to her touch. She bent down to inhale a near-suffocating sweetness.

Suddenly Elliot came to mind, specifically the deep chestnut curls adorning his chest and pubis, curls thick and musky sweet in which she had reveled in whipping her nose back and forth – except, of course, during the couple's last months.

Gretchen had spoiled Elliot with what he'd called her 'monkey lust,' springing from one part of his body to another, inhaling, licking, stroking, sucking, wanting to take through her senses the parts and the whole he would not give to her any other way.

It was several months into their relationship before Gretchen realized that he allowed her to 'make' most of their lovemaking. While she'd explored him like a Vasco de Gama of the bedroom, heady from the contrast between say cinnamon-redolent chest hair and tangy, slightly sour anus, Elliot had been content to let her enjoy and, for a few seconds, he'd tug at her nipples, touch a finger or two to her engorged pussy lips and clit, then thrust his purple-headed cock into her generally dripping hole.

Gretchen closed her legs tightly, shamed by sopping panties but now unnerved by another image of Elliot, legs splayed on her bed, erect icicle in place of turgid penis. She clamped her legs still tighter and, this time, shuddered.

Things would have to change, she thought. Then Gretchen remembered that things would never get better – and they'd never get worse. Elliot had accomplished that last night.

A tear escaped Gretchen's left eye, made its way down her cheek, and swayed from her chin before dropping onto an uncovered blackberry in her open *Fong's* bag. She flicked a fingertip across the fruit then raised it to her tongue. The coupling of saline and sweet made her thirsty and eager for more.

The painter closed her eyes. Suddenly she wanted to crush berries inside a tight fist. She wanted to smear them over her face. She saw her neighbor Frank bend his head to lick seeds from her eyelids, to lap at juice on her cheeks. She saw him unscrew his lens cap, adjust the light meter, and position himself and his Nikon to achieve the best shots of her berry-stained neck. Now Elliot swatted at Frank. Her most recent ex wanted to suck juice from Gretchen's darkening clavicles, but a determined, stronger Frank thrust Eliot aside. This bolder Frank was unbuttoning her blouse. He was bending down and snapping photos as blue-black juice made its way to her breasts.

Gretchen blushed in her bus seat. She could imagine Margaret chastising her, 'Now Gretchen, this is what you get when you go too long without eating. This is what happens when you waste time traveling for dinner while decent food is right around your corner'.

No, Margaret, this is what happens when you go too long without love, without reciprocated heat. Gretchen lowered her head, the better to inhale the berries, as well as to dab at another nascent tear. She prayed her own juices had not noticeably dampened the crotch of her jeans, hoped her mascara-tinged tears had not left telltale raccoon eyes. She looped the handles of her plastic *Fong's* bag. Gretchen stood up. This was her stop.

CHAPTER TWO

Feeling stuffed with excitement over the prospect of working lighter, of working better, for herself and for Frank, Gretchen postponed her fruit-only lunch. She would begin a study for *Still Life with Berries and Wine*. Gretchen assembled her box of stubby charcoals, her tray of chalks. She impatiently thrust aside other boxes of colored pencils, Conte crayons, filled and unfilled fountain pens, and bottles of ink, in search of her new, full-length charcoals.

Why was she so disorganized? It was only with Margaret's help that Gretchen had, a year ago, categorized and labeled her supplies and fit them into boxes large and small. Now Gretchen had to search for laundered rags. Margaret had chided her last month about organizing those, too. Maybe Margaret could store in neat, color-coded boxes all of Gretchen's scattershot belongings. Gretchen could hire her best friend to put into clear storage units and place on sturdy wooden hangers Gretchen's emotions and rationalizations, too. Margaret would love that! If only Margaret could make Gretchen focus on the task, the beginning of this creation, right now.

Gretchen knew she had to rely on herself this time. She knew she couldn't keep turning to others – like Margaret, like men – to make her life happy and whole. Gretchen would find the new charcoals later. She'd work with what she could grasp at this moment.

And so the revitalized painter threw on a well-worn sweatshirt, zipped up acrylic and oil paint stained jeans, and wound a ponytail holder around her lank hair. She set a large drawing pad on her easel and placed several charcoal and chalk pieces on the grooves in front of the pad. Now all she had to do was compose the fruit and wine on one of the decades-old mahogany tables she used for her still lives.

She loved the water stains and nicks in this mangy assortment of wooden pieces. The artist often lost herself in variations in hue, sun-bleached tabletops, legs striated by scratches from, she imagined, some ex-owner's cat. She believed that the 'lives' these tables had led, the people they had 'seen' and served, added to the richness and texture of her paintings.

Gretchen loved the tables the way she loved her chalks, charcoals, and crayons; tubes of paint; fresh, aromatic berries; and as-yet-unopened bottles of wine before her. She cared for these implements and subjects as much as she'd cared for Elliot. Maybe, Gretchen thought, she loved them even more – because they unstintingly gave her so much in return. Inanimate objects could give, thought Gretchen, in a way some people never could. Objects had nothing to lose, and so could yield themselves willingly.

She felt her eyes begin to water. Oh, no, she would not waste more time weeping over Elliot. She straightened her spine. Instead of pining for Elliot, she completed a moderately Byzantine arrangement of blueberries, blackberries, strawberries, and errant peach slices on a tray, along with uncorked bottles of a Sicilian Rubio, plus two etched, unfilled wine glasses, all atop a fraying thrift-shop scarf that looked torn from the back of somebody's nana. No, she would not cry now. The two tears she had shed over Elliot minutes before had dried on her cheek. There was nothing to wipe away.

Gretchen narrowed her eyes and pursed her lips. She studied the curves of the bottles and fruit, the shapes of the spaces between them, and the shadows thrown on the scarf and aged oval table. In an amount of time she couldn't have quantified if she'd tried, she had made her way through three knobby charcoals and one pinky-sized chalk. She had black and white smudges on her cheeks and brow. Wisps of ash-brown hair had fought free of their pony-tailed prison and were now attached to moist forehead, cheeks, and neck. Her first study for Frank's painting was taking shape on a page of this oversized sketchbook.

Gretchen was blissfully engrossed pushing back strands of hair with a chalk-flecked thumb, when she realized her doorbell was ringing. Then the ringing stopped and knocking ensued. Who could it be? She hoped whomever it was would stop and then vanish, thus allowing her to return to this blessed, semi-trance state.

No, the person choosing to annoy her would not stop. She turned towards the front of her apartment. What if it was Frank? Surely he would be thrilled to know of her progress on his commissioned work. Gretchen heard a muffled 'It's me' and, without thinking – about her drawing or about her scruffy appearance – she rushed to open the door.

CHAPTER THREE

He bent down, his six feet-plus to her five feet, five inches, and she almost reeled from his scent, like moist, burnt umber earth, as he kissed the top of her head. He reached behind to shut her door. He moved with her, or, rather, he moved her, until they reached a wall. Then he backed them against it.

Gretchen knew she should say something, should acknowledge what was about to happen, but she couldn't. Maybe it was the brush of his day-old beard against her cheek. Maybe it was fumes from paint and turpentine that had seeped into her brain. Whatever the reason, all she could do was stand, barely, and accept, with her mouth open, what was to come.

And now Gretchen's mouth received his tongue, his very warm, very wet tongue shimmying up hers and flicking at her teeth. Then his lips were flattening hers, and his teeth were nipping and tugging at her top and bottom lips.

She wouldn't have reconciled these actions with him, wouldn't have imagined he would do these things to her, now. She still could not manage to close her mouth, and so he took this opportunity to place a finger inside it. Almost involuntarily she sucked this finger, her mouth needing it like a parched brush tip requiring water. His skin tasted of perspiration and soap, though not a soap she would buy for herself; this was not a bar exuding lilac or lavender, this scent was sylvan and almost harsh.

She wanted more of him. As if reading her thoughts, he pushed a thumb against her lower lip, opened her mouth wider, and thrust two more masculine digits inside her accepting mouth. The painter felt her insides start to twist around, especially as he'd begun to knead her left breast over her sweatshirt.

He kissed her art-marked face, and at once she began a wordless protest about her current messy state as she tried to pat charcoal and chalk off her face. She grappled with sweat-lacquered strands of hair that had fallen out of place. He grabbed her wrists, he pinned her arms up against the wall, and then he told her she was beautiful, that in this light and in this studio, amid her art, she glowed. He had not seen until this moment how she glowed.

And then they were on the floor, he in bleached blue jeans and pressed white shirt, she in paint-splotched dungarees and pilled fleece sweatshirt. They were rolling onto clean and dirty rags. Then they bumped lightly into her easel, which alarmed her and deposited clouds of charcoal dust over each other as well as her floor. Gretchen craned her neck to make sure her sketchpad and Study were standing unharmed.

Then she dismissed *Still Life with Berries and Wine* because he was kissing and nipping at her neck, telling her how elegant it was. He was lifting the sweatshirt over her head. He was pawing at her breast through her bra. She wished she had worn a newer, prettier bra, but a moment later she forgot to be self-conscious, because he had already taken it off.

He was telling her again how beautiful she was, his breath falling hot on the tips of her breasts, and then he was pulling at her nipples, almost too hard, causing them to turn the shade of her favorite red globe grapes. He was causing her nipples to swell, making her want to ask him to lick them, to flick his fine tongue over and around them, to take them, one by one and then together, inside his mouth, and suck them so deeply that she would feel the current between these points and her now flowing-with-juices hole.

She didn't ask him, though, because Gretchen remembered that he had never done this, had always been a finger and cock man – mostly, in fact, a cock man – not a lover who, below her neck, freely employed his mouth. Then Elliot was using his mouth to tell her how lovely she was, to tell her he had missed her, but he would not move his mouth from above her breasts to on top of them.

And now Gretchen did not know if she wanted this, if she wanted

Elliot. Still, here they were the two of them stained with sweat, chalk, charcoal dust, and lust, and, a moment ago, even hope. She was too far gone; she was soaked from the inside of her very responsive pussy, to her engorged labia, to the tops of her inner thighs, and she saw that Elliot was too hard, his member huge and almost menacing, to let this go.

So she swooped onto hiss chest and licked and suckled his tiny dark nipples; she felt them grow as hard as his ever-ready cock. Then she licked that, too, as much to taste it as to drive all thoughts out of her head.

Her ex-boyfriend thrust two fingers inside her, he strummed his thumb across her cherry-colored clit, and just as she was about to come, he stopped and rammed his demanding penis inside her. She felt her cunt contract around this plentiful package; she felt the betrayal of her own pussy, but it was, at best, a betrayal incomplete, because her orgasm started to ebb almost as soon as it had started.

And then Elliot was, in quick succession, off her; on his back, next to her, not holding her; turned away from her. He was saying how great that was and God, oh, God, he had missed her.

She watched him wipe perspiration from his forehead, bend to pick up his clothes, and walk swiftly to her bathroom. She half-listened to the noises of his ablutions: slamming back the toilet lid, clearing his throat three times in a row, waiting, then clearing it again, rifling through her medicine cabinet in search, perhaps, of a man's toiletry she no longer possessed.

Gretchen knew the sounds Elliot made. She must have recognized his voice before rushing to let him in. She must have known that knock, as well, the insistence, the entitlement of it. She must have known, and yet, she had hurriedly opened her door. It was when she heard Elliot gargle and fiercely expectorate that she pictured herself spitting him out of her life.

CHAPTER FOUR

Gretchen had let Elliot ruin her concentration as an artist, and what had remained of her dignity. She'd made libidinal hunger her *raison d'etre* – other times, surely, but especially today – and it had left her sad, sexually frustrated and, worst of all, parted from profound creative flow.

The still-life painter sat on an old stool, rapidly applying a tissue but losing the race with the tears rushing down her washcloth-scrubbed cheeks. She had told Elliot to leave, she'd said in a voice she wished had been stronger, that she couldn't do this again. After he attempted to sweet-talk her in twenty words or less, after he donned his clothes far quicker than she thought was kind, she ran to the shower stall. She nearly hurt herself with forceful, punishing strokes of her soap (a soap that smelled nothing like Elliot's.) She spent over forty minutes in a steaming shower; she used half a bar of lavender soap to remove the charcoal, chalk, sweat, tears, and the hateful mingled stink of her and her ex.

Afterwards, she rubbed her skin pink with the bath towel, making sure she felt this pain; making damn sure she'd recall how much Elliot could hurt her with her consent. She wanted to remember not to give her consent again. Still, she could not erase his scent from her nostrils, that scent that made her wild and single-minded or, more precisely, mindless, like a canine bitch in heat.

And here she was, almost relishing the discomfort of the shaky stool under her terry-robed rear, tissues at more tears rolling down her stupid face. Would she ever resist the questionable charms of Elliot? Would she always let a man interrupt her work? Would she ever find a man who respected as well as loved her? A man who gave of himself in bed as much as she did? Would she ever stop talking like a soap opera voice-over?

'Funny, Gretchen'. She could hear Margaret loud and clear. Gretchen needed to hear the common sense and wisdom of her best friend. 'Gretchen, keep your sense of humor', she imagined Margaret would tell her, 'but keep away from Elliot, too. Look at what happens when you let a selfish man get the better of you or, in your case, the best'.

Gretchen knew Margaret loved her, but she often felt that Margaret married scolding with love like alcoholics mix rum with cola: free and easy utilizing the former, downright parsimonious using the latter. The painter backed away from her phone. Wasn't she chiding herself enough for two people?

Then a different face popped into her head, and a feeling of warmth suffused her down to her bones. She closed her eyes. She saw Frank hugging her, coming from behind, but not in a dominating fashion. She pictured his strong arms wrapped around her waist, then her hands on his, their fingers interlocking, their souls in embrace.

This is what she wanted. She held herself tightly, and then opened her eyes. Oh, she thought, touching the black terrycloth robe, this is one thing, at least, that I can change quickly. I want to wear clothes that will comfort me, that will lift my spirits with color. I don't want to be enshrouded.

Then she remembered Elliot had given her this robe last Christmas! She shuddered, untied it, and let the garment drop to the floor. Even standing naked, she felt warmer than before.

Right now, before Margaret's voice could tell her that tossing aside a well-made, useful gift was wasteful, before Gretchen would lose her own newborn resolve, she strode to her broom closet and removed one of many neatly stacked, large-handled shopping bags. She winced, recalling that her best friend had supervised this much-needed organization of her closets.

She held her mouth firm and opened the bag. Then she folded Elliot's gift and placed it inside. This would be welcome at Goodwill.

* * *

Gretchen sat at her hunter-green Art Deco kitchen table. She smiled as she surveyed the speckled Formica top and gleaming aluminum trim. She *did* have something green, and silver, too!

Elliot had thought this table quaint, a colorful relic of an era that boasted too many symbols of flights of fancy to suit him. Elliot preferred the clean lines and simple silhouettes of mid-twentieth-century or modern furniture. She remembered him remarking, at a recent museum exhibit featuring the work of great twentieth-century architects, that he admired the utilitarianism of *Mies van der Rohe*.

Yes, Elliot was (had) been all business. Elliot was smart, magnetic, almost annoyingly sexy, but, ultimately, all business at his job, in their bed, and everywhere else.

Gretchen tightened the amethyst-colored robe around her. She caressed one sleeve and nodded approvingly. She owned purple, too! She'd found this lounger at the rear of her clothing closet, almost crushed. She remembered opening this holiday gift from Margaret; she remembered how delighted she'd been with the jewel-like color and velvety texture. Margaret had given this to her nearly three years ago! Only after a diligent purge of her closet for Elliot-related items had Gretchen unearthed this beauty, and many other lively pieces of attire that had been relegated to the back of that closet during her two years with Elliot.

She lifted both legs and crossed them at the ankles over an adjoining chair. She had a plate, paring knife, and Winesap apple before her. As she pierced the skin and watched milky liquid ooze onto china, she thought, *I could call these last couple of years my 'Elliot Period.' I will remember intensity, compulsive creativity, and frenetic lust, a period of stunningly elaborate, almost mid-nineteenth-century, arrangements of fruit nearly pulsing with ripeness.* As she slowly sucked a thin slice of tangy apple into her mouth, she said to herself, in her best pseudo-intellectual tones, *The Elliot Period should be appreciated, understood, and then gracefully – and gratefully – left behind.*

CHAPTER FIVE

Near the last of the Winesap, Gretchen had forsaken the gentility of the paring knife. She realized she was ravenous, and so had downed the remainder of the apple with ferocious bites. She'd even swallowed some of the core and bitten down into two seeds, experiencing the almond-like bitterness that awakened her to the fullness of her hunger.

Gretchen did not want to spoil the arrangement that she hadn't completely captured on her sketchpad, but she was exhausted from her artistic *endeavorus interruptus*, the shameful lust-fest with Elliot, and her subsequent soap-and-towel attempts at self-flagellation. She was simply bone tired, and could not will herself to draw any more that day.

So she gathered the now room-temperature, fragrant peach slices and berries into her large wooden fruit bowl. Gretchen lightly pressed her wooden mixing spoon against the berries in order to release sweet red, blue, and purplish-black juice. Then she spooned a generous portion of *Fong's* heavy cream into the bowl, and mixed it all with the large spoon, careful still not to bruise or flatten any fruit. Gretchen brought the bowl and spoon to her kitchen table, along with a corkscrew, bottle of Rubio, and wine glass. This would be a satisfying meal.

* * *

It was after midnight when Gretchen awakened. Her head was resting on the sparkly Formica tabletop, to the right of the bowl she had eaten clean of cream and fruit. Her right arm had encircled her head, and now the arm felt heavy and dull. To her left on the table was the half-full bottle of Rubio and a drained wine glass.

Her purple robe had fallen open. Her moon-white belly, thighs, light-brown bush and left breast were fully displayed in the night. She didn't know if it was the thrill of being exposed, the chill in the air or the voice of Frank that had filled her ears during her sleep, but she was feeling very aroused. Her left nipple was delightfully swollen and hard. She touched a finger to it and sighed as she saw the pink tip grow longer.

Half asleep and half inebriated still, the artist imagined she heard Frank guiding her. *Touch your breast for me again, Gretchen. Go on, yes, like that.* Frank's deep, Midwestern twang filled her head. *Pour a little wine into your glass. Go on. I want you to dip your fingers into the glass.*

As Gretchen's eyes gradually adjusted to the darkness, they followed her fingers plunging into the deep red liquid. She awaited further instructions from Frank.

Do you see how full and ripe your little bud looks now? Gretchen nodded, as if Frank were present in the air around her. *I want you to caress your breast with the wine*, he continued. *Yes, go ahead.*

Gretchen moved the robe aside to allow herself full access. She lifted her left breast towards the moonlight then moved wine-dipped fingers all over her own white and pink orb. Her areola immediately puckered.

Now, Frank's voice continued, *I can see that felt good.* Gretchen blushed in the dark. *Put your fingers in the wine again. Coat that luscious nipple with more wine. Now, gently squeeze it for me.*

Gretchen was breathing hard now. She felt a churning in her lower abdomen, and she watched her now scarlet nipple react to her own and Frank's attentions.

Take your nipple into your mouth, Gretchen. Imagine it's my mouth. Gretchen shivered as she sucked her left nipple. She imagined it, grape-fragrant, blood-warm, a dark red pearl pulsing in Frank's mouth. She felt her pussy contract as she continued to suck the engorged tip of her left breast.

These are my fingers, Gretchen, Frank was saying, these are my fingers in the wine again and now inside your pussy. These are my big fingers circling your clitoris.

Gretchen sucked the tip of her other breast now. She felt it stiffen as soon as she took it into her mouth. She wanted Frank's lips on her breasts, Frank's fingers on and inside her and Frank's knowing cock pushing hard inside her tight, welcoming folds.

She pictured his aqua eyes watching her, and all at once Gretchen felt a rippling within, the likes of which she had never before experienced. She could only hope that her escalating sighs would be duplicated in a real-life lovemaking session with Frank. She could also only hope that these so-called sighs would not lead anyone to knock on her door or call the police.

The artist smirked at her joke. Then she slowly stood up and tied her robe at the waist. She concentrated on breathing, slowly, deeply, evenly, thereby steadying herself. Gretchen picked up the wooden bowl and spoon and walked to her kitchen sink, squirted liquid detergent into the receptacle, filled it with hot water, and made her way to bed. She felt satiated, lonely, but more than a little hopeful.

* * *

It was Frank's voice. Minutes ago it was Frank's hand, his long, broad fingers encircling bananas, offering the upward-curving fruit to her with downcast eyes and a smile. And hours before that it was Frank telling her where to place her fingers on her own body, making her feel special because he desired and knew how to please her.

Was that true? Had it been Frank? This was Frank now on her answering machine. Groggy from too much wine and too little sleep, Gretchen shook her head back and forth like a damp spaniel and quickly reached for her telephone.

'Frank? Is that you?'

The photographer cleared his voice, too loudly, in Gretchen's ear. 'Oh, you're there. I was just about to hang up.'

She sat up in her bed. She glanced down at her nakedness and immediately covered herself with her blanket. Then she laughed.

'Gretchen? What's so funny?'

The artist turned pale pink, deep pink, medium-red, and dark red, in rapid succession. She wondered if Frank could hear the embarrassment in her voice. No, she didn't think he had enough clues to come to that conclusion. And if Gretchen were smart, she wouldn't give him any.

'Gretchen?' Frank cleared his throat, again too loudly for this hung-over artist. 'Did I wake you up?'

That was it! Frank had handed her phallic fruit *in a dream*. Frank had told her how to touch herself… had that been a dream, too? She would sort it out later, but she'd talk to him now, or Frank would think her rude, or possibly demented. He would decommission his painting, and, to top it off, abandon any interest he may have had in her up until this conversation.

'No, no, I wasn't sleeping. I was just…'

'Just what? Unable to form a sentence? Unable to respond to a question?'

Oh, this man had been in New York too.long.

'OK, you caught me. I was sleeping.'

'I knew it. You're the first person in New York to fess up to having been awakened by a telephone call. What is it about this town? Why can't you people admit it when you're asleep? Do you think sleep is a sign of weakness?'

'Sleep is simply a physiological need, Frank. New Yorkers, however, need less of it.'

'Hey, that's pretty quick for a sleepy New Yorker.'

'And you're pretty sophisticated for a guy who says 'fess up."

Frank laughed into the phone. She didn't care if it hurt her ear. Gretchen was happy to hear him laugh. Frank's laughter was like strawberry juice trickling down her chin. It was like a Conte crayon opening up one's notion of a sky, making a portion of that sky not quite the violet it truly was but precisely the violet it ought to be.

'Gretchen, did you go back to sleep?'

The painter blushed again. 'No, I was just…'

'Unable to form a sentence again?'

Now Gretchen laughed. 'Such acerbic wit for a man from Indiana!'

'We're not all rubes, you know. And fess up, were you falling asleep on me?'

If only she were! If only she were falling asleep on what Gretchen imagined was a chest positively overrun with curly, cozy blonde hair, she would be the happiest still-life painter in Manhattan, the happiest fruit buyer at *Fong's*. Hell, she'd be the happiest woman she knew – anywhere! 'I know you're not rubes, not a bunch of bumpkins. And I was not falling asleep. I was thinking, I was thinking… how nice your laugh sounded.' Oh, no, why in the name of *Fong's* fragrant fruit had she said that? Now there was silence on Frank's end, silence from which Gretchen would probably never recover. 'That's what happens when you speak to someone before you're fully awake, before you have control of yourself'. Oh, Margaret, annoying, insightful Margaret.

'Gretchen, that's a very nice thing to say; very disarming.' Frank cleared his throat. 'Thank you.'

'You're welcome.' Now what?

Frank spoke again. 'I rather like your laugh, too. Hmm, I think I'm forgetting why I called.'

Would that be a bad thing, wondered Gretchen? She would like to hear him talk a lot more about her laugh.

'Ah, I remember. How is *Still Life with Berries and Wine* coming along? Anything come to fruition?'

Gretchen laughed so readily that she had no time to be disappointed. Besides, she had no tangible reason to feel let down. After all, Frank had commissioned a painting from her. That did not, of course, preclude talking about anything else he might like about her, but she did have to act professionally. And she did have to answer his question. 'Well, I've been working up studies for it, and I think I'll be ready to start painting in two or three weeks.'

'That's great news! I'm not rushing you, by the way, so take more time if you need it. This is your area of expertise.'

'I was going call you about it, Frank. I am planning on keeping you up to date.'

'That's all right. I don't mind calling you.'

Oh, was 'don't mind' close to 'like'? She had to stop this. She had to concentrate on the here and now. And here and now working on the painting for Frank was what mattered. It was what mattered most. Anything else would be like whipped cream on a bowl of already enticing berries.

'Gretchen, I'll let you get back to sleep, if you need it, or to work. Oh, one more thing: it occurred to me, just last night, that I'd like to come by and see a study or two,' Frank paused, 'when it's convenient for you. Bantering aside, I'm excited about having a painting by Gretchen Collins hanging in my apartment. You are a very talented woman.'

In her own apartment, Gretchen Collins felt her insides tumble round, which might have felt pleasant if she hadn't hoisted back over half a bottle of Rubio the night before. What had she been thinking last night? Or, more to the point, why hadn't she been thinking? 'Frank…'

'You're still there! Listen, important, sleepy painter. It's impolite to leave a person hanging after he tells you something like that.'

'I'm sorry.' Why did she have the IQ of stretched canvas this morning?

'All right, Manhattan woman, leave this Goshen guy feeling like a… rube.' Frank was laughing. It was a laughter that followed his words too quickly.

'Frank, I didn't realize…'

'I know. But now you do, though I think you probably did before. Now get to work so you'll have some studies to show me. I'm going to chalk up your conversational skills to too much turpentine and not enough sleep. Have a good day, Gretchen.' Frank hung up before she could offer another pathetic rejoinder.

What had just happened? She wanted to call him back. She wanted to go back to sleep. She wanted to finish the bottle of Rubio. Instead, the artist did the next thing – the first smart thing – that popped into her foggy head. She decided to shower and go to *Fong's*. She would buy fruit for a new study for *Still Life with Berries and Wine*.

CHAPTER SIX

On the bus to *Fong's*, Gretchen thought of what she and Margaret would say during their next telephone talk. First Margaret would chastise Gretchen for not calling sooner. Then she would thank Gretchen for calling. She would tell Gretchen she missed her. She would question Gretchen regarding her progress with her artwork.

Gretchen would not respond to Margaret's expression of caring. She would evade Margaret's question. She would not ask her best friend how she was faring. Then Gretchen would feel guilty. She would think about buying more black clothing. She would tell Margaret about her conversation with Frank, how it was the first talk she had had with him in two weeks, and how it had been even longer since she'd seen him.

Margaret would say that it had been at least that long since she'd seen Gretchen. Gretchen would ignore that and tell Margaret that her discussion with Frank had been scary but exciting.

Gretchen's head began to pound. This faux communication was too much and not enough simultaneously. She took from her coat pocket her emergency-use-only-for-reasons-known-only-to-Gretchen cell phone and called Margaret.

'Gretchen, is that you? Oh, my God, how are you? Wait, let me…'

'If this is a bad time, I'll hang up.'

'You're not getting away that easily. Besides, what makes you think I want you to hang up? Just hold on.'

Gretchen held on. She read her shopping list:

Blueberries

Peaches

Greengage plums

Raspberries

Blackberries

Kiwis

Limes

Short ribs

Bliss potatoes

Asparagus

One head each Bibb & Boston lettuce

Vine-ripened tomatoes

Green onions

Baby Portobello mushrooms

Elephant garlic

Bottled water

Mission figs

This was the list of a woman with an appetite. This should be the list of a woman giving a dinner party.

Gretchen smiled and continued to hold on. Wait... the list had red meat on it! Was this wise? Gretchen would have to go to a butcher; so much for one-stop shopping. That wasn't the issue. She wasn't thinking clearly. Why had she thought of meat? And where was Margaret?

No one had told her not to eat red meat. Not her doctor, not her nutritionist, not the latest healthy lifestyle magazine article. After Gretchen had stopped eating red meat, two, maybe three years ago, she had felt better: lighter, healthier, cleaner, and, best of all, virtuous.

She had purged herself of desire for any kind of protein that bled. Even soy protein doctored to smell and taste like chicken or beef no longer made it onto her skillet. Now she wanted meat back. She wanted it like she wanted cerulean blue oil paint on her palette. Like she wanted a lemon-yellow, cinched-waist dress in her closet. Like she wanted a purple lace teddy on her body. Like she wanted to climb on top of Frank.

Margaret! Where was Margaret?

'Hi, Gretchen. Sorry I took so long. That's what I get for having two kids, huh?' Margaret let out a husky laugh. 'So, Gretchen, are you painting? Are you in love?'

'What? What are you talking about?'

Margaret laughed again.

Gretchen had forgotten how her friend's laughter sounded. Funny, everyone was laughing lately. Oh, that was funny, too!

'Sweetie, I haven't heard from you in quite some time. I decided to leave you alone, because I knew you have your commissioned painting to work on. Honestly, though, I was worried. Then I remembered Frank. And I thought, who knows, maybe he's been keeping you busy in more ways than one.'

'Margaret!'

'So, do you two...?'

'I don't know.'

'You don't know? First, how are you? Are you taking care of yourself?'

'Yes,' Gretchen dutifully replied.

'Are you painting?'

'I'm working on studies for *Still Life with Berries and Wine*.'

'Studies? Drawings? Is that good? Is that where you should be now?'

Bless Margaret for her caring and for her bluntness – which is exactly why Gretchen shied away. Sometimes Margaret was too much to take. She was, however, always what Gretchen needed.

'Gretchen, are you there?'

'Yes, and one of these days you are going to tell me how you are.'

'Well, how sweet of you! I'm fine, thank you very much for asking.'

Gretchen thought she'd heard a quiver in Margaret's voice. Had it been that long since she'd asked about her friend?

'We're all fine here,' her friend continued.

'Margaret?'

'Yes?'

'I spoke with Frank again and I'm scared. It was good, it was... energizing, talking with him. I sounded like an idiot, because I was half-asleep. Still, he respects me as an artist and he is so warm and open, he's like a cornfield in his home state.'

'You told me that Frank is from Indiana.'

'So?'

'Cornfields are in Iowa.'

'I thought so, too, but Frank told me they grow corn in Indiana, too. I always get those "I" states mixed up, though.'

'As long as you don't get Frank mixed up with anyone else. Thanks for the agriculture info, by the way. Good to know! And, by the way, Gretchen, when you're in the company of a man who is strong and secure what you get is a man who is open and accepting.'

'Not like Elliot.'

'Certainly not like Elliot.'

'Margaret, I'm on my way to *Fong's*... and don't tell me I don't have to go to *Fong's*.'

'If you're happier with fruit from *Fong's*, go to *Fong's*.'

'Oh.'

'Gretchen, as much as I love talking to you, I'm busy, and you're busy, too, or you should be, so tell me what you wanted to tell me before you reach *Fong's*.'

Had Margaret always been like this or had the real Margaret been subsumed by Gretchen's idea of Margaret? Like the real Frank had been subsumed by fantasies, dreams, reveries, of Frank?

'Gretchen?'

'I don't... I don't know what to do about Frank.'

Margaret laughed again. Then she made a tsk-tsk sound. 'Why do you have to do anything? What would happen if you concentrated on that commissioned painting for him? Then, see if anything comes after that.'

Oh, this was why Gretchen loved Margaret. This was whom Gretchen wanted to be when she grew up – minus Margaret's life as a single parent, plus Gretchen's own life as a painter.

Now Margaret's youngest was pulling at her mother's pantyhose. Gretchen's greengrocer was two bus stops away. The artist thanked her friend repeatedly and hung up.

Gretchen was fortified for *Fong's*, bloody ready for a butcher, and aching for what might come after. Gretchen personified Mr. *Fong's* oft-repeated description of any new shipment of fruit, 'good and ripe.'

* * *

Gretchen told herself to think of nothing but arrangements of wine bottles and fruit. On her way through *Fong's* automatic sliding doors, past a stock boy with dark blonde hair and blue eyes almost as clear as Frank's, the painter admonished herself to get back on track.

With this in mind, Gretchen decided to splurge on a taxi ride home. She associated the bus trip from *Fong's* with carnal reveries involving Elliot or Frank, and did not want to succumb again. Gretchen knew her imagination served her well – as a painter, naturally, and surely as a lover – but it led her, too, to procrastinate, or to detour with steamy, meandering escapades.

Like Margaret with kids in tow, she had to formulate plans to accomplish her goals. Like Frank with Nikon or Leica and subjects, she had to focus. So she hailed a cab on Sixth Avenue, determined to make her uptown trip productive.

As soon as she slid onto the lumpy back seat and informed the driver of her destination, Gretchen visualized herself placing two bottles of Rubio three inches from each other, perhaps this time on her octagonal-topped, cherry wood table. The linear qualities of the furniture, she reasoned, would contrast nicely with the curved shapes of the bottles and fruit. In addition, the tabletop sported several water stains and dark blemishes, adding character to the wood.

And then Frank appeared to her, specifically the two small, brown-madder moles beneath his right eye. She remembered one time when they'd conversed, by the fourth-floor stairwell in their building: he'd asked her about the advantages of oils versus watercolors, and while listening, enrapt, to her response, he'd left the moles alone. Once attention had turned toward him, however, for example, while informing her why he liked to shoot outside right after it rained, or while he was telling her that his hometown, Goshen, was famous for its maple trees, at those times, Frank had covered or rubbed the small tags of dark flesh.

At first, Gretchen had assumed his habit a vestige of small-town shyness. Later, however, when he'd told her that Goshen was, in fact, a small city, she thought he must be like her: self-conscious about his own imperfections, eager to learn about someone or something else. With Frank, Gretchen intuited this was less a desire to retreat from himself than a yearning to know, and, through this knowledge, come to understandings, artistic as well as philosophical, about the world and himself.

Instead of her still-life composition, Gretchen thought of the planes and colors of Frank's face: high cheekbones reflecting Manhattan light; full, pale, almost peach-hued lips; angular, patrician nose; clear, swoon-worthy aqua eyes; and those tiny, troublesome – to him – moles.

Gretchen wanted to see him. She wanted to bang on his door, rush inside, stand on a stepstool before him, and touch those moles. She longed to kiss those distinctive features, and to tell Frank that he needn't cover them, that those marks on his face were as beautiful as the rest of him.

At this point the cabbie turned his head slightly and asked, 'This corner or the next?'

Suddenly she was home, and still she had not fleshed out ideas for today's study. She did, however, have tears forming in both eyes, as well as a lump in her throat – plus a stronger resolve to start this study, her second, one she would be proud to display to Frank.

CHAPTER SEVEN

Before Gretchen would pick up a stick of charcoal, she had to know she'd be able to concentrate. She wouldn't be able to draw with tears in her eyes, an ache in her throat, and, despite all that, a persistent tingling in her loins.

She dried her eyes. She refrigerated the berries, lettuce, potatoes, short ribs, and vegetables, and arranged in her favorite wooden bowl the kiwis, limes, peaches, and vine-ripened tomatoes. She placed the deep purple Mission figs and light violet Elephant garlic far apart from one another on her kitchen counter. She carefully folded and put away *Fong's* plastic bags. She removed all of her clothing and laid it on the back of a bedroom chair. Then she walked to her bed. Gretchen pulled back the cover and climbed on top of her sheets.

Only when she was calm and naked in her bed did Gretchen imagine herself again with Frank, in this bed, facing each other, metal container of mixed berries between them. Frank had just fed her a raspberry and a blueberry, and she'd greedily downed both as well as licked his fingers immediately afterwards. He was softly touching her fingers with his; then his hand was back in the bowl. He was feeding her again, sliding berries and then berry-stained fingers into her mouth. She sucked each one of his fingers thoroughly, then licked the spaces between his digits, plus the inside of his palm and his wrist.

Gretchen felt a vein pulsing under the skin of his forearm, she felt her heart sounding loudly in her chest, and then she knew her own rich juices were running freely. They were embarking from her rounded pussy hole, soaking her full labia, announcing to this lovely man, *I have been waiting for you. I am ready for you now.*

She closed her eyes. She felt Frank climb on top of her, felt him steady himself with one broad palm to the left of her head and one to the right. He had a blackberry in his mouth, which he deposited on Gretchen's closed lips, surprising her with the contrast between the fruit's cool, bumpy surface and his warm, smooth lips. She lifted her tongue to the berry, but it toppled onto her breast. She heard Frank laugh, and she smiled at that delightful twang. Then she felt the berry atop her nipple. Frank took berry and nipple into his mouth, sucked on both deeply, repeatedly, with his moist and pliant lips.

Gretchen was breathing heavily, and Frank felt heavy, but perfectly right, on top of her, placing his berry-tart tongue in her mouth, swirling it lazily inside. His hard, crispy-curly haired chest was on her breasts, his nipples squashed against hers, and his long, lean thighs pressed onto her own. She became aware of his hard cock against her, but he was not rushing her to take it in.

He began, in fact, to tease her face with it, and then her breasts. He ran his wonderfully firm but soft-skinned member against her eyelids and across her cheeks. She moved her head and opened her mouth to take it in, and it was better than any kind of berry, it was tastier than wine. It was Frank, tasting at once light and substantial, faintly earthy and scrubbed clean. It was Frank's penis filling her mouth, driving into her mouth as she knew it soon would drive into her pussy.

All at once he pulled his cock out of her mouth. He whispered in her ear that he didn't want to come, not yet, he'd been waiting to give her pleasure. With that, she pictured him creating a path down her body, licking with pointed tongue her neck, her breasts, her stomach, then, Lord have mercy, her inner thighs. He was spreading her thighs as she was spreading her own lower lips. As she circled her warm, slippery clit with her fingers, he was darting across it with the tip of his tongue. He was licking around and around, and, again, across. She was plunging a finger inside herself, wishing it were Frank, and then she was thrumming her stiff clit with drenched fingers.

She felt Frank deep, very deep, within, further in than anyone had been. He was reaching her G spot, no, he was up to her H. Gretchen was laughing, then she was whimpering. Finally, her fingers came to rest on her throbbing pussy and clitoris. For the next five minutes, Gretchen was too exhausted to move.

Gretchen would take a shower. Now she would be able to concentrate, to devote herself to fruit and wine bottles and charcoal and chalk. She had temporarily freed herself of this animal lust so that she would be able to work, alone, on a passionate rendering of inanimate objects – for that liveliest of subjects, Frank.

* * *

The notion first came to Gretchen, as did so many of her ideas, in images: Gretchen standing in front of her easel, feet bare on hardwood floor, lifting her naked arm to the study on her easel; Gretchen, unclothed limbs in pale contrast to the purplish-blue, cherry, and claret hues of fruit and wine before her; Gretchen, torso free of any constrictions save light-peach-tinted cotton bra and matching bikini panties.

Gretchen, drawing lengthy shadows thrown by wine bottles, would be clad not in jeans stained with oils from previous artistic efforts and sweatshirt hampering her elbows and wrists, but in underwear alone. Gretchen would be wearing these items of clothing only to keep errant air currents from stirring her sensitive, uncovered nipples and titillating her easily aroused, exposed vulva.

As soon as the artist began working in her underwear, she felt more connected to the tender surfaces of the berries, the easily bruise-able peaches. Particles in Gretchen's studio could alight on her flesh and cause reactions barely visible, even to her. Fruit might be exquisitely sensitive, too, and Gretchen wanted to communicate this to the viewers of her completed *Still Life with Berries and Wine*.

Gretchen wanted Frank, and anyone in the vicinity of Frank's commissioned work, to imagine the sweet pungency of the slices of Freestone peach. She wanted them to gasp when realizing that the scents that wafted into their nostrils were not perfumes of women nearby, but the piquant, early-season juices of raspberries, blueberries and blackberries waiting to be released. Gretchen wanted the dark, maturely salacious Rubio, the heft of the table, the nicks, and the rich hue of cherry wood to be palpable, too.

As Gretchen worked in peach-toned bra and panties, she knew that the lines she had drawn were more fluid than any she'd drawn before.

The charcoal and chalk seemed like extensions of her arms and fingers, as well as her mind and her soul.

* * *

Late in the day, after hours of drawing during which time she'd taken no sustenance but swigs of spring water, one Jonathan and one Winesap apple, Gretchen prepared a stew of short ribs enlivened with balsamic vinegar and crushed Elephant garlic. The now-famished artist steamed asparagus, squirted the elegant stalks with lime, and placed the vegetable on a white china plate. To these she added a small portion of boiled bliss potatoes. A glass of her friendly Rubio rounded out the meal.

After dinner Gretchen dreamily washed the pot, pan, plate and utensils. Hot water and suds caressed her lower arms, and nurtured the fingers that had determinedly directed charcoal and chalk. Gretchen marveled at how industrious she'd been that day.

Why, she wondered, was it almost painfully difficult to get started at times, when she always felt better after her workday was done? A day like today made her feel virtuous, proud, and thrilled to be in her own skin.

Tomorrow the painter would be ready to review the fruits of today's labors. Tonight she felt tired from her exertions as well as from the red meat. Gretchen needed air. She needed people. She needed to step outside of her studio.

In minutes Gretchen was pounding Manhattan concrete. She was keeping an eye out for uneven sidewalks, sidestepping heterosexual and homosexual couples with strollers, silently admiring strapping young men in leather jackets walking their giant Labs. So much revolved around what was on her sketchpad, or in front of it, or in her art-filled brain, that Gretchen knew she needed the stimuli of the city in addition to the exercise.

She also needed to see Margaret more often. She needed to propel herself to art exhibits again, and to replenish her painting and drawing supplies. Gretchen had to remind herself to fill her life with more than *Fong's* fabulous produce and her own alarmingly enjoyable erotic reveries. And now, after more than a mile of very brisk walking, Gretchen needed a shower.

* * *

Gretchen closed her eyes and felt hot mist envelop her body. Then she imagined Frank taking the washcloth from her hand. He began rubbing her lavender-scented soap into the center of the fabric. Without looking, she knew the floral creaminess was overtaking the cloth, just as these thoughts of Frank were causing her to flood the tops of her thighs with her own aromatic juices.

Frank was asking her to raise one arm. He was lovingly stroking her armpit, then running the cloth along the length of that same limb.

'Now the other one,' he urged his shower-mate, and she lifted her left arm for him. Again she felt the thrill of his warm hand guiding the slick cloth.

'Turn around, Gretchen, that's right,' Frank said. She was facing him, soapy and vulnerable. He gently cleansed her neck and breasts.

Gretchen opened her eyes. She looked down at her full breasts, lathered by her own hands, and saw that thoughts of Frank had caused her nipples to swell. She squeezed them with sudsy fingers, and watched as they darkened and stood out further. Oh, she wished Frank were standing amidst this pelting water, exquisitely manipulating her drenched and swollen orbs.

With that her pussy pulsed. Gretchen moved the cloth to her clitoris, made fragrant, frothy circles around the throbbing nubbin of flesh. In her reverie it was Frank applying the precise amount of pressure she needed. And, she smiled to herself, delivering the precise amount of pleasure, too.

'Gretchen,' Frank was murmuring in her ear, 'let me do that for you. Keep your eyes closed and concentrate on that wonderful feeling between your legs.'

Again she pictured him in her shower, rivulets of water rushing over the two beautiful moles on his cheek, down his taut-muscled torso, and flicking off the head of his member, the clearly appreciative member pointing up at the naked woman clearly entranced by him.

As she imagined his hard, dripping cock entering her, she fingered her clit faster, then aimed the showerhead stream directly at her swollen bull's-eye. Her body jerked. Just as she started slipping, she grabbed onto the faucets behind her.

She sighed, from relief at staying vertical as well as from her imaginary romp with Frank. Now she'd need a second shower, this one, cold, to help her recover from the first – and to still the throbbing between her legs.

CHAPTER EIGHT

The next morning, refreshed and determined to complete her second study, Gretchen arose at eight a.m. At eight-thirty, attired in banana-colored lace bra and matching high-leg briefs, she stood in front of her easel. She eyed her arrangement of fruit, peered at the unfinished study, and then looked back at the tableau before her.

This study was an improvement over the first. The peach slices looked fleshy, the raspberries moist and ripe. She approved of how she'd repositioned the wine glasses, too. The spacing among all her objects was now more harmonious.

Gretchen was about to peel a kiwi when the telephone rang. She was pleased to hear Margaret's voice and to report her own progress. She was bent, however, on keeping the call short.

Margaret understood. 'Sweetie, I'm busy, too. Next week I'll be taking the girls to their father for a four-day weekend, so I'll have some time for myself – and for us, too. How about we busy women have lunch together the following Friday?'

This was balance. This was worth striving for – work, friendship, love – along with a thriving career and a real sex life to rival the oh-so-active one in her head!

And so Gretchen made plans with her best friend Margaret. She asked her how her daughters were. Gretchen knew she had to remind herself that life existed outside her studio walls.

All day Gretchen worked hard. By the end of the day, her skin and under things were nearly coated with charcoal and chalk dust. Still, she wouldn't return to sweatshirts and jeans, at least not for these still-life drawings. In fact, she looked forward to producing many charcoal- and chalk-dusted bras and panties over the course of painting *Still Life with Berries and Wine*.

Her second study was done. She didn't want to overwork it. She did, however, enjoy analyzing her drawing. Moving the raspberries to the right of the wine bottles would enhance the repetition of these tones in the coming painting: the raspberries would pick up the ruddiness of the wine, which could further be reflected in the empty glasses. She saw that two or three slices of a paler peach, along with slices of deep golden ones, would offer a subtle continuum of these not-quite ocher hues, as well as play up the contrasts amongst all the colors in her finished work. The artist hurriedly wrote notes for her painting. It was now very late afternoon. This had been another day well spent.

* * *

As soon as Gretchen finished writing her notes she became aware of deep pangs of hunger. She glanced at the wall clock, a modern square affair, black background with skinny white numerals and hands, which she had bought while shopping with Elliot. It was 6:30 pm. Gretchen made a mental note to replace the clock. She would rather have one with color and curves – like fruit.

The painter grinned, thinking that a clock shaped like an actual piece of fruit would be a nice piece of whimsy on a kitchen wall. Then she prepared a snack of sliced strawberries, peach chunks, and *Fong's* heavy cream.

After she'd eaten, Gretchen felt even more fatigued. It was time to rest again. She wriggled under her bed sheets and smiled, sated from a fruitful day.

* * *

Now she was at *Fong's*, shopping for apples and oranges with Frank. Once on line, they amused themselves by kissing. Soon Frank was sectioning pieces of an orange to feed Gretchen the succulent fruit. Orange juice was dribbling down her lips and chin. Frank was rushing to lick and finger it off. A middle-aged woman behind them shook her head. A teenaged boy in front turned and smirked. Gretchen was enjoying the attention.

Suddenly she and Frank were at the head of the line. A curly-haired, handsome man in his thirties lifted their bag of navel oranges onto a shiny scale. The cashier was Elliot.

Gretchen said to Frank, 'Oh, no, we have to go.' She didn't want Elliot checking her out. The panicked painter grabbed the clear plastic bags of navels, Winesaps, and Macouns, yanked the photographer's hand, and headed for another line, any other line, far away.

Gretchen woke up. She caught her breath. What was that about? Was she not yet over Elliot? If Elliot were a piece of fruit, she could take large bites and quickly make him vanish. She knew she didn't want Frank to disappear. She hadn't even begun to see him as much as she'd like to. Which is not to say that she wouldn't. She desired Frank the way she desired a tangy Winesap – a tangy Winesap on her lips and a twangy-voiced Frank on her lap!

Oh, Gretchen was groggy. Of this much, though, she was aware:

1. You couldn't compare Elliot and Frank:

    a.Elliot was someone to walk away from while still clutching one's bag of fruit.

    b.Frank was someone to walk toward, someone to whom you'd gladly offer your produce.

2. *Still Life with Berries and Wine* was just one example of the abundance Gretchen yearned to share with Frank.

Her creativity and hard work would bear fruit. *That* Gretchen would guarantee.

CHAPTER NINE

Gretchen was repositioning the two empty wine glasses in her still-life study when the telephone rang. Unlike her behavior most days, this morning Gretchen let her answering machine handle the call. This morning she would not employ a telephone conversation to shy away from work.

Then she heard his voice. 'Gretchen, are you there? This is an impulse call. Some of the best things in my life have happened when I've acted on impulse. Funny, I just realized that. If you're there, please pick up. I guess you know who this is. It's…'

Frank! Gretchen sprinted to the phone. 'Frank? How nice to hear from you.' *How incredibly, phenomenally, heart-stoppingly nice*, she thought. Could it be? Frank was asking her out to lunch.

'I hope I'm not disturbing you, not taking you away from your work, but I hear that even oil painters have to eat sometimes. Photographers, too.'

'Yes, I'd like to meet you for lunch.' *Yes, I'll meet you at a French bistro. I'd accompany you to the cleaners. I'd wait for you at the dentist. As long as I could hear your voice, look at your twin moles, and get lost inside your luscious aqua eyes.*

'Gretchen,' she could hear Margaret loud and clear, 'you've gone gaga'.

* * *

They were to meet at 1 p.m. at *Le Petite Cochon* on Great Jones Street. Gretchen had never been there, though she dimly recalled glancing at a review of the place in the back pages of *New York Magazine*.

Given its name, she hoped the bistro wasn't partial to pork. Gretchen was still accustomed to tofu or fish. The short ribs had already been a jolt to her system. Pork roulettes might do her in!

Gretchen strode to the small cherry wood table. She finished setting up the still life, but not before pondering what chemise to wear to lunch.

* * *

Her lavender shirtdress and strappy cream sandals were pretty and flattering, she had finally decided, but not overly fussy. The artist didn't want Frank to think she'd spent more time dressing for him than working on his painting. Though Gretchen had put time and effort into getting ready for this date, she had devoted most of the morning hours to setting up and drawing *Still Life with Berries and Wine*. Gretchen was delighted by this realization.

Gretchen checked her watch. It was 12:50. She walked into a massive discount drug store to check her makeup. Out came her mirrored compact. If, right now, anything on her face looked askew, this was the site for emergency repairs.

The painter peered into her small round mirror. The hint of peach blush brought natural-looking color to her light skin; the fawn mascara widened her blue-gray eyes. The light brown pencil defined the subtle arch of her brows, and the coral lipstick accentuated her very full lips without making them the focal point of her face. Gretchen brushed aside a couple of lightly gelled strands of hair. She thought, *Today is a good day to look directly into a mirror.* What looked back at her was very fine.

'Now, Gretchen', she heard Margaret's voice, 'you can do better than that. Maybe Elliot would say you look fine. Don't take his words to heart. You look beautiful, Gretchen. You look radiant, and just in time to be admired by a good man'.

Gretchen grinned so broadly that the stock boy near her stared. She pushed the heavy exit door with ease and walked two blocks to *Great Jones*.

* * *

You're right, Gretchen,' Frank said, after swallowing his forkful of *pommes frites*. 'I've always been curious about people. My folks back in Goshen are, I wouldn't say close-mouthed, but not exactly hopping to volunteer information about themselves.' Frank speared several crispy strips of potato.

'Is that why you're always asking questions?'

'Gosh, I guess the more you hold back on a person, the more the person yearns to dig. This person, anyhow.' Frank hurriedly swallowed. He looked deeply into Gretchen's blue-gray eyes with his own aqua ones. 'It's not just that, Gretchen.'

She stopped chewing her poached skate. 'What do you mean?'

'I have a disorder. Innate.'

'A disorder? What kind of disorder?' She could feel the blood drain from her face.

Her date tapped the side of his bread plate with one finger. 'I am a congenitally nosy man.'

Gretchen wadded up her napkin and threw it at Frank's chest. 'Creep!'

In seconds Frank's face was deep pink from laughing. He was stamping one foot and laughing into his dinner plate. Then he tossed his head back and laughed louder. He followed that by tossing Gretchen's napkin back at her. 'The Indiana rube had you going, huh?'

Gretchen put down her utensils and folded her arms in front of her plate. She felt Frank's earnest gaze, then looked away to the golden ochre strands on his sweet Midwestern head.

Frank grazed her wrist with his thumb. 'Aw, come on, Gretchen,' he said softly. 'You're not angry with me, are you?'

Could he believe she was truly angry? No wonder he was so sensitive and considerate. His family must have had little tolerance for one so curious. Frank must have learned early on to investigate the world on his own, perhaps at a distance: behind a camera, a lens, a filter. Gretchen wanted to gather this man into her arms like a bunch of thin-stemmed flowers.

'Gretchen, Earth to Gretchen. Can you read me?'

The artist shook her head. She shook loose near-thoughts of pity. Yes, this man was sensitive. He could, however, take care of himself. He had a sense of humor for that, and great big arms and... 'I'm sorry.'

'I was just about to say the same thing.' Frank was smoothing a knife over the remainder of his hanger steak, spreading pink and black peppercorns evenly across its surface. 'I shouldn't have joked with you that way. Sometimes I do that when a person I like gets under... under...'

A person he likes should help him out, thought Gretchen. 'Under what? Under the weather?' Gretchen poked at her jade-green *haricots verts*, then smiled up at her lunch companion. 'Underwear?'

Frank stopped playing with his steak. He straightened up in his chair and started laughing again. 'Thank you, yes. When a person I like gets underwear, I have no choice but to make a joke.'

'You must have seen your share of funny bras and panties.' Did she really say that? If Gretchen had her compact open, no doubt it would have displayed a face not too far from crimson.

'Ah,' Frank nodded his dark blonde head and flicked a finger across his moles, 'fun, flirty, talented, smart – you are a delight. And I'm relieved that you're not angry with me.'

Angry? No! For all she knew, Gretchen's face could have matched the bistro's terra-cotta-colored floor tiles. That was the degree to which she was embarrassed, thrilled, and happy, oh yes, happy, too.

CHAPTER TEN

Gretchen was not sure how she'd ended up where she was, in front of a storefront lingerie shop on Eldridge Street, fingering the two *Le Petit Cochon* matchbooks she'd snapped up from the mahogany bar before exiting the bistro.

The painter and the photographer had attached themselves to their wrought-iron chairs for over two-and-a-half hours, their waiter Alain filling and refilling their water glasses, and periodically asking if there would be anything else. They placated him with orders of coffee and *Crème Brulée*. Neither of the two wanted to leave.

Over the course of their lunch, Frank had disclosed to her the origins of his love for photography, how excited he'd felt when first turning the pages of a book of Edward Weston's natural studies, a life-changing collection of black and white photographs someone had mistakenly left behind near the geography section in a Goshen public library.

Frank had been eight years old, dutifully studying for an elementary school exam, when he'd glanced at the book left on his rickety table. After he viewed a bell pepper that looked as smooth and inviting as the back and hips of a woman, after he saw halved kale become a gossamer otherworldly landscape unto itself, how could he trust his previous perceptions? If a simple shell could be transformed into lush, pulsing newness, then all things formerly deemed workaday could be rediscovered for their truer essences. At that age Frank believed he'd never again see the world in his same old ways.

And he hadn't. Frank told her how he'd begged his parents for a camera for his ninth birthday. His parents seemed relieved when he was poking a camera in front of cut honeydew and gleaming toasters inside the house, and at clotheslines and school buses outside, instead of pushing his face into theirs with queries about the first and second wives of his paternal great-grandfather or the sex life of his collie Rex, always asking anything and everything that came into his mind, topics that turned his parents' faces the range of powder puff pink to scarlet.

As he grew older, Frank continued, caressing her hands during the telling, he'd traverse his neighborhood after most school days were done, taking random shots of sites and people, compositions that appealed to him for reasons no one understood. His neighbors didn't mind, though, Frank said. In fact, some of them started to pose for him, like Ethel Yoder, who filled prescriptions in *North Main Drugs*, or scrawny Mr. Hess, always searching out treasure amid junkyard scraps.

Eventually they forgot he was there and just went about their business. That was, Frank leaned forward to confide, when he got his best shots, his 'candids'. That was also the genesis of a project to which he'd been devoting his time when not making a living as a studio photographer.

Since high school, Frank had been making candid portraits of people at work. Frank felt people revealed themselves at work more readily than in a typical studio set-up. Often his on-the-job subjects talked to him, and he talked back, though mostly he listened. Sometimes his subjects were silent. Either way, he was communing with them, and finding something true beneath the surface.

It was enthralling to Gretchen, being in the company of someone else who loved to experiment, to explore, as much as she did. The two talked about how they loved to create, how they *lived* to create. She told Frank how her favorite portrait artist, Alice Neel, had spoken to her subjects, too. You could see that in her work, Gretchen explained, in the way the people she painted – an old man, a young Spanish boy – all looked animated, involved, and often infused with colors that no other portrait painter Gretchen knew of would dare to employ.

Gretchen wished Frank would invite her to see his photographs. She wanted to invite him to see more of her paintings. She brought up neither idea. She did say, however, that she'd be ready, within the week, to show him two studies for his commissioned work. Frank grinned the biggest grin this side of Indiana when he heard that.

At the end of their lunch, by which time their waiter Alain was rolling his eyes whenever he'd pass their table, Frank was running his fingers lightly over hers. Then he was telling her how much he was looking forward to seeing her studies. Now, though, they had both better get back to work.

And then Gretchen found herself, feet hurting after walking in high-heeled sandals from the West Village to the Lower East Side, touching a tiny pink pig on a matchbook, thinking of Frank caressing her hand, and eyeing the deep violet teddy that graced the mannequin in this downtown, upscale shop.

* * *

Frank is wearing teal blue boxers, which offset beautifully the pinkish undertones in his skin, the vivid blue of his eyes, and the dark straw hues of his hair. Gretchen is enjoying the movement of his long thighs beneath the silk. Too, she appreciates the care he took in the selection of his smoking jacket – silk like the boxer shorts – navy background with teal, burgundy, and deep gold paisley swirls.

Frank has tied it loosely at the waist, but the robe is beginning to fall open, and Gretchen can't help but admire his solid abdomen, firm chest erupting with golden curls, and, most entrancing sight of all, his phallus curving upward behind the teal silk.

He is walking toward Gretchen, and the closer he gets, the wetter she becomes, especially as what appears to be a very generous-sized tent rapidly builds itself beneath his shorts.

Behind her new violet teddy, embroidered with lacy grapes over the now-warm snap crotch and across the under wire cups, Gretchen's nipples are erecting themselves in sympathy with her lover's cock. She feels her nipples tingle as they push against the satin; she believes they would talk to Frank's cock if they could. They would say, *I know how you feel, I know whom you yearn for.*

Frank's cock, as fluent and as turgid as Gretchen's nipples, would respond, *Oui, oui, mon petit cochon.*

231

Gretchen woke up laughing in her overstuffed chair, violet teddy across her lap, bistro matchbooks fallen by her feet. Then she groaned as she touched her pussy, a pussy that had rendered her panties and pantyhose soaking wet. Gretchen arose to go to bed – sans teddy, sans Frank – determined to wear that purple satin for the deserving photographer very soon.

CHAPTER ELEVEN

She's got them precisely how and where she wants them: the plump raspberries, now in two small dark wood bowls, are glistening with drops of water the paper towel missed. One pale peach remains whole, surrounded by several slices of a richer, riper one, as well as a sprinkling of the mighty raspberries. The lush blueberries, resplendent in a saucer, will amplify the smoky blue in the shadows of the wine glasses and bottles, as well as shades of that blue in the wine itself. All hues will be repeated in the print of the *nana's* tabletop scarf.

Gretchen is itching to paint. She has decided, however, to complete this third study. By the time it is done, she reasons, she'll be more than ready to paint *Still Life with Berries and Wine*. She will be almost bursting, like the rotund fruit before her, like the grapes crushed for the Rubio, like her frustrated, bountiful breasts and needy nipples, her untouched torso and thighs, her poor, lately almost-always-pulsating pussy and clearly clamoring-for-attention clitoris.

Determined to get her brain – and the rest of her – out of the bedroom, Gretchen dressed in old gray sweats and a long-sleeved T-shirt to work on her drawing. She would not let this lust get in the way of her work.

She transferred her passion to her drawing. She concentrated on the light and the shadows. She let her subjects communicate to her how they filled the bowl or plate or bottle, how they felt on a tray, or draped across a table. She welcomed them to become on her page what they were on the table, all their disparate slopes, smells, textures. By the end of the day, they had one voice, and with that voice they sang to her, through her chalks and charcoals.

By the end of the day, Gretchen was as exhilarated as she was fatigued. She decided to shower and walk to *Fong's*. From now on, she would always walk to *Fong's*. In this way she would think about the painting while on her way; she would exercise her mind as well as her body.

Today she would compose her list of groceries while walking, and make sure that list contained the scrumptious fruit she'd need for Frank's still life. And, as a special treat, she would purchase her favorite red globe grapes. Gretchen could imagine her teeth tearing through the taut skin, her tongue savoring the sweet, watery flesh right now.

*   *   *

Gretchen was rolling a wine-red grape on her tongue, then nipping at the tart skin with her teeth, when it occurred to her to share this fruit with Frank. She remembered he'd said he seldom finished a meal without an apple or an orange. Perhaps Gretchen could convince him to substitute these firm, dulcet red globes instead. Gretchen was sure his palate would appreciate them, and she hoped he'd appreciate her sharing them, as well.

With that she tore off half of a large bunch she'd bought at *Fong's*, rinsed a plastic container, and placed these beauties carefully inside. Frank and Gretchen could discuss the progress she'd made on *Still Life with Berries and Wine* while feeding each other grapes! What if this wasn't the most original thought going? It would nonetheless make apparent her continued interest – in him *and* his commission. The hopeful artist reapplied face powder, brushed her hair, and headed across the hall to Frank's apartment.

Only after she rang his bell did Gretchen question herself. Sure, Frank might benefit from acting on a whim, but would she? Besides, didn't proper etiquette dictate calling before a visit? If there was anything her mother had taught her – and even though it had been years since they'd spoken, Gretchen would never forget her mother's oft-repeated lessons on decorum – if there was anything that had successfully been drilled into her sorry head, it was 'Don't simply drop by'! And here she was, doing just that!

Gretchen was so caught up in self-recriminations and worry that she realized Frank had not yet answered the bell. Gretchen was about to walk away, especially after thinking of her mother's admonitions, when she recognized Frank's voice.

'Coming!' There it was; that unmistakable twang.

And then she heard a woman's voice. Gretchen heard the softer tones of a woman emanating from Frank's apartment.

How many times have I told you, Gretchen? Think before you act! Suddenly she felt ill: from the pan-fried trout she'd hurried down for dinner; from the castigating voice she knew was not her own, not Margaret's, but her mother's; from the knowledge that her photographer friend was clearly not alone in his apartment.

She clutched her container of grapes and moved away from Frank's door. With any luck she'd make it back to her place without Frank finding out she'd come to call. Oh, no, her mother's words, 'coming to call'.

The artist's key was in her apartment door when another door opened behind her.

'Gretchen!' Frank placed a hand on her shoulder. He practically spun her around. 'I'm guessing that was you at my door. Gosh, this is a surprise. Please come in.'

* * *

She is tall, this woman, and pretty, with ash-brown hair that falls gently to the middle of her back. She must be at least five-ten, Gretchen thinks, even though she is slouching slightly, next to a large round table laden with food.

Gretchen knows she has passed through a hallway, long like the one in her apartment, lined with photographs presumably taken by Frank. She understands, too, that it is Frank's hand on her shoulder, propelling her towards a large, well-lit space. For a moment Gretchen focuses on the platter of steaming apricots, prunes, and couscous on the well-appointed dining room table.

All she fully takes in, however, is the striking woman chewing on an apricot and absently combing through her hair with tapered fingers.

Gretchen doesn't remember the name of the woman Frank intro- duces. She doesn't recall if Frank has asked Gretchen to join them, but he must have, as he's pointing to a chair to the left of where the attractive interloper has now sat down. Gretchen doesn't remember shaking the woman's hand, either, but she probably did, because this tall female in Frank's apartment is smiling at Gretchen and lowering the hand that hadn't held the piece of warm fruit.

Gretchen dimly recalls Frank smiling, too, but she can't fathom why, and then she is thrusting the bowl of red globe grapes in his direction. She is barreling past Frank, away from the rich smells of cinnamon and cardamom and cooked fruit, away from the woman tapping lacquered fingernails on a plate. Gretchen is barreling down a hallway that seems to tunnel on forever.

Gretchen is out of this hell, she is back in her apartment, she is crying in her overstuffed living room chair. She is akin to a vat of red globe grapes – crushed, liquid, under that woman's feet.

* * *

You foolish, foolish girl! What made you think this charming boy would be interested in you'? Her mother's voice was obliterating Gretchen's own, Margaret's, Frank's, the voice of anyone kind and empathetic in Gretchen's life.

Gretchen pictured her mother standing over her, her mother as an adult, Gretchen as a child. 'Why would he spend time with you except to ensure that you give him what he wants'?

'Mother,' Gretchen was talking aloud, seeing this woman, hands on hips, narrowing her eyes at Gretchen, 'he told me I was talented, funny, and smart.'

'Honey, don't you think he says that to all the girls? I wish you were smart enough to see that'.

'Gretchen, get a grip'! Ah, Margaret. The artist sniffled and blew her nose. Thank God for Margaret. She should call Margaret right now. No, one of her best friend's daughters was having a sleepover at Margaret's place. Gretchen bothered her friend too much already.

'Gretchen, see what happens when you listen to someone other than yourself? You really can't be sure what tonight's events with Frank meant. What you need to do is rest – and tomorrow, get back to work on your still life'.

Gretchen blew her nose once more. She wiped the back of her hand across her tear-soaked face. Margaret would have said that, and Margaret would have been right: Gretchen didn't have all the facts with which to judge tonight's fiasco with Frank. Still, the bedraggled artist couldn't help thinking that perhaps Frank had been so warm and flirtatious because that was the way Frank was. It didn't mean he'd been insincere, just primarily concerned with the progress of his commission. She couldn't fault him for caring about a piece of art he would be displaying in his home, a piece of art that would be setting him back two-thousand dollars.

There was art, Gretchen thought, and there was commerce. And there was friendship, and there was romantic love. Mingling all four was bound to be foolhardy. Gretchen was too sad and confused, however, to know if this was truly her belief, or one attached to her mother – or Elliot.

If Gretchen were wise, if she had learned anything useful over her twenty-eight years, she would try not to muddy her life with the complications of love. If she wanted to relieve her sexual frustration, for example, she could simply act on her lust.

This was what Elliot did. Gretchen felt an ache behind her eyes, an ache, as well, in her heart. The painter dabbed at a fresh profusion of tears. She tried to block out an image of her mother towering over her, arms akimbo, scowl hardening her face. She tried to erase images of Frank with that woman, trading forkfuls of hot couscous and fruit, Frank excitedly taking shots of her in various stages of undress, Frank and that willowy woman rolling around in his bed.

Gretchen pulled her legs in under her and hugged her body close. She shut her eyes and remembered Elliot, his dark, curly chest hair, his musky smell. She wanted his arms wrapped tightly around her, his mouth mashed against hers, then his grunting, deep, primordial, in her ear, spurring her on.

She needed to open wide for him, to feel his thick cock stretching her welcoming pussy walls, to know nothing but him, pounding, mercilessly, into her dripping cunt. She longed to spasm, to shiver, to cry out loudly beneath him.

Without further thought, she picked up her phone and dialed Elliot's number. Elliot answered on the second ring. Gretchen heard him say hello, twice. She bit her lower lip and covered her mouth. Then she hung up.

CHAPTER TWELVE

Early the next morning, Gretchen decided to walk to *Fong's*. Her step was lively after four blocks, her shoulders and neck less tense after eight. At the tenth block, the perked-up artist stepped inside a diner for coffee. The warmth trickling down her throat helped her to herald a new day.

She freshened her makeup in the ladies room, determined to will herself into feeling better, or, barring that, to look better than she felt. Gretchen smiled. A sense of humor, under-eye concealer, beige foundation, russet lipstick: all these could perform magic for her day.

Now, on to *Fong's*, for what would improve her mood even more and, more importantly, give special meaning to her day: the meticulous selection of delectable, deep-hued, earth-blessed berries and peaches for the completion of her final drawing. After this, she would begin painting *Still Life with Berries and Wine*.

* * *

Gretchen got goose bumps viewing the latest arrivals at *Fong's*. Mr. Fong himself grinned broadly at his very reliable customer, nodded his head and tipped his cap. After he espied her staring at the raspberries, he said, 'Nice, yes? They're our freshest yet!'

Gretchen breathed back, 'They're gorgeous,' and grabbed a red plastic carrier from the many stacked at the entrance to *Fong's*.

Raspberries, strawberries, blueberries, blackberries, star fruit, papayas, peaches, persimmons, Gretchen wanted to gather these to her flaring nostrils and deeply inhale. She wanted to buy more than she needed just to be sure she'd have all she wanted.

She yearned to fill one carrier, no, two carriers, and then her kitchen counter, treasured wooden bowl, crystal bowls, and refrigerator shelves and compartments with all the soul-nurturing, taste-bud-tantalizing fruit she could charge on her almost-at-the-limit charge card.

Then she received her second set of goose bumps. Gretchen turned her head, slowly, and spotted Elliot, waving at her. He was standing next to the zucchini, probably wanting shoppers to compare and contrast. Gretchen laughed at her joke, in spite of the urge to bolt. In two seconds she would have left to buy her goodies elsewhere, an Epicurean misdemeanor under any other circumstances. In two seconds, however, Elliot was at her side.

How could this be happening? Elliot, sex-loving, money-grubbing Elliot, was telling Gretchen that he knew she had called him last night; he had Caller ID. Why had she called him? Elliot said he'd wondered. Gretchen must have wanted a rerun of their last time together, must miss him the way he missed her.

He remembered how much she loved *Fong's*, in fact, if she recalled, this was where they'd first met. So Elliot took today off from work, a rare occurrence, that. He called her this morning at nine, hoped that, since she wasn't in, she might be on her way to *Fong's*. It was a medium- to long- shot, sure, but he had made it his business to run into her today. If he hadn't located her at this produce market, he would have found her somewhere else. That, he told Gretchen, was how determined he was to see her.

That, Gretchen believed, is why she had to leave. Still, she felt frozen, like plastic-bagged blueberries and raspberries she wouldn't be caught dead buying. Then Gretchen was moving. She let herself be taken by the hand to the young men bunching flowers in the front of the store. Every day, all day long, three nephews of Mr. Fong brought together flowers with palette-brightening colors and hard-to-remember names and wrapped them in thin, patterned paper. Elliot selected three of the largest, showiest bouquets from the dozens standing in tall, water-filled mini-tanks in front of *Fong's*.

Elliot reminded the numbed Gretchen that his apartment building was five short blocks away. He told her how beautiful she looked. He ran his sandalwood-scented fingers through her hair and said he'd return with her, *afterwards*, to buy her fruit. He knew how much she adored *Fong's* fruit. Elliot would buy her all that she desired; he'd fill her belly with fruit.

How did Elliot know she felt empty inside? Gretchen feared he'd read it on her face. She found herself holding cadmium-yellow, passion-pink, alizarin-crimson petals to her nose. Next she found herself in Elliot's elevator, she and Elliot, no one else inside. The flowers landed on the floor. Elliot's tongue filled her mouth, explored where no tongue had been since his on that day in her studio.

She watched him press the stop button. She felt his cock hard against her. She wanted his knee right where it was, rubbing her soaking crotch. She didn't, however, want to crush the flowers. She toed the bouquets to the far side of the elevator floor.

Now his fingers were on her nipples. Elliot had deftly unbuttoned Gretchen's blouse, had undone her front-clasped bra. Her pussy was flowing, but her brain interrupted with worries about residents needing the elevator.

'Elliot,' she forced out between kisses, 'what if someone wants the elevator?'

He responded by kissing her harder, by pulling, squeezing, twisting her nipples between thumb and forefinger, by shushing her, by thrusting two fingers into her sopping pussy.

She didn't want him to stop; she urged his hand back onto her engorged, stretched nipple and felt him pull it again. Then Elliot rushed her hand to his zipper and helped her tug it down. He pushed her onto her knees.

She had Elliot's cock in her mouth. This felt wonderful. This felt wrong. She opened her eyes to flora strewn and trampled around her. She worried aloud about his aged neighbor not being able to negotiate stairs.

Elliot barked, 'That's the old man's business.' Then he pushed her head back onto his penis.

This was Elliot, Gretchen thought, all business – his own business. Then she knew, way too late, that she had no business being here. She got off her knees. She felt sickened by the sweet balsamic scent of his cologne; saddened by the crushed bouquets, the lot of them making an even more dizzying aroma; and, especially, poker-hot mad at herself for being here like this with Elliot, for wanting this man, still.

Gretchen, despite her ex-boyfriend's protests, stepped back from Elliot. She rearranged her clothing and hair as best she could. This was the last time; she could never do this with Elliot again.

'It's good that you dumped me,' Gretchen said as she re-buttoned her blouse. 'You're not good for me,' she told him, as she wiped off the remainder of her lipstick with her thumb.

Elliot shook his head, no doubt in disbelief and anger, and zipped his pants as she repeated, as much for her ears as for his, 'You're not good for me, Elliot,' she added, 'you're just good-looking.'

Then she pressed the button for the closest floor. She rushed off as the door opened. She almost didn't mind the stares of tenants massed by the elevator door.

* * *

Really, Gretchen, you could have called me,' Margaret lightly scolded her friend. 'It hasn't been that long since I've been in the company of a man. And I can remember that special kind of hurt.'

At a local restaurant, Gretchen told of her encounter with Frank and his guest. Gretchen hadn't the heart to speak of her 'encounter' with Elliot. She didn't know if Margaret would understand – or even if she should – and Gretchen didn't want to bring upon her own shoulders a disgust the likes of which her mother might have tendered. The artist didn't want to keep confusing Margaret with her mother. She also didn't know that this was the time to figure out how to disentangle them.

Gretchen resolved to think about her behavior with Elliot later and, with time, to forgive herself. She knew it wasn't wise to forget.

Now she chose to give her full attention to Margaret. Margaret spoke of the surprisingly amenable discussion she'd had with her ex-husband after dropping off the girls. Gretchen was pleased to hear this, for

Margaret's sake, as well as for the sake of Gretchen caring for someone other than herself.

Margaret deserved a fulfilling life. She deserved to be out in the workforce again, something Margaret had lately talked about a great deal. Margaret should have a good man, too. And she deserved a friend as worthy of her as Margaret was of Gretchen.

While the artist was musing about her friend, her friend surprised her by cutting their lunch short. One hour was not unreasonable, Margaret pointed out, especially as she had a job interview this afternoon.

'No wonder!' Gretchen burst out. 'No wonder you look so put-together!'

Margaret looked warmly at Gretchen, and then spoke of the supervisory position available at a friend's place of business. It was similar in scope to her last position, but much better paying.

'And now,' Margaret announced, 'it's time to leave for my appointment. Isn't it time for you to return to work, too? That commission won't finish itself.'

Slave driver. Gretchen loved this woman.

Margaret studied her reflection in her pocket mirror. Gretchen told her she looked professional as well as very pretty. She hugged her best friend and wished her good luck, feeling grateful for the love that warmed her veins.

Margaret rose to find a taxi to her interview. Gretchen stood up to take a walk: first to *Fong's* to purchase fruit, then to Diamond Paint Downtown for oils and solvent.

Gretchen would not allow pain from Elliot to keep her from *Fong's*, just as she would not permit uncertainty about Frank to keep her from her finishing his commissioned work. Whether anything substantive happened with Frank, or with any other man, Gretchen knew that painting and friendship would sustain her – not, of course, that she didn't want more.

CHAPTER THIRTEEN

It had been two days, she believed, since her debacle with Elliot, three since her disappointment with Frank. Gretchen hadn't the stomach to speak with either of them, so she'd turned down the ringer on her telephone and thrown a towel on top of her answering machine. She hadn't wanted to see or hear evidence of calls from either.

However, today – fortified by her lunch date with Margaret, a triumphant return to *Fong's*, and a productive trip to *Diamond Art Downtown* – Gretchen felt steady and brave.

She'd received two calls from Frank, zero from Elliot. As if from an analyst's chair, Gretchen observed how she felt wounded by the lack of contact from Elliot, even though she didn't want it, even though it was safer for her this way.

She had felt her heart jump and her skin tingle when she'd recognized Frank's telltale twang.

Call number one: 'Gretchen, how are you? Are you there? Thank you for the grapes. I'm sorry you didn't stay to eat with us. You didn't have to rush off, you know. This is Frank, of course. Call me, OK?'

Call number two: 'Gretchen, it's Frank. Are you all right? I'm wondering, um, if you're angry with me. Please give me a call. I hope all is well.'

Dear Frank. She pondered whether he had a clue and, if not, why not. Still, he'd sounded concerned. Perhaps he had feelings for her after all. Or perhaps he didn't know whom he cared for, which was why he sounded clueless in the first call and confused in the second.

Gretchen sighed. Naturally she would return his call. Part of her longed to speak with Frank this instant, part of her was scared to find out where she stood. If she didn't call, she couldn't know. Ignorance was, if not bliss, then preferable to full-on pain.

She would paint instead of calling Frank. She had already arranged the bottles and glasses, and the bowls of *Fong's* fresh fruit. She had dusted the table legs and smoothed the old-world scarf. Donning her old-paint-splattered clothes, cleaning her brushes, stretching her canvas, smoothing her hands with protective cream, mixing her beloved paints – these were the rituals that calmed and energized her.

In moments, Gretchen was immersed in capturing the lushness and sweet pungency of the fruit. At several points over the next few hours, viewing her work as well as the fruit tableau, her mouth began to water. Once she used a clean rag to wipe away a line of drool that had dribbled onto her chin. Gretchen laughed at herself. If she reacted this way, there was a chance that *Still Life with Berries and Wine* could evoke similar reactions in others. That would be hilarious – and immensely gratifying!

She labored through the day. She applied layer upon layer of paint, striving for luminosity of tone, fullness, depth. She wanted this piece to embody the objects as well as transcend them. She desired: her college professors to praise her technique; her mother to drop arms from hips and nod her head in approval and awe; her agent to book her another gallery show, better than the last; Margaret to clap her hands at the outcome of this painting and share in her joy; Frank to hold her close and whisper in her ear that he loved it.

Gretchen stood back to view her canvas. Again and again, she looked from object to painting and back again. She bit her lower lip in concentration. This… this was good!

The artist cleaned her brushes. She stretched plastic wrap over her palette and placed it in the freezer. Then she stepped into her shower. Under the soothing spray, Gretchen thought of devouring the deepest blue blueberries mixed with *Fong's* heavy cream. She would study her day's work and decide whether she'd made as impressive a start as she'd initially thought. After that, she'd call Frank. She knew she could speak with him now, without the threat of tears.

* * *

Gosh, Gretchen, is that you? I'm relieved to hear your voice. You had me worried.'

He really does care, thought Gretchen. Her shoulders relaxed, her breathing slowed. 'I didn't mean to worry you,' she said.

'You know, I stopped by a couple of times, but you weren't home. I almost left a note under your door, but didn't want to be a pest, what with the two phone messages I'd left and all.'

'Oh, Frank, I'm sorry.' She was truly sorry she'd caused him to worry, but also a tiny bit thrilled to hear how much he cared.

'Gretchen, I wish I had a telephone number of a friend of yours, or a family member, just so I could have known you were OK. Maybe whatever we have here doesn't warrant that, I don't know, but I do know that I wish you hadn't worried me like that.'

'Frank, oh, I'm so sorry.' Gretchen started sobbing. 'Hold on, please.' She placed the receiver down and reached for a box of tissues.

'Gretchen, are you there? I think I'm the one who should be sorry. I didn't mean to make you cry. Gretchen, um, my sister is still in town. That's who you met when you came to my apartment five days ago.'

Five days? And that was his *sister?* 'Your sister?'

'Yes, and it occurred to me that you might have thought otherwise when you rushed out. Funny, it was my sister who pointed out this possibility to me yesterday, when I finally told her I was concerned.'

Gretchen started crying again. She couldn't help herself.

'Gretchen? You're crying again! I'm coming over. Don't go away. I'm coming over, OK?'

Gretchen wasn't going anywhere.

* * *

As soon as Gretchen let Frank in, as soon as he was hugging her so tightly she thought she might die a delightful death, Gretchen realized that the unfinished, uncovered *Still Life with Berries and Wine* was in this very room, at the far wall, directly across from Frank. As soon he let go of her he would see it. It was too late for her to cover her work in progress and, besides, there was no way she wanted to free herself from the warmth and comfort of his arms.

'Gretchen,' Frank whispered, his eyes closed, his fingers smoothing her hair, 'I realized after you fled my apartment how much I care for you. I was rotten to my sister for three days straight after you left, but was afraid to tell her why. I was sullen and sulky with her. Finally she sat me down and made me fess up. She's the only one in my family who does that – and I'm grateful to her for it.'

Frank opened his eyes. Here goes.

'Gretchen!' He stood back. 'Is that it? Is that *Still Life with Berries*?'

'Yes, that's it, unfinished. I hadn't planned for you to see it yet.'

'Please let me see what you've done so far!'

This was so sweet. Frank was smiling ear to ear, like an awestruck little boy, or the village idiot, she wasn't sure which. How could she not let this man view close up what clearly already thrilled him from afar – especially after what he had told her?

'Oh, Frank, how can I deny you now?' She took his hand, felt that strong and warm hand fully in hers, and led him to her easel.

'So, Photography Man,' Gretchen lamely joked, hoping to calm herself, 'what do you think?'

Frank walked up close. He walked to the left of the painting. He walked to the right. He kneeled in front of it. He squinted. He stood up. He stepped back. He stepped further back. All this time he was smiling.

Now Gretchen couldn't keep from smiling. This rube could make her happy!

'Gosh, Gretchen, gosh, you are so… it is so… good!'

Oh, the smile on Frank's face! Forget 'available light'. The light from Frank's face was the finest light possible. She could paint by the light from his face! 'Frank,' she managed to say, 'I'm so glad you like it. Remember, though, I have layers to go before I sleep.'

'Gosh, Gretchen, Gretchen Collins *Frost*, you are so funny, and so smart, gorgeous, and, gosh, talented. You have me stammering and, um, totally at a loss.'

Gretchen thought he was doing very well. She thought she could listen to a lifetime of goshes from this man from Goshen, this man so honest, and so caring, appreciative, and joyful!

The artist rushed over to the photographer and hugged him as hard as he had just held her. 'Frank,' Gretchen said to him, 'I care for you, too, very much.'

* * *

Gretchen had finally made it to Frank's studio, and she hadn't invited herself! The painter was growing accustomed to the slower pace of what was already becoming a fruitful relationship.

Frank was unlike any man she'd known, most of whom she had given her heart, to say nothing of her body, way too soon. Frank rewarded her interest and affection in many ways. He: asked about her life as an artist, respected her art, and encouraged her to work; paused to think after she'd ask him a question, never responding glibly; stroked her fingers or arm while listening to her talk; grinned and tapped his foot when happy or excited; and was full of emotion when telling her about and now showing her his photography. Yes, Frank rewarded Gretchen in so many ways, she was sure there'd be even richer rewards in bed.

And now she had evidence of this man's talent. She peered at the black and white shots on the walls, framed simply, of Goshenites at work. All had captions: *Mrs. Yoder typing a medicine bottle label, North Main Drugs; Mr. Strom, obituary writer, Goshen Times-Maple City Gazette; Miss Lulu Smith, Paddle Canoes for Rent, Elkhart River.* These photographs were so expressive that even the inanimate objects – dusty tubes of ointment on pharmacy shelves; newspaper office chairs sporting scuffed leather; headband askew on Miss Smith's head – seemed to have as much to tell the viewer as Mrs. Yoder, Mr. Strom, and Miss Smith.

There were other shots, recent, of people at work in New York. Gretchen thought she recognized a dollar-toy vendor in the Union Square subway station, a tattooed woman performing with her snake by the Cyclone roller coaster in Coney Island's Astroland Park.

More than the cropping, which she deemed thoughtful, or the composition, inspired, or even the subjects, certainly not run-of-the-mill, Gretchen thought that Frank felt in his gut the elements of a good shot. He had the curiosity, the love of life, the innate visual sense to make the ordinary special, and the special extraordinary. This man's being possessed art.

Frank had been working in his darkroom. He was about to show her photos he'd taken of his sister, then, if she'd like, he'd present to Gretchen landscapes of Goshen, and portraits of his mom and dad.

If she'd like? She'd like, she'd like! She had not yet slept with this man – though she felt it was imminent – but already she felt more intimate with him than during all her time with Elliot.

After she looked at more of his soul-satisfying work, before she went back to paint, Gretchen would give Frank the longest and most passionate kiss of his life.

CHAPTER FOURTEEN

For two days, Gretchen had been in and out of, mostly in, her painter's trance, starting at dawn, working eight- to ten-hour days. Her threadbare jeans were almost entirely covered with oil paint: old spots layered with splotches from yesterday's work, yesterday's dried patches overlaid with golden ochre, bismuth yellow, blue-black from today.

When Gretchen stepped away periodically, to refresh herself with herbal tea or spring water, or to tame hunger pangs with star fruit or salmon fillet, she was struck each time she returned by how much progress she'd made. Near the middle of the second day, Gretchen assessed that *Still Life with Berries and Wine* was halfway done.

At this juncture, the telephone rang. Knowing that she hadn't been loafing, and therefore feeling worthy of an extended rest, the artist reached for the phone.

'Gretchen, Sweet Kolinsky (he had nicknamed her after her favorite sable paint brush) I had another impulse today. Naturally, it involves you. First, tell me, am I taking you from work? I don't want to do that, you know.'

Gretchen laid two worn beach towels over her overstuffed chair and sat down. 'Listen, Henry Hasselblad,' she purred into the receiver, and then paused as they both laughed, 'I happen to be on a break. You'll be pleased to know that I've been working diligently on your commission. I trust you've been working hard, as well.' She crossed her legs and twirled a lock of hair. She couldn't remember having this much fun before with a man outside of bed.

'As a matter of fact, I have. I catalogued most of my people-at-work photos, for Indiana and for New York, and came up with a pithy working title, if you'll pardon the pun: *Goshen to Gotham: Photos of Progress in Work.* One of my subjects put me in touch with an editor, and it looks like a book deal might be in the works. Oops, another pun! And this morning, I thought, gosh, she's really busy, but why not ask Gretchen to be in my book? That, um, was my impulse.'

Wow, thought Gretchen, stunned into silence. Wow!

'Gretchen, are you there? You don't have to make up your mind right now. I know I don't have a book deal yet, but I'm close!'

'I'm here, I'm here.' Gretchen blinked back tears. For the first time in months she was crying from joy. 'Frank, I'm so happy for you. This couldn't happen to a better, or more deserving, photographer! And I love your book title.'

'That means a lot to me, Kolinsky. You have no idea.'

Oh, yes, she did. And she'd better come up with a term of endearment superior to 'Henry Caseload.'

'Gretchen, will you be one of my subjects? I can start shooting today!'

She loved the enthusiasm of this man, like she loved – him! 'I'd be honored to be one of your subjects, whether the photo appears in a book or not. I think I'm done painting for the day, though, plus I'm meeting Margaret for a very late lunch. Do you think you can make it tomorrow?'

Tomorrow, at eleven a.m., Gretchen would ascertain whether art, commerce, friendship, and love could produce a felicitous blend.

* * *

At *Le Petit Cochon*, Gretchen's choice for lunch, Margaret led with news of her supervisory job. 'What luck! My first interview in eight years and I landed the job!'

Gretchen shook her head at her best friend. 'I'm not surprised, and you know it wasn't luck that got you the job.' Then Gretchen asked the waiter Alain to bring their finest champagne.

Gretchen turned to Margaret. 'I've always wanted to say, 'Bring me your finest champagne!" Now the artist had a reason to do so. She thought there'd be more celebrations in the near future. Hmmm, Gretchen could get used to drinking champagne. Champagne could become her new Rubio.

After finishing her glass Margaret said, 'Gretchen, you're glowing. And I think it's more than this bubbly. Come on, tell me. What's up?'

Gretchen chewed her *Steak au Poivre*. Her desire for red meat reasserted itself as soon as she'd coasted through *Le Petit Cochon's* doors. 'I'm glowing? Really? It must be my progress on *Still Life with Berries and Wine*,' she swallowed the very rare meat, 'or the fact that I spoke with my agent today about getting another show. Or it could be my progress with Frank.'

'Oh, my God,' Margaret leaned closer, 'tell me what's happened.'

Gretchen was about to spill and spell when she heard a familiar twang. She turned her head to search for its source. At the farthest wall, at what must be a coveted table, Frank, dining alone, was talking into a cell phone. She opened her mouth and stared.

Now Margaret was staring at him. 'Who is that? Is it your photographer? Is it Frank?'

Maybe Frank's radar was working especially well. Maybe he sensed the none-too-subtle Margaret. As soon as he flipped his cell closed, he looked in Gretchen's direction.

'Gretchen! Kolinsky!' Before the startled artist could tend to her best friend's bewilderment, the photographer was at their table. Introductions were made.

Frank was surprised but thrilled to see her, and he was glad to meet her best friend, too. He looked at Margaret, told her he'd just been on the phone with his sister, the sister that Gretchen will never forget. He glanced at Gretchen and grinned. He said he'd told his sister all about Gretchen. He shared the champagne. He gushed to Margaret about Gretchen's talent, her beauty, her intelligence. He stroked Gretchen's arm and fingers.

Gretchen blushed repeatedly, and with each blush her face got darker. By the time Frank left them to finish their lunch, she was sure she matched the alizarin crimson she'd been mixing for the raspberries in *Still Life with Berries and Wine*.

'Gretchen, he's adorable! He's kind, articulate, handsome, and very sweet. And he's obviously smitten with you!' The newly hired supervisor clapped her hands and lifted her champagne glass. 'Not that you need my approval, but I heartily approve! To my job and me! To you and your painting! To you and Frank! I think we're ready for another bottle, sweetie!'

Gretchen motioned to Alain. It was time for a second bottle of *Le Petit Cochon's* finest.

* * *

For the first time since they'd met, Gretchen was angry with Frank. It was eleven-thirty, she noted, glancing at that awful black clock she'd been too busy to replace. Frank was half an hour late.

The artist had been at work since eight a.m., having lost a ridiculous amount of time making herself up for this event. Ordinarily, the artist did not apply brown-black, mink-oil-enriched mascara, 'Smokin' Blue' eyeshadow or 'Sensational Sienna' lipstick before painting a still life. Generally, she did not fuss over whether a certain pair of paint-splotched jeans made her *derriere* look even rounder than it was, or whether her mauve sweatshirt accentuated her blue-gray eyes but stretched too tautly across her very ample breasts. Nor did she usually prepare a fruit salad tossed with coconut, mandarin orange juice, and rum.

Ordinarily, of course, Gretchen was not being photographed for a book by a passionate, immensely talented man with whom she was falling in love. A man who was now thirty-five minutes late. She put down her brush. Maybe Frank was too good to be true.

'So, you've finally come to your senses! Don't you think you've fooled yourself long enough'?

No, Mother, thought Gretchen, I'm not going to listen to you. I'm going to prove you wrong – and get you out of my brain. I don't need you in there, Gretchen finally understood. I don't even need Margaret in my head. I want all the room in there for me!

Then she heard her doorbell ring. The artist breathed deeply, smoothed her hair, and opened her door to Frank. He was grinning sheepishly, leaning perilously to the left under the weight of a bulging equipment bag on his shoulder, sporting two Nikons around his neck, and holding in his right hand an aluminum-foil-covered casserole dish, the sweet and savory contents of which were titillating her as much as the tardy, tasty presence of the man himself.

'I should paint a big scarlet L across your face,' Gretchen quipped, and opened her door wider. 'L is for late. It's eleven-forty, mister!'

'Oh, I know, Gretchen, and I'm sorry! I wanted to make something special for you,' he said, holding the dish before her. 'It wasn't cooked through by eleven, but I couldn't call because that would have given away the surprise. It's my couscous with Cornish Hen and apricots. Promise me this time you won't run away!'

Gretchen shook her head in mock annoyance and laughed. She placed Frank's casserole dish on the kitchen counter and brought her nose close to the foil. His food smelled so delicious that she wanted to eat it right now. Of course, *Frank* looked delicious. Talk about food for thought! O.K., Gretchen, behave yourself, for the sake of this man's book if for nothing else.

When she came back into her studio Frank was retrieving lenses and filters from his big black bag. He saw her tense up, and suggested she try to forget he was there (fat chance!) to simply go back to what she'd been painting. They could talk if she wanted, of course, but that was up to Gretchen.

The flustered artist tried to ignore the tall, aqua-eyed Hoosier with the two beautiful facial moles as she returned to painting her Freestone peaches. If she weren't aware of his muscles straining under his denim shirt, if she weren't entranced by the melding aromas of strong man and moist hen, if she hadn't been tantalized so recently by his fingers alighting on her sensitive skin, if, if... If she didn't start concentrating he'd be on to her. She half-expected him to ask 'Gretchen, are you here?'

In minutes, however, though aware of his presence, she lost herself in capturing the essence of the still life before her. Too, she became absorbed in the concept and practice of Frank photographing her as she worked. She moved right, then left, to ensure she was painting the peach curves correctly; Frank moved as well. He was nimble, pivoting, squatting, stretching the length of his body onto the floor, moving any way he could to achieve the best shots of Gretchen plying her craft.

It was exciting, no thrilling, working with each other, working *off* each other. Today each worked independently, but each was a vital part of if not a reason for the other's work. Her painted peach was a magnificent specimen, her paintbrush a glorious vessel, and she and Frank together were afire with their art. She was incredulous at the quantity of photographs he'd taken: the photographer had to be on his third or fourth roll of film by the time she'd put down her brush.

They hadn't the need of talk while fully engaged. Anyway, Gretchen sensed they were beyond talk. Frank put aside his camera after she put down her brush. He rushed up to her, began to say how much he loved working with her, then mumbled 'Gosh', took her head in his hands, and pressed his mouth to her lips.

She stumbled, he laughed, and they both fell atop the towels on her overstuffed chair. Gretchen had never felt lips so moist, so giving, moving so creatively on hers. She felt she could kiss him forever, but of course she wouldn't. Gretchen wanted to know, see, taste, all of him. After all, she had waited so long.

Then Gretchen unsnapped his denim shirt, and was surprised to see a chest that was nearly hairless; he was not as she'd imagined him. This was different. This was better: there were few hairs to get in the way of this body that beckoned to her. As she lowered his briefs, his teal-veined cock jumped and hardened even before she touched and tasted him. She had never had a lover who tasted so pure yet utterly manly at the same time.

Gretchen removed his clothes and he let her without rushing to rip off hers. Then he slowly, meticulously, nearly torturously, removed every item of her clothing, gently touching each new area of skin revealed to him as he did so.

Frank carried her to bed. No man had ever carried her to bed. She felt light and pliant while aloft, then in bed, like terrain he would come to know without benefit of camera. He was his camera. He explored her curves, his long, supple fingers on her full breasts, which felt larger and softer, yet with nipples harder, redder, longer then ever before. All parts of her rose to meet his touch. Her pussy widened, quivered, gushed for his digits, lips, tongue, mouth, cock, as if made expressly for Frank, every part of Frank. They made love – it was not merely foreplay and fucking – for hours, stopping only once, for water and fruit.

She asked if he was hungry for the hen and couscous or fancy fruit salad, and he told her they could eat it later. Tomorrow. Whenever. Finally they arose and then sat naked at her table imbibing Rubio; feeding each other the fruit she'd composed for *Still Life with Berries and Wine*. Frank wanted to be sure that this was acceptable.

'Don't worry,' Gretchen told him, 'I always replenish my fruit.'

He told her he could hardly wait until the painting was finished, hanging in his apartment, and they were sharing this fruit in front of it.

'Perhaps,' he offered, 'our painting can hang in another place altogether – in a house, with two studios where we can work on what we love, every day, and be with whom we love, every day.'

Gretchen started to cry.

'Gosh, I'm sorry if I overwhelmed you.'

She fed him berries. 'It's too late to be sorry, Goshen. You made your bed or rather you unmade mine, and now you'll have to sleep in it with me.'

'Kolinsky,' he reached across to kiss her, 'that's perfectly fine with me.'

Gretchen climbed into Frank's lap, smiled, and licked the raspberry juice drizzling down his chin.